The Tailor of Giripul

Bulbul Sharma is a painter and writer. She is the author of several books, including *My Sainted Aunts*, *The Perfect Woman* and *Anger of Aubergines*, *Banana-Flower Dreams*, *Shaya Tales*, *The Book of Devi*, *Eating Women*, *Telling Tales*, and *Now That I am Fifty*. Her books have been translated into Italian, French, Finnish and Spanish.

She has also written several books for children including – *Book of Indian Birds*, *Fabled Book of Gods and Demons* and *The Children's Ramayana*. She has been conducting art and storytelling workshops for children with special needs for the last fifteen years.

The Tailor of Giripul

BULBUL SHARMA

HarperCollins *Publishers* India
a joint venture with

New Delhi

First published in India in 2011 by
HarperCollins *Publishers* India
a joint venture with
The India Today Group

Copyright © Bulbul Sharma 2011

ISBN: 978-93-5029-105-4

2 4 6 8 10 9 7 5 3 1

Bulbul Sharma asserts the moral right to be identified
as the author of this book.

HarperCollins *Publishers*
A-53, Sector 57, NOIDA, Uttar Pradesh – 201301, India
77-85 Fulham Palace Road, London W6 8JB, United Kingdom
Hazelton Lanes, 55 Avenue Road, Suite 2900, Toronto, Ontario M5R 3L2
and 1995 Markham Road, Scarborough, Ontario M1B 5M8, Canada
25 Ryde Road, Pymble, Sydney, NSW 2073, Australia
31 View Road, Glenfield, Auckland 10, New Zealand
10 East 53rd Street, New York NY 10022, USA

Typeset in Cambria 11/14.8
Jojy Philip, New Delhi 110 015

Printed and bound at
Thomson Press (India) Ltd.

This book is for my five grandchildren
Naina, Samara, Shivam, Prithvi and Shiv.

I hope they will grow up to love the mountains
as much as I do.

The mountains held their breath and looked down at the village still covered in darkness. The moon hovered uncertainly above the highest peak and a dim light flickered in the hut hidden by the shadows of the deodar forest. The winds too remained still, as though they did not want to disturb the cold silence of the winter night. When the baby was finally born, the deodar trees suddenly began to shiver though the air was quiet and still. It was a bad omen, and even though a boy was born, the women did not celebrate and the men stood outside, grim-faced and afraid. The old women began to wail and beat their chests with clenched fists.

The newborn lay naked in the moonlight. He was a strange, ugly child and his birth could bring only shame to the village. His skin was the colour of milk gone sour and his hair was matted, like threads in a rotten cob of corn. He did not cry lustily like all healthy male babies do, but mewed like a sickly kitten, his tiny white hands covering his face as if he was ashamed of being born. His mother, a young girl still in her teens, turned her face to the wall and closed her eyes. She never woke to see the dawn. The father hid his face in shame, then cursed his dead wife for giving birth to a monster.

The midwife muttered a prayer and cast her eyes towards the dark sky. She burnt a few red chillies to ward off the evil air that hung over the hut like a heavy, ash-laden cloud, and threatened to spread to the hills. Outside, in the forest and on the hillside, in the caves above the stream, dark shadows hovered and the villagers huddled together in the light of the breaking dawn to pray that the darkness would ebb when the sun rose, and take this freak, this half-baked creature with it.

The sun rose, travelled across the sky, and set beyond the hills, yet the albino child lived.

Dawn floated down, touched the hills lightly to wake them, and then swept over the rest of Giripul. As the mild sunlight danced over the rooftops, the village yawned, snapped its fingers over its mouth and shrugged itself awake. Smoke from wood fires, fragrant with butter and milk, began to float out of the kitchen windows. The winding, dusty street that divided one side of the village from the other was still empty except for a few stray dogs.

A group of monkeys sat in a patch of sunlight and watched Janak as he bent down to open his shop. He pulled up the iron shutters with one hand. In his other hand he held a pink satin blouse with a single golden sleeve. In the cold wind, unusual for this time of year, the amputated blouse fluttered sadly, like the banner of an army in retreat. Janak tucked the blouse firmly under his armpit and slammed open the shutter. The monkeys, startled by the sudden noise, so early in the morning, bared their blood-red gums and bounded into the forest.

A few pigeons flew down from the roof and settled on the steps leading up to the shop. Janak scattered a handful of seeds on the ground and began cooing to them. The birds started picking up the grains greedily, but as usual, his favourite bird – a brown and white one – did not respond to his cooing and, like every morning, he felt hurt by the bird's aloof behaviour. He believed in his heart that one day, the bird would look at him and coo back in gratitude. Just like he believed his wife would, one day, look deep into his eyes and declare her love for him.

A lame hill crow waddled up to him and, giving him a sympathetic glance, began pecking at the leftover grains. Janak scooped out some more and threw them closer to the bird, almost hitting its head. With an offended caw, it flew away.

Janak, who was called Janak Tularam Bolan according to the village voter's list, never came to the shop this early, but today there was an emergency. And since the legend above his shop, painted boldly with a flourish of decorative font, flanked by two giant, shocking pink roses, announced *Giripul Pink Rose Ladies Tailor*, followed by *Emergency Service Available* in smaller letters, Janak could never refuse a customer, especially a woman. It would not be right and, moreover, what would the village people say.

Once you had written something down, that too in such fancy handwriting costing Rs 150, not including transport for the sign painter who came all the way from Simla, you had to stand by the words. Janak was thankful to the gods that he had not added *Day and Night Service* for an extra fifty rupees, as the painter had suggested.

He dusted the table lightly and then bowed his head to the calendar which had the picture of a smiling Lord Ganesha on it. Muttering a quick prayer, he lifted the cover off his sewing machine and gently stroked the shiny black and gold body like a lover waking up his beloved. With a contented sigh, he fixed a reel of new thread and began to turn the handle, slowly at first, and then with gathering speed. The cinnamon sparrows chattered outside and the water pump behind his shop gurgled as the women came one by one to fill their pots.

Slowly, lane by lane, Giripul awoke. The houses looked up at the sky above the mountains where a few white puffs of cloud played, and then turned their gaze below to survey the fields bathed in fresh summer sunshine. Janak hummed an old film song as he turned the handle of his sewing machine. It was a peaceful morning, and so far he had nothing to worry about. He did not know that this would be his last morning of peace for many months to come.

The air got warmer as the hills slowly turned their faces to stare at the sun. The cinnamon sparrows outside Janak's window were now arguing, unwilling to share their seeds with the pigeons. He could hear Balu the beggar coughing and muttering as he tossed and turned in his shed. The sunlight fell in an arc on Janak's window, and though he did not lift his head from his sewing, he knew one of Lala's boys was peeling a hill of potatoes and throwing them in a tin drum; he could hear the potatoes clank loudly as they fell, like soldiers dying in battle. The huge, battered saucepan for tea had not yet been put on the fire since the first bus would not arrive for an hour. Only the monkeys, the birds and the good hardworking wives of the village went about their business, while most of the men still yawned and struggled to get up. Janak's faithful dog, Tommy, was still asleep under the water tank, though he opened his eyes from time to time to see what his master was up to.

The shop was cold and a ball of damp air clung to the back of Janak's neck like a clammy fist. He wished he could have a cup of tea. A cup of hot masala tea would warm his throat and clear his head of the strange dreams that still hissed in his ears and danced before his eyes. In the bright clear light of morning, however, he was less afraid of them.

Last night he dreamt that his father, who had been missing for twenty-five years, had come and stood by his bed, asking him for a loan of five hundred rupees. It was a small sum, but for some reason Janak had refused. Now he was feeling bad about it. A missing, possibly dead parent asking for money meant you had done something wrong and should ask for forgiveness. But whose forgiveness should he ask for? It was a real worry, adding to various other worries that sat on his shoulders all the time.

He rubbed his eyes and looked out at the quiet street, longing once more for some tea, but he had not dared to wake up his wife before leaving the house. He had sneaked out like a thief at dawn with the half-finished satin blouse.

He knew there were many men in the world who woke up roaring like lions, shouting for their first cup of tea, and then gargling and spitting and cleaning their teeth so noisily that the entire village could hear them, but he was not one of them. When Janak woke up, not even a sparrow took notice, and when he left his house, creeping out of the door like a ghost, the only one who looked at him was his father, from his portrait on the wall. Sometimes he wondered if it was really his father's photograph or a stranger's, which his late mother had found in Raja's Fancy Goods Shop and hung on the wall to impress the neighbours. After all, very few people in Giripul had ever seen his father and the two men who had, were both quite old and senile now. He had never questioned his mother about it, though.

Janak, a frail, gentle man with large eyes, crooked ears and nimble hands, was not the kind of man to question women, especially his wife, Rama, whom he loved more than his life. Let women do what they want. It is the best way to keep peace in the house, he always told himself. He had realized this after watching other men in the village cope with screaming wives and angry mothers and mothers-in-law. If you let women say and do what they wanted, they left you in peace. It was a simple truth, but surprisingly, most men did not seem to understand it.

Many women came to his shop everyday to get new clothes stitched, but they all wanted more than just a

new blouse or kurta. They wanted to unburden their
deepest thoughts. At first it was frightening to listen to
their little secrets, their tiny dreams and hopes. Some
began to cry as they spoke and others laughed without
reason, beating their chests with bits of leftover cloth.
Janak just sat quietly and listened, and over the years he
had got used to them. It was all right as long as you let
them have their say.

But sometimes he worried about what their husbands
or fathers would say if they found out they were talking
like this to him, a tailor – an outsider. So far, no man
in the village had said anything to him and the women
always left the shop with their heads covered, their eyes
modestly cast down as if they had not, only moments ago,
sat on his bench and revealed to him their very soul. So he
let them talk. He did not have to do anything, just listen
and nod, listen and nod. Sometimes he hummed a tune
while they spoke, but they did not seem to like that and
looked at him accusingly. They wanted to hear only their
own voices echo in the tiny shop, so they spoke without
pause, softly and clearly, like the mountain stream. Soon,
he forgot what they said. All he could remember was his
wife Rama's face and her angry abuses.

Janak often wondered about his father's picture. His
mother used to hang a garland of marigolds around the
chipped wooden frame every morning, say a prayer, and
circle the photograph with an incense stick.

Now after her death, he did not feel like continuing with
the garlands and prayers because he did not believe this
man, with mean, close-set eyes and a sharp nose, could be

his father. The garland had withered around the picture, but he did not have the heart to throw it away, nor could he throw the picture away. What if it really was his father? One should always be cautious about such things.

'Be cautious' was Janak's motto in life. He was always treading carefully on the uneven path that life had rolled out for him. His soft, gentle eyes were wary and his body poised to escape in case of danger. He cared only for his sewing machine and his wife. He had been married for three years now and they even had a two-year-old son, yet when he saw her each morning his heart still filled with love and thumped madly against his chest as if he were seeing her for the very first time. He could not take his eyes off her as she walked around the house, doing her chores. Sometimes, when she caught him gaping at her, she hissed at him. How beautiful she looked when her cheeks turned pink with rage. He wanted to hold her tightly in his arms till she cried out breathlessly, 'Tailorji, tailorji, please let me go. People will see!' But so far nothing like that had happened.

His mother had chosen her for him and he had not even known her name until the day of the wedding. He had seen her properly only after they got married, when she came with him to Giripul. She had lifted her veil and looked at the house, but not at him. For the first three months, she had not spoken to him or even sat alone with him, behaving just like a new bride, and then one morning, when his mother was not around, Rama looked him straight in the eye and said, 'Will you have another chapatti?'

That was the moment he fell in love with her. He had not noticed until then how beautiful she was, how lovely her large doe eyes, how tiny her waist and how delicate her rosebud mouth. He was the first man in Giripul to fall in love and he hoped and prayed each day that no one would ever find out his guilty secret. It would bring shame to the memory of his dead mother and missing father. The entire village would think he was mad, falling in love like a modern city man. He would be cast out of Giripul at once. Rama would send him away and he would die of shame as well as a broken heart.

It had been a mistake to write *Emergency Service Available* on his shop signboard, a mistake that had cost him fifty rupees extra. Janak sighed as he carefully pushed the flimsy satin under the needle. This was an important customer, the village headman's third wife. He had promised to finish the blouse for her by Tuesday night and it was Wednesday morning. But she had made the job difficult by buying only seventy centimetres of pink satin, which had arrived by the evening bus from Simla, the last bus that stopped at Giripul. The bundle of satin had arrived, dusty, crushed and smelling of diesel fumes.

'There is only enough cloth here to make half a blouse,' he had told her and thought, just enough to cover your two plump breasts, and may they remain plump by god's grace.

He did not look at her or her gorgeous breasts, but he knew them well because he had measured them just a few months ago. Like two ripe, but not over-ripe mangoes, they had resisted his measuring tape, bouncing about happily inside her blouse.

She had laughed coyly and told him, 'You can do it. You know you can, you are a magician tailorji. Please, please make the cloth stretch.' She had run her bejewelled fingers across her forty-inch chest.

How could he refuse when a woman looked at him like that – all sugar candy and pure milk ghee. So he rummaged through his trunk and found scraps of golden silk left over from a bridal blouse he had stitched last summer, and sat up late at night, stitching strips of golden silk to the pink satin blouse by hand. Thank god his wife had gone to bed early with a headache, otherwise she would surely have had something to say. She always had something to say. When he got home late in the evening, she would say, 'So how many women came to the shop to show you their breasts today?' and then walk away, her long plait dancing like a cobra on her generous hips. Could she not hear his heart thumping in his chest? Could she not feel the storm raging in his heart?

Rama had a high-pitched, nagging voice and her rosebud mouth was always moist and shiny. She had a strange habit of licking her lips as she spoke, as if she was savouring each and every word. Even when she was scolding him for something he had not done, which was usually the case, her mouth looked as juicy as a ripe plum. If only she knew how much he loved her. She was the only woman in this world for him, the rest were just bees that buzzed around in his shop and then flew away.

Janak sighed as he thought of Rama's soft, sullen mouth. He tore the thread off with his teeth and placed the blouse on the table next to the sewing machine. It was almost done, except for the eyes for the hooks which he could do in the afternoon when Rama was having her afternoon siesta.

He hoped she would not be in a bad mood today. Rama's moods were very finely tuned to the waxing and waning of the moon. On full-moon nights she was as gentle as a cow, mooing softly, snuggling up to him, her large black eyes dreamy and soft.

But just as the moon began to shed its roundness, she would get into a bad mood. At first she would be irritable and sullen, with short outbursts of temper. Then as the moon got thinner, her anger would rise to a crescendo and the entire house would be filled with her high-pitched accusations. On some dark, moonless nights she howled like a she-wolf that had lost its cub, her eyes narrow and blazing with rage.

And just when Janak, got used to her moon moods, she changed them. Now the moon affected her moods the other way round. Full-moon nights made her bad tempered while on moonless nights, she became loving and docile – the perfect cow-like wife any man or his mother could wish for.

After their son was born, she had calmed down a bit and she no longer howled on dark nights though her temper was still quite mercurial and Janak never knew what she would say or do. But whether she smiled or scowled, whined like a mosquito or whispered softly in his ear, his love for her grew stronger each day and wrapped itself around him like a tight silk rope. She was his entire world, from the Giri river to the snowcapped peaks. She was the reason he had been born a man and not some insect in this life.

He held up the blouse and the golden sleeves puffed up like wings. The sunlight streamed through the window and the blouse shimmered for a moment as if it was on fire. He placed it flat on the table and pressed the seams down with his hands, thinking for the briefest moment of the magnificent breasts his creation would soon cover.

The tiny, almost invisible stitches would wrap the satin around the third wife and it would be almost as good as embracing her. Not that he would ever do such a terrible thing. Touching another man's wife was a sin, but thinking about it did not harm anyone. After all, he was a man and a man had to think of other possibilities however unlikely.

Janak switched on the old electric iron and after touching it with his fingertips to see if it was working, he began to iron the blouse gently. Rama's face appeared before him and he began to stroke her gently as he moved the hot iron over the blouse, taking care to go over the newly-done stitches firmly. He would make a satin blouse for Rama too, but in a different colour. Women hated it when other women wore the same item of clothing and that was why there were so many clothes shops in the world and thousands of tailors like him catering to the whims of the women.

He was pleased that he had finished the blouse well before anyone in the headman's house was ready to come out. From his window he could see the tall, slate-roofed house, gleaming in the morning sunlight. Two goats nibbled a paper bag near the verandah and the headman's pajamas swayed on the clothesline. Someone must have forgotten to take them in last night and now they would be damp with the early morning dew. The third wife was obviously not doing her household chores properly.

All beautiful women were like that; if you wanted good household service, you should marry a plain woman. Anyway, it was too late for Janak. He was only a poor tailor with a small house and he could barely afford one wife, though it would be nice to have a plain wife to do the chores efficiently, as well as a beautiful one to admire, love and hold in your arms. His wife Rama belonged in the second category – women who forgot to bring the washing in – and Janak often wore a damp, dew-drenched kurta at night.

In Giripul, tucked into a corner of the mountain range that surrounded Simla, all the houses looked into each other from some door or window. Like old friends they stood side by side with their arms around each other, whispering, quarrelling and sharing secrets all day and night, through the seasons. All the children knew each other from the time they were born and called every woman 'didi' or 'chachi'. When a new bride came to live in Giripul, she was called 'bhabhi' by all the children and 'beti' by all the older men, even those whose greedy eyes followed her swaying hips.

Janak's house was one of the smallest in Giripul, but it had a backyard that opened out into the forest. While most of Giripul had sloping fields, Janak was fortunate to possess a flat piece of land, a precious luxury in the hills. He had gradually cleared out a large area, by digging out strips of forest land that actually belonged to the government. This vast, illegal patch, unevenly cut like a badly-fitting blouse, was once used by his mother to grow vegetables in spring and summer. She wanted to sell them from his shop, but he did not want the newly-stitched clothes to be stained by damp spinach and muddy potatoes and they had often argued over this.

After she died, he felt sorry he had not allowed her to sell vegetables from his shop. He wished he could call her back and say, 'Ma, here is a new table. You can put all your vegetables on this now. I do not mind if my clothes get muddy,' but it was too late. You cannot call back the dead and apologize for all the things you have or have not said to them. There would be so much traffic going to and fro from heaven and earth. The gods would not like it.

Now the garden he had stolen from the government-owned forest was a desolate patch where jackals sometimes came and sat in a circle and howled at the moon. His wife had no interest in growing vegetables, but she liked watching the jackals and sometimes left food for them which they never ate. He told her the jackals did not like vegetable curry and only ate raw meat, but she did not believe him. Janak was afraid she would start howling with them on her bad nights, but thank god she never did, except on one bad night, when she screamed the house down and the jackals howled back from the forest. He still got gooseflesh thinking of her shrill cries echoing all over Giripul. People must have thought he was beating his wife.

He could not imagine any man doing that. The thought of even scolding Rama made his stomach ache and his breathing became faster. If the village people knew how much he loved his wife, they would think he was possessed by a mind-eating magical spirit and needed to go to a faith healer like Bengali Baba. In Giripul, a man could show his love for his parents, his land, his sons or his cattle, but to love one's wife openly was something no one ever did. It would be a shameful scandal and your name would be mud.

Janak dropped the iron on the table with a loud crash. He stared out of the window, shock and horror on his face. Rama, his beloved wife was in a strange man's arms. They were kissing with abandon. They were kissing right in front of his eyes, standing shamelessly in the house across the street from his shop. Rama was wearing her blue suit, the one he had just stitched for her last week. How ... Why? Janak felt a sharp pain in his heart. 'Rama... Rama...' he tried to shout, but no sound came out of his throat. His feet were slowly sinking into the ground. Suddenly, he could smell smoke and looked down. The iron had singed a patch of cloth on the table and he quickly picked it up. When he looked out of the window again, Rama was not there. There was no one, except a blue suit hanging in the courtyard of the house facing the shop. He picked up the blouse and began ironing again. The tiny room was filled with the smell of burnt cloth. 'I must stop seeing Rama everywhere,' Janak said loudly to himself.

Giripul had twenty-one houses, if you included the ruined, haunted house where the beautiful English lady ghosts danced and played with their dogs. They said, there were more dog ghosts than human ones and that was why no dog from Giripul would go near the house, even if you were to throw a dead goat inside. No one had ever done it, of course, what with meat being so expensive, but everyone believed the story. You had to believe stories about ghosts, lest they felt offended and haunted you. Everyone in the village had a good ghost story to tell about the house or its wild garden where the plum trees still gave the sweetest fruit. Janak's mother used to say the fruits were made sweet by the English ladies' tears. How plums could be made sweet by tears that were salty, Janak did not know, but he believed her and so did the rest of the village.

Four hours away from Simla, Giripul was neither a village nor a small town, but an odd, in-between place, where dozens of paths ran down the high mountains to merge like lines in an intricate embroidery. There was a main street, uneven and dotted with potholes, and the doors of all the houses opened onto this street. Ever since the old bridge over the Giri had been made pucca, buses came rattling up from Kalka and Simla, giving Giripul a fleeting sense of importance. Three times a day they disgorged dusty, weary, bandy-legged passengers out on the main road right outside the three main shops of Giripul. There was Lala's tea shop which served aloo pakoras, fish curry and rice, but only between noon and two. Lala also served home-brewed jaggery wine, but only to the residents of Giripul, who were allowed to sleep on the long wooden benches for as long as they liked or until their wives came to take them home.

Next to Janak's ladies' tailor shop was Raja's shop, which stocked rice, lentils, jaggery, mustard oil, chappals, incense sticks, soap, matchboxes, notebooks, pencils, betel nuts, rope, chalk, slates, birdseed, and a few odd things that only the bus passengers needed but no one in Giripul ever bought. City things like bread, cold cream, potato chips and bras.

The women of Giripul flocked to this shop every afternoon to buy ribbons, bindis, kajal and jasmine talcum powder. They paid furtively, taking the notes out from their blouses and quickly hiding what they had bought in the folds of their duppattas. It took them months to save the money, pinching loose change from their husbands' shirt pockets before they washed them. They had to be as quiet as pickpockets because their husbands did not like them spending money on useless city things.

Three buses stopped at Giripul at three-hour intervals and people would set their time by these buses, though they were usually late. Janak opened his shop with the arrival of the morning bus, expect on emergency days, like today, when he had come to the shop at dawn. Raja came to his shop only when the noon bus arrived and so did Lala, though he was up and about at dawn, ordering his servant boys to peel potatoes, chop onions and knead a huge bucket of dough for chapattis.

At three-hour intervals, the sleepy, lopsided village perched on the bend in the river would be shaken out of its stupor and voices would rise, people would run about for no reason, and a hidden radio would blare out film songs. Dogs would bark endlessly and old men would come out of nowhere to cross the road. When the bus left, its musical horn honking out a loud farewell, Giripul would sink back into slumber.

How Giripul became the main bus stop no one knew, since there were quite a few villages on the road to Simla where the bus stopped, though only for a minute or two. Raja's uncle said that Giripul became a main bus stop because of the bridge, that stretched shakily across the river, linking the two mountains. He also said that many years ago people had to cross the river by boat and they often drowned, though no one really believed him because it was such a shallow river.

'It was very deep when I was a boy,' he insisted, thumping his stick on the ground angrily.

Later, a wooden bridge was built by the English sahibs who came to the river to catch fish. One of them drowned, according to Raja's old uncle. 'He wanted to catch the biggest fish and the Giri river took him along to the sea where the biggest fish in the world lived,' he said with a crooked smile.

A small stone temple was soon built under the bridge by the village people to make peace with the river goddess, and bus drivers stopped there to throw coins to the idol, which was made up of battered tin boxes cut into the shape of a woman. So first came the bridge, then the temple, and then Giripul became the main bus stop.

Not everyone agreed with this reason for Giripul's fame. Some of the villagers said it was the heady aroma of Lala's fish curry that made the bus drivers stop and it soon became a habit, even with the vegetarian drivers who ate only cucumbers with black salt at the shop. Whatever the reason, the people of Giripul were happy that their village had been chosen as the main bus stop and all the other villages were very envious of them. Gradually Giripul would become a bigger village and, who knows, maybe a town, with cement-roofed houses, a hotel with glass windows, and a cinema hall of its own.

The second bus came rumbling into Giripul as the afternoon sun rose high above the hills and shadows appeared under the pine trees. Flocks of parakeets flew in waves across the sky and occasionally swooped down the hillside to search for wild berries that grew on shrubs tucked behind the rocks. On the tall pine tree behind Janak's shop, a pair of spotted owlets woke up, stared briefly at the ground, their large yellow eyes alert and wary, and then glided deeper into the forest to seek quieter, shadier spots for their day-long rest.

Janak folded the blouse and placed it carefully on the shelf. He lit an incense stick and, after waving it about, placed it under the calendar with Ganesha's picture on it. It was torn at the edge and was dated 1988, but Janak's mother had insisted on hanging it in the shop because she thought it was lucky for them. Janak had bought her a very handsome brass Ganesha figure with an umbrella that lit up when you pressed a button, but she preferred the calendar. Now she was dead and he could not remove the calendar. It would certainly offend her soul. Once people were dead you had to respect their wishes, whatever happened.

He was amazed that till this day none of his customers had noticed the year. Very often he would look at the old calendar with a frown and say, 'I cannot give your kameez on the nineteenth. See, that is only three days away,' and the women would nod and look impressed. The older women, of course, could not read, but the younger ones had been to school – they should have noticed that the calendar was almost twenty years old. Women were like that. They noticed little things like burps and farts, when you looked at another woman, what you had promised them five years ago, but they ignored important facts like dates, time and measurements.

Janak, being the only ladies' tailor in Giripul, was very much in demand not only in his own village, but also in the neighbouring villages. Women from the villages perched on the highest ridge of the mountains walked down to his shop, carrying bundles of material on their heads. The reason why he was so popular was not only because he was a skilled tailor who could sew intricate salwar suits in the latest fashion, but because the men trusted him with their wives and daughters. They knew he would not take any liberties when he was measuring them, like tailors did in other villages. If only they knew what wicked thoughts churned in his mind when he strung the measuring tape around the women's chests. But Janak always kept his eyes modestly downcast even when some of the young girls giggled and pretended to be ticklish when he measured their waists. How easy it would be to give them a gentle pinch.

Girls of today were not what they used to be in his youth. How bold they had become. Travelling alone by bus, talking to boys on the street, looking straight into their eyes and laughing loudly without caring who saw or heard them. His mother and wife had never been anywhere alone and he was sure that if he'd had a daughter he would not have allowed her to travel by bus alone either. Even if she sulked and argued he would just not allow it. One had to be firm with women in these matters – whether they listen to you or not.

Janak got up from the chair and folded his hands in a namaste to the sky. He did this a few times each day, in case a passing god was looking down at Giripul. It also helped to soothe his free-floating anxious thoughts.

After Janak's father disappeared, for almost a year his mother had waited for him everyday, putting his string cot out and placing a plate with food and a glass of water next to it. The crows would swoop down to eat the food and the cats would lap up the water, yet she did it day after day.

When she died, her sisters dressed her like a bride though her husband had not been seen for twenty years, because she could not officially be declared a widow without a dead husband who had been properly cremated with all the religious rites.

'You are not a widow unless you produce a dead husband's body,' said the head priest and Janak's mother agreed.

Some people in the village said that a gypsy woman had lured his father away and some said a bear had hugged him to death. A woodcutter said just last year that he had seen him in the forest, an old man with long white hair, talking to the trees. Janak and his mother had consulted the Shadow Chaser – the great Bengali Baba – but he said he could do nothing to help.

'Your father is neither late nor living, so it is beyond my powers, my son. I only deal with dead spirits who are lost, not with real bodies who have disappeared,' he said, and gave Janak some incense to burn, free of cost. 'It will clear his room of any shadows that may be thinking of taking up residence there, seeing it is unoccupied. Best to be prepared.'

Janak feared he would wake up one morning and find his father sitting on the cot that still sat outside the house. He would demand his food and Janak, being the only son, would have to look after him. His wife would not like it, but it was his duty and he would always do his duty, come what may.

He saw himself lying on the floor, his body covered with marigold garlands. One by one the village people came to pay their last respects to him. 'This was a man who did his duty,' they said, as they filed past his body. The women sat outside, many of them wearing the suits he had stitched for them with such loving care, each hook perfect, each seam as straight as an arrow. They shook their heads and said in a sad tone, 'He was a good tailor and did his duty.' Yes, when he would die, they would all say that about him.

Maybe he could get that written on a piece of pine wood in neat letters. It would not cost more than fifty rupees if he kept the size small. There was no need to add any fancy writing or flowers since it was a solemn sign to make people think about him long after he had gone. Maybe he could give it to his son, with instructions to put it under his photograph, garlanded with fresh marigolds and lit with incense sticks. But his son was only two and might not understand all these instructions. He would have to think of some other plan to ensure that the signboard was placed properly and given due respect.

The sun was now behind the headman's house, and cast a dull glow on the white walls. A pumpkin vine trailed over the roof and giant pumpkins sat on the slates like green footballs. Janak could see his friend Shankar, coming up from the river bank, carrying a basket full of fish that still looked alive. Any minute now, Lala would meet him at the top of the street, near the big elephant-shaped rock, and they would begin their daily haggling. Shankar kept trying to sell the afternoon bus passengers the biggest fish he had caught, but Lala would not allow him to do that. Everyday they argued and struggled, each trying to pull the biggest fish out of the basket.

Once, they had both rolled down the hillside, Lala clutching a giant mahseer fish by its head and Shankar grabbing it by the tail. The news about the mighty fish soon spread through the village and everyone rushed to the river and placed bets to see who would win. Lala made off with the fish as usual and Shankar retired hurt to Janak's shop. All through summer and spring, this battle for fish continued, stopping only when the fishing season ended, when the rains filled up the river and the fish hid in the deep, muddy pools.

Not once had Shankar managed to get past Lala, no matter how early he came up from the river. He had once tried to avoid confrontation by coming up another path, but had slipped all the way downhill and the fish, still breathing, fell back into the river, much to their surprise and joy.

This was not the only problem Shankar had to face. His wife was a strict vegetarian and would not allow him into the house till he had bathed and changed his clothes. So he kept a set of clothes in Janak's shop and went there to change after fishing and battling with Lala. He was always exhausted, even before the day had begun, and would mutter all day to himself about giving up fishing and finding a new profession.

But Janak knew it was not easy to change your calling in Giripul. If your father was a woodcutter or a fisherman, you had to grow up and be a woodcutter or a fisherman.

Raja's father had been a shopkeeper and Shankar's father, a fisherman. Janak was fortunate that his father, who had been a farmer, had disappeared, leaving Janak free to choose his own calling. He could never have become such a famous tailor if his father had been around. He would be ploughing fields all day long and planting potatoes, ginger and corn.

The sun had moved to the second-highest peak so Janak knew it was almost noon. The street was crowded with people, some residents, others passengers who had just got off the bus. They would have a quick cup of tea at Lala's shop and start walking to the remote villages on the higher mountains where they lived. With them would go all the gossip and news of Giripul and the other villages situated closer to the road. Many of them were Janak's customers and would be carrying newly-stitched blouses and petticoats for their women. Janak had never seen these women, but he knew their measurements quite well and was told by their husbands that the fitting was always perfect.

Janak put the iron back on the shelf, stretched and raised his hands above his head, yawning. He could see Shankar coming out of Lala's shop. Shankar and Janak had grown up together, they had gone to the same school on top of the hill, Shankar always trailing behind, taking short clumsy steps with his bandy legs. They were married to girls from the same village across the river. Their sons were the same age too, and lived together like brothers. In fact, Janak's son often slept in Shankar's house and had to be forced to come home in the morning. Sometimes Janak thought that his son liked Shankar's wife more than his own mother, but he never dared to say this aloud. Rama would thrash them both.

Shankar often sat in the shop with him while he hemmed a kurta or turned the neckline of a blouse. These tasks did not require too much attention and Janak liked having someone to talk to, but only a man, not a woman.

You could not stitch a button or do even a simple running stitch when you were talking to a woman. You might say or not say something, and then there would be hell to pay. One day he had made the mistake of saying 'yes' while biting the thread off a blouse he was hemming, and Rama had hit him with a rolling pin. He still did not know what he had said wrong.

Shankar did not say much and brooded most of the time, but he was a good listener. He always said yes and no at the right time, encouraging one to talk freely. Though occasionally, he would get into a talkative mood, and then he talked and talked until he fell down, exhausted. After that he would be silent for days. Janak felt that there was something locked deep inside Shankar, trying to come out. It was like the scorpions they used to trap in matchboxes when they were boys. They would lie curled up and absolutely still, as if dead, and then suddenly jump out and give everyone a fright.

Janak's and Shankar's conversations were, and had been since boyhood, about women.

'I measure them everyday, feel the soft flesh on their neck, arms, breasts, waist and hips, feel the bones on their wrists and ankles, but I do not know what goes on in their heads,' Janak would often say. Shankar's replies were always the same, unless he was in a talkative mood. On silent days he only grunted or nodded his head.

'What do you think? Am I right?' Janak would prod.

'Yes,' Shankar would say.

'What do these women think of us? Do they really have any feelings for us?'

'No.'

'They say you must look them straight in the eye to understand them.'

'Yes.'

'But I cannot look them in the eye, I could not even look my own mother in the eye. I get a funny feeling in my forehead, you know, as if someone was tickling me there. Do you get it too?'

'No.'

No matter how close he was to Shankar, Janak never dared to confess his secret love for Rama. Shankar would be shocked and, worse, might tell Raja and Lala about his passion for his wife. He would become the laughing stock of the village.

But it was Shankar he confided in when the third wife confessed her strange, frightening dreams to him. He had tried not to think about it at all, hoping her dreams would vanish if he ignored them. But today, as he looked at her satin blouse peering out of the shelf, he suddenly felt he had to tell someone. Of course, a week later he would regret it, but how could he have known that Giripul was going to be shaken and his life would be upturned like a newly-ploughed field?

'I must tell you about the headman's wife,' said Janak, watching his friend carefully. 'You know, the pretty, third one. You are the only person I can tell this to, since I know you will never breathe a word to anyone.'

'No,' said Shankar, and looked up. His tiny eyes suddenly began to gleam and his nose seemed to be twitching like a tiger sniffing prey.

Later, Janak thought that he should have been warned by that nose and that look, but he ignored it and carried on. 'Yesterday she came to me with this pink satin cloth – only seventy centimetres, too small for a full-sleeve blouse, and after she had explained to me what kind of neckline she wanted, she sat down. "I do not need to measure you, sister, you have only gained some weight on your arms and I can adjust the seam accordingly," I said, but she kept sitting and staring at the wall, looking at the Ganesha picture on my calendar. I thought she was praying or thinking about God and life. You know, something noble like that. Her eyes were not blinking at all. That always means women are thinking serious thoughts.

'Then she spoke. "I want to tell you something, tailorji, since you are a decent man and will not tell anyone else. Last night, I dreamt that I killed my husband, the headman, chopped his head off with the new grass cutter," she said, her eyes glittering with fear.

'"Our handsome headman will not look good without his head," I said, but she did not laugh. She picked a thread from a newly-stitched blouse, but I let her. This was a serious matter, I realized, and I could redo the blouse later.

'"This is the seventh time I have had this dream. My mother, who knows about these things, says a dream that comes more than three times always comes true," she said, tears glinting in her pretty eyes.

'"Better wear the pink blouse quickly before you become a widow," was all I could say to make her feel better. Did I say the wrong thing?'

'Yes,' said Shankar. Then he put on his clean, non-fish-smelling shirt, and went outside.

The third bus had arrived in a cloud of dust. The invisible radio began to sing. Janak looked out, and to his amazement he saw his wife's mother get off the bus. Her head was covered with a white shawl, the same one he had bought his wife last winter from the Simla fair. She was clutching a big cloth bundle. The old witch had come to stay, that too without warning. Her scrawny arms stuck out of her loose white blouse like an old chicken's feet. And then she turned and he saw the brass cage gleaming in her hand.

Janak got up from his sewing machine and peered out of the window. She had brought her bald parakeet along. That meant she would stay for a month or more and eat him out of house and home.

'I never eat in my daughter's house,' she would say in that glass-breaking, sharp voice of hers, and slap ten rupees down on the table. Ten rupees for ten cups of tea in a day, half a kilo rice, dal, vegetables, papad, dollops of pickle, a big bowl of dahi and at least three pieces of mithai, along with endless supari. Ten rupees was all she paid for this. Not that he wanted her money. The old hag and her wretched parakeet – parasites, the two of them. How such an ugly woman had produced a beautiful daughter like Rama, he would never know. Maybe she was adopted. Janak hoped she was, because he could not bear the thought that his beloved wife with her rosebud mouth would one day become a scrawny chicken. Sometimes, on the days when her mood was foul, a mean glint would flash in her eyes or she would twist her neck in a strange way, and the startling similarity between mother and daughter would give Janak a terrible fright.

Janak rose, squared his shoulders and went out to meet his old enemy. The third bus rolled away, leaving behind a black trail of fumes. The village dogs chased it, barking loudly. The light changed as the sun rose higher above the hills and the ill-fated pink satin blouse with golden sleeves lay quietly on the table, waiting for a murder to take place.

2

More worries for Janak; Headman brings pink satin for secret suit; Balu the beggar reads an uncertain future in the truck legend

For years no one saw the pale, silver-eyed child. He seemed to merge like a lizard into the white, lime-washed walls of the hut during the day, and at night he burrowed into a pile of old quilts stored in the loft. The women of the house fed him from time to time and because he cried very rarely, they often forgot to feed him. Yet he grew.

A year passed and then another. He grew quietly, like a weed, drawing sustenance from the rainwater that gathered in the window sill, from the shreds of discarded fruit and roti that the mice brought into the loft, and gradually he became quite strong.

Sometimes he crawled to the door but the men shouted at him and he got frightened, not by their loud voices, but by the strong sunlight that almost blinded him. His father's new wife cursed him every morning and prayed to the gods to take him away.

His dead mother's family sent him some old clothes and came every few months to see if he was still alive. His grandmother had come once. She threw hot water on him to clean him, chanting prayers all the time. She made sure her hands did not touch him.

Most people in the village had forgotten about him, though sometimes the children peered into the hut to gape at him. If he happened to be near the window, they threw stones at him, which made him laugh, even when they hit him. He waved his pale arms at them and they ran away, shouting, 'Ghost's shit ... devil's baby!'

By the time he was six, he had grown quite tall and greedily ate all the food that was thrown at him. The men laughed when he jumped up to snatch away the scraps thrown to the dogs. 'He eats like a mule. Make him work like one,' said the women, so his uncles showed him how to clean the cowshed, and soon he was sleeping there every night. When everyone in the house was asleep, he would go out and look at the mountains, and inhale the scent of the night sky. The owls would hoot and he would hoot back at them. Once, he walked to the edge of the forest but quickly ran back when he heard the jackals howl. He did not try to mimic them.

Though no one spoke to him, he learnt to talk by listening to the people in the house, repeating each word till he knew it by heart. From his corner in the cowshed, he watched the women in the house carefully. By the time he was seven, he could sweep the house, though the broom was bigger than him, and he could wash the dishes and light the fire. They did not let him come into the kitchen because that would pollute the food they were cooking, but he was allowed to stay in the courtyard and wash their clothes and clean their shoes.

The cowshed was his entire world. He knew the markings on every beam, every crack in the wall, every hole in the stone floor. The broom and the bucket of cow dung were his toys and he often pretended they were alive. The cows loved his small, soft hands stroking their heads, and allowed him to milk them without making a fuss. He talked to them as he took thorns out of their ears and cleaned their hooves with water. He milked them at dawn and carried the pails into the house one by one, never spilling a drop. He took care no one saw him. His grandmother left thick chapattis with some dal on the steps for him and he ate them as fast as he could. As the sun rose, he crept back into the cowshed and stayed hidden in his dark corner. He had not been given a name and no one thought he needed one.

Janak's house, which perched lopsidedly on the left side of the hill, where the land was studded with glistening mica rocks, had been built by his father just before he vanished into the forest. It was as if he had set himself a target: finish the house and disappear. He did not even wait for the house-blessing ceremony, his mother had lamented to Janak everyday until she died.

'I had to explain his absence to the entire village and make the arrangements for the ceremony all alone. I had to peel an entire sack of potatoes with my own two hands, grind the masala all by myself. And there was no corpse lying in the courtyard, to bring sympathy to my aching soul either. They all came and ate, but none offered any comfort. How could they? Did they know for sure whether he was dead or just visiting the next village? Oh, your father did me great injustice by disappearing like that. Men leave their wives, it happens all the time, but they tell you and go. Then the wife gets the sympathy of the entire village. Men also became sadhus, but they announce it to the whole world. And everyone respects thier wives then. No one just vanishes like this, and on the very day I needed help with the potatoes,' she said as she served Janak dinner every evening.

Janak was not sure what had offended his mother more, her husband absconding, having to peel a sack of potatoes by herself, or the lack of a dead body to cremate with full rites. It was a combination of all three, probably. It was difficult, Janak realized, for her to be suspended like this, neither widow nor wife.

For years he had watched his mother pace up and down, trying to decide whether to wear white and take off her gold bangles or to stay in a coloured sari and wear a bindi, in case her husband turned up suddenly and took offence when he saw her wearing white. It was a very bad omen if a husband saw his wife as a widow while he was still alive. It could strike him dead at once.

After ten years, Janak's mother decided to be a widow on alternate days, but she continued to complain to Janak about her half-wife-half-widow state till her dying day. Even when they laid her out on her funeral pyre, dressed in a red sari like a bride, Janak could read the disapproval on her face. That face stayed with him

long after the flames had burnt her body to ashes but
now, oddly enough, for the last one month, when he
remembered his mother, he always saw her dressed in
a widow's white sari, a gentle smile on her face. He did
not remember her smiling at him like that when she was
alive. Maybe after she had died and gone to heaven, she
met his father and was now happy and content because
she knew for sure that her husband was definitely and
irrevocably dead.

The house too had never got over this betrayal by
its owner, and over the years, it had acquired a moody,
sullen outlook which changed everyday like his late
mother's saris and his young wife's temper. On some
days it looked open, sunny and brimming with good
humour. The windows winked at him like old friends
when he went out into the street, the steps shone, the
doors smiled and gently creaked a fond farewell.

But the very next day its mood changed. The walls
darkened at noon, the windows glowered, and the doors
mumbled abuses over and over again as they slammed
shut on their own. When Janak sneaked into his room
quietly, taking care not to upset the house, the floor
trembled under his feet in anger and the walls caved
in, trying to suffocate him. The red and green glass
panes on the window, so cheerful just a few hours ago,
crackled with malice. He ran out, afraid the house would
fall down on him and crush him to death, but nothing
ever happened and he went inside again, feeling foolish.
Only Tommy felt this sudden change in the house's mood
and refused to enter the house on bad days. He stayed in

the backyard, whimpering. His wife and little son never seemed to notice anything at all.

Over the years, Janak had learnt to ignore it, but he checked the walls and the windows carefully every morning to gauge their mood, just as he examined his wife's face as soon as he woke up to check what kind of a day he would have. If her eyebrows were curved smoothly like a new moon, he knew she would be sweet and mellow, and may even smile at him, but if her eyebrows met across the bridge of her nose, like two dark, hairy caterpillars about to mate, he knew he had better come back home quietly in the evening to avoid being thrashed with a broom or a rolling pin, whichever was handy.

The jungle crows called from the pine tree as Janak walked slowly towards his shop, followed by Tommy. The monkeys were not around today, maybe they had found an orchard of ripe fruit to raid, or a field of potatoes. The poor farmer would wake up to find his crop destroyed.

Life was so uncertain, each day bringing surges of joy or fear or horror. You could win the lottery or be run over by a bus. A mad man might throw a brick at you as you leave the house or you could receive a letter from the bank asking for repayment of a long forgotten debt.

The shop was not far and Janak stopped to look up at the clouds floating in from the north, hoping they would bring rain. The fields were dry and the spring near his house had run dry over the past one week. The gods would have to send a few showers and maybe it would also improve Rama's mood.

Everything around him waxed and waned: the moon, the clouds, the street dogs, the river, his house, his wife. Only his beloved sewing machine remained calm and untouched by the rise and fall of tides. The mountains around Giripul stayed still too, just as they had done for thousands of years, and the dense deodar forest stood like a calm sea of green. The higher hills of Simla gleamed far away, turning white in winter, and the fields changed their colours with the seasons, but he knew exactly what they would do, unlike his house and his wife.

In winter the ground around his house was dull brown, with a few clumps of yellow grass, but in spring, hundreds of wild flowers came up to cover the hills. By the time summer arrived, the entire hillside was emerald green, and every shrub weighed down by wild fruit and berries. Huge blue and green butterflies floated around his house and sometimes came into the shop and settled on a brightly coloured piece of cloth. The air was fragrant with a musky smell that stayed in the head long after summer had gone. This year summer had come early and the hillsides had quickly got ready with their new colours. There was so much grass everywhere that the women did not have to climb to the higher peaks to cut grass for the cattle. They could just stroll to the edge of the hill near the bridge and find tall stalks with juicy stems and soft tips, which the cows loved.

Life was easy during summer and the women had spare time to indulge in idle gossip. That was why they kept coming to the shop with scraps of cloth and fancy trimmings. Summer came only for two months in Giripul, and once the warm sunlit days, when everyone had so much time on their hands, were over, the women would calm down. The cold would make their minds quieter and they would think only of feeding the cattle, keeping their homes warm and their children safe from the bitter cold. Maybe it was all right to let them have a little happiness for a month or two.

Janak stood in front of the shop, admiring the sign glistening in the gentle sunshine. One day he would have a bigger shop where he and his son would sit side by side and work on brand new sewing machines.

He said a quick prayer and opened the shutters. A pigeon, not his favourite one, flew out from its roost on top of the shutter as Janak took his slippers off and entered the shop. Everything was neat and clean and a faint scent of dried roses and machine-oil hung in the air. He took the cover off his sewing machine, gave it a gentle pat and began to thread the needle. The scent of stale roses, for some reason, suddenly jolted his memory and he remembered how last month Channa barber's wife had turned up at the shop and insisted on telling him about her aches and pains. She had lifted her kurta and showed him her pale gold belly button, and then looked at him with pleading eyes, like a cow about to give birth. Why had she done that? What did she want him to do? He was not a vaid or healer. He was not Bengali Baba, the Shadow Chaser. He was just Janak – the only ladies' tailor in Giripul.

It had been a difficult moment. All he could do that day was nod and tell her to drink hot water with fennel and then he had taken her measurements.

She had gone away looking quite pleased, but after a few days she had sent her two sisters, who were visiting her from a village on top of the mountain. They told him that they got bad headaches and always woke up with a strange singing in their ears. Both were very pretty girls, with healthy, plump hips and rosy cheeks, like all the women in that village on top of the mountain. He took their pulse like he had seen the vaid do and they giggled happily. Then they selected some blue cotton for a salwar kameez, asked him to edge the sleeves and neckline with pink piping, and left. Janak sat and watched them for a long time as they raced up the hillside like two young mountain goats, their dupattas streaming in the warm summer breeze. Yes, now he remembered, there had been a strong scent of roses floating in the air that day.

After working for a while, Janak came out of the shop to see if the first bus had arrived. As soon as he stepped out, the lame hill crow came out of its hollow under the mulberry tree and Tommy began to bark. Janak stepped carefully over the lemon and green chillies someone had thrown on the street not far from the mulberry tree. Tommy and the hill crow did the same. They knew these were used to ward off the evil eye and one must never step on them. Lala was always doing this to protect his tea shop, which made a lot of money now. The bus drivers ate there and even packed huge tiffin boxes to take back with them to Simla. Lala was now talking about building a bigger tea shop, which he was going to call 'The Giripul Standard Hotel and Tea Shop'. Janak and Shankar were worried he might stop giving them tea on credit then. Fortunately, it was still at the talking stage and nothing had really been planned. He had not even called the signboard painter as yet, so Janak knew it would take a long time for Lala's hotel to be built.

Janak took out a stale chapatti from his pocket and gave Tommy a few pieces. Then he broke some smaller pieces and put them in front of the lame hill crow. Tommy ate his share in a gulp and watched the hill crow's pieces hungrily but he did not come forward. He knew his chapatti had to be shared with this bird. Why, he did not know, but Janak wanted it this way and Tommy had to obey. Balu the beggar fed this bird too, giving it tasty titbits from the food the people of the village gave him.

Just as Tommy gulped down his chapatti, a loud bang went off over his head. He jumped back, almost choking. Janak too was startled. A gun shot! He quickly ran inside and shut the door, making sure Tommy was safely with him. The shot seemed to have come from Lala's tea shop. Janak opened the door just an inch and peered out cautiously. A group of old men were playing cards as usual. They had not heard the gunshot it seemed, but then, they were all quite deaf. As Janak watched, hidden behind the door, sweat pouring down his face, Lala appeared on the verandah of the tea shop. He carried a country rifle and was very drunk.

'Bastard! Stealing my sugar! I will not let you get away this time,' he shouted, waving the gun in the air, trying to focus his bloodshot eyes. He was staring at Janak's shop.

'Lala ... Lala, my friend, I have never stolen your sugar. Please, please, put the gun down before someone gets hurt,' Janak shouted from behind the door. He suddenly saw bodies lying all over the tea shop. The four old men, shot through the head, the playing cards strewn over their blood-splattered bodies.

'What? How dare you argue with me, you old monkey! You sugar thief!' he yelled, aiming his gun towards the sky.

Janak realized that Lala was not looking at his shop, but at the roof. He heard a noise and knew, at once, the old monkey, the leader of the pack, was sitting there. He must have stolen sugar from Lala's storehouse.

Janak took a deep breath and opened the door. Tommy whimpered as he watched him step out to face Lala. A drunk man with a gun is more dangerous than a she-bear with cubs, he tried to warn Janak.

'Lala, calm down,' said Janak, walking very slowly towards the shop. The country-made rifle could go off on its own any minute and injure him badly, but he had to control Lala. 'Give me courage, oh devi,' he muttered as he went near Lala.

Lala looked at him with surprise. Then he slumped down on the road, the gun beside him, and began to wail.

'Oh Janak, save me from this dacoit. He has taken all my sugar stock in one swoop. I am a cursed man, a poor man now. You know how much sugar costs now

in the black market. Thief! Bandit monkey! Kill him!'
he sobbed.

Janak sat down next to him. He patted him gently,
taking care not to thump his back too hard or to startle
him. You had to be very careful with a drunk man,
especially a drunk man with a loaded gun who believed
he had been robbed.

'There, look … the monkey. Look, he has not taken any
sugar. His hands are empty,' he said in a soothing voice.
Fortunately, the old monkey had licked all the sugar off
his hands and now sat glaring at them. As Lala lifted his
head to glare back at the monkey, Janak quietly picked up
the gun and placed it under a stone, pointing it towards
the hills. He did not know how to handle a gun and hoped
it would not suddenly go off. When he turned around,
he found Lala fast asleep, his head resting on a sack of
potatoes. The old monkey gave a snort and bounded
away while the men continued to play cards.

Janak and Tommy sat on the steps waiting for Lala to
wake up, and put the gun away safely into its wooden box.
These guns, made by a blacksmith in the neighbouring
village, using bits of scrap metal, old pipes, gunpowder
and wood, were very dangerous. Only Lala and the
headman knew how to use them. They often went out into
the forest to shoot jungle fowls and partridges and loud
gunshots would shatter the peace of the village at odd
hours. Janak hated these guns and so did the monkeys.
He felt a surge of anger as he watched Lala snoring, his
mouth wide open, the lethal gun lying innocently next to
him. He would sleep till the effect of the rum wore off.

Janak could hear Balu chanting his prayers in the shed, unaware of the danger outside his door.

'Life is a deep, dark ocean where your ship can sink anytime,' he muttered to Tommy. Neither he nor Tommy had ever seen the ocean, nor had anyone in the village, but they knew it existed because the Goddess often swam in it and Hanuman had flown over it to Lanka. People of Giripul had not seen many things: oceans, straight roads, aeroplanes, mango trees or ice cream, but they knew about all these strange and wonderful things.

Balu was a self-made beggar who had once been a farmer with twenty bigha of fertile, terraced land that gave a rich harvest of mustard, potatoes and corn every year. He used to give his fields out to landless villagers on 'adhai', which meant they would give him half the crop they grew. Balu would sit all day in the tea shop and tell people stories about the old days, when Giripul was part of the great forest. Like the oldest man in Giripul, Balu remembered the days before the bridge was built and the drowning of the English fisherman. And he knew interesting stories about wild animals, ghosts and tiger-hunters.

Then fate, which does not like to see people content and sipping tea all day, struck him a cruel blow. He lost everything he owned: his home, his wife and his land. It was then that he decided to give away the rest of his possessions and become a beggar. He built himself a shed with a battered tin sheet, four cardboard boxes and two old truck tyres cut into neat strips. He found a sturdy wooden packing case which he made into a door by tying it with some wire and cattle rope with bells attached to it. When he opened the door it sounded as if the cows were coming home.

The shed was small but comfortable and everything was within reach. Not that there was much to reach for. All that he kept from his old life were an old radio and his wedding photograph, and on the tin roof, which was surprisingly solid, he kept a flower pot with a tulsi his wife had planted long ago.

The people in the village said he had a lot of money in a bank in Simla, but no one ever saw him leave Giripul to get any money or give money to anyone.

Once he had recovered from the slap of fate and become a beggar, Balu worked out a perfect plan to deal with the uncertainties of life. Every morning when he woke up, he looked through the chinks in his packing-case door to see what was written on the back of the truck parked near his shed that day. If the legend said *Ma ka ashirwad*, it meant he would get a proper meal today, just the kind he liked, so he should go and wait outside. If the truck legend said *Duniya matlab ki*, he would curl up and go back to sleep. On the days when there were no trucks, Balu would stay in his shed, talking to himself.

People passing his shed swore they heard many different voices within, laughing and chatting, but they never saw anyone come out. It was yet another one of those inexplicable things that happened in Giripul and people accepted it. Feed Balu and he will not harm you, in fact he will bring good fortune to the village. They also thought of the money in the Simla bank, but did not say anything. It did not look good to say such things aloud. You could think greedy thoughts in your head, but it was best to stay silent. Envy, greed, lust and other evil thoughts should always stay hidden from other people, only the gods could know that you were thinking these evil thoughts, but they ignored them because they themselves were greedy, jealous and lusting after another god's wife or daughter.

Janak went back into the shop and sat down to work again. He pushed the cloth under the needle and began to turn the handle. Soon he was lost in thought. Yes, the gods knew everything and they saw to it that life remained a mystery and played endless tricks on you. You never knew what was waiting for you around the corner, especially when the road of life took a sharp blind curve.

His mother-in law's arrival had really shaken him and he had to stay calm and keep his wits about him.

A truck roared up the hillside and Janak jumped up at once. He peered out of the window. *Malik hai mahan par chamcho se pareshan*, said the sign on the truck's back fender, above a black and red painted face. God is great but fed up of his hangers on. 'How true,' muttered Janak.

The pigeons began to coo above his head as if they agreed with him and he smiled, feeling happy for the first time all day.

Janak loved birds. He fed the pigeons, sparrows and doves that sat outside his shop window, but for some reason his mother-in-law's parakeet frightened him.

This bald bird, with its faded green feathers, looked like a human – one who had led a life of great cruelty in the past and had now been born as a parakeet. The pujari of their temple had said you had to be born 7,80,000 times before you could become a human again. Or was it 8,70,000 times? Janak was not sure.

But Janak sometimes wondered if Mithoo the parakeet could read his mind, and he always tried to keep his thoughts pure when he was in the same room as the bird. He never looked at his wife's breasts even when they surged out of her blouse as she sat on the floor, cooking. He took great care to ignore her swaying hips when she swept the backyard, especially when she was right below the bird's cage. In Mithoo's malicious, gleaming eyes, Janak could see years of evil doings; sometimes his claws seemed bloodstained. Janak was sure he turned into an evil spirit at night and flew around the village, making people fall sick or harming the cattle.

Janak stopped the machine and placed his hands on the table to rest them. He thought about his mother-in-law with a stab of irritation. The old woman and her parakeet had been here for a week now and showed no signs of leaving. They seemed to be spying on him all the time and she even came into his bedroom and sprawled on the bed, spitting marijuana seeds which the two of them munched all the time. Tiny pellets dotted the bed and Janak wanted to strangle them both. No, that was going too far. He could never kill anyone, no matter how much he hated them. Maybe he would snip a few inches off the bird's tail with his new scissors.

'Mithoo, sweet son of mine, come and have your chilli,' his mother-in-law's shrill voice rang in his ears as he began to work on the machine once more. Janak's own mother had never spoken to him so lovingly. Perhaps he should pray to be born a parakeet in his next life.

The kurta he was sewing was almost finished and Janak stopped the machine and stood up. He rubbed his back and took a few quick steps around the room. He was tempted to go out to talk to the birds, but he had to finish cutting a new suit. He sighed loudly and spread the suit piece on his table and began marking it with chalk. 'Neck, arm-hole, sleeves, chest, waist,' he chanted aloud. The pigeons cooed outside his window and the white and brown one lifted its head and looked at him. Janak stood still. This was his favourite one. He got up slowly, reaching for the tin of bird seed. The pigeon watched him, bobbing its neck up and down to encourage him. He took a handful of seeds and very, very carefully stretched out his hand. Just then Tommy barked and the bird flew away, alarmed. 'Never mind, this was an important step. One day she will overcome her shyness and take the grain from my hand,' Janak mumbled to himself and scattered the seeds out of the window. He was sure the white and brown pigeon was a female.

He went back to cutting the cloth and when he reached the neck, he wondered what his mother-in-law was doing. Now he would have no time alone with Rama till the old woman left. He could not even look at her in front of her mother because Rama said it was not proper. 'You keep staring at me as if you have never seen me before.

What kind of behaviour is this for a married man with a son? What will my mother think? As it is, she has a poor opinion of you.'

The only place he had some privacy was the wooden shack in the backyard, which he had built as a bathroom and toilet. Most people in Giripul bathed in the river and did their morning business before sunrise on the hillside where the raspberry shrubs grew thick and close together. But Janak's wife suffered from severe constipation and could not defecate in the open air. Even when she was a child, the women of the house had to hold up a bedsheet as a curtain for her every morning and make encouraging grunts to enable her to have a bowel movement.

Rama's entire village participated in this morning ritual and the details of her bowel movements were discussed by the women when they went to fetch water at the spring. Each woman narrated stories of the different kinds of constipation in her family; one elaborated on her gas problems, another talked at length about her piles and heart burn.

'All day long I let out sour belches and then feel a burning sensation in my heart,' Janak had often heard his mother-in-law lament. If only she would eat less, he thought. But it was not polite to say that to your mother-in-law, no matter how much you disliked her. That was the rule.

When Rama got married and came to live in Giripul, the news of her morning rituals came to an abrupt end, but for many years people from her village would ask about her bowels. 'Does she go regularly in Giripul or is it still difficult? Is it easier now that she is a married woman with a child?' they would say whenever they visited Giripul. Janak hated discussing his wife's bowel movements so publicly but you could not be rude to someone from your wife's village. It was another one of those harsh and cruel rules of life one had to obey.

So Janak built an outdoor toilet for Rama, the first one in Giripul, but she hardly ever used it and preferred to go to the hillside at dawn with the other village women. The shack was Janak's haven now, and would remain thus as long as the old witch stayed. It was the only place he was safe from the old woman.

Sometimes green grass snakes would glide in or a pair of doves would build a nest outside the window and their constant cooing would fill the shed. Balu's shack was like Janak's too, but it had a special roof made with a battered tin sheet which was difficult to find in Giripul. Janak had cut up several old wooden packing cases which he had found discarded in Raja's shop, and joined them together to make his toilet.

He liked reading the English writing on the boxes as he squatted – *Pure Butter Cookies for that Special Moment* or *Enjoy the Strong Aroma of Taj Tea*. It was a good way to practise his English. He knew English was the language that made you rich and important; it was too late for him, but he would certainly send his son to an English-medium school. Then he could become a clerk in a government office in Simla, and maybe rise to a head clerk's position. People would respect him and call him 'sir', and bring him small bribes like boxes of sweets, and material for pants and shirts.

Janak had placed an old chair in the corner and kept a magazine hidden in a box underneath it. Some passenger on the bus from the city had left it in Lala's tea shop and Lala had hidden it in the tea chest before anyone could see it. It was the only glossy magazine in Giripul and they had to take good care of it. Only the headman, Lala, Janak and Raja knew about it and they took turns to look at it. Shankar was not included because he would make the pages smell fishy, but he was allowed to look at the magazine when it was in Raja's shop, as long as he did not touch the glossy pages. They heard later that Raja had started charging other men in the village ten rupees to look at it, but they could not do anything about it since Raja denied it and it was difficult to prove.

They guarded the magazine and kept it safely hidden where the women could not find it. Each of them got to keep it for a month only. It was all very secretive.

It was Janak's turn this month and he had only ten days left, hardly enough time to look at all the pictures. He liked looking at the pictures of these foreign women, not just because they were pretty and happily half naked like babies, but also because they wore such delicate undergarments. Those flimsy things they wore on their breasts and lower regions were like cobwebs of silk, like dewdrops on roses, pink and white, gold and silver. He wanted to touch those silky fragments of silk and lace even more than he wanted to caress the women.

But these women with strange pale eyes and golden hair lived in some other world, far, far away from Giripul. Which was a good thing, Janak reflected, because if they came to live in Giripul they would make his life even more difficult. He would have to repair those silky strips of lace that barely covered their breasts and he was not sure he had the skills or matching silk threads.

Janak finished cutting the suit, folded it neatly and put it on the shelf. He stood at the window and watched the sparrows glean seeds from the street. How brave these little creatures were to face the busy street where they could be run over any minute. He wished he had a bit of courage in his heart too. Every morning he thought of asking Rama how long her mother planned to stay but when he looked into her beautiful eyes, his courage failed him. He knew she would start crying.

'You do not want my mother to come to my house,' she would say. 'You want me to be an orphan like you. I will leave this very moment, pack my bags and take her with me. We will beg on the streets.'

Janak allowed himself a brief moment of delight by imagining his mother-in-law and the parakeet begging on the street, maybe even fighting with Balu for leftovers. No, one must not think badly of one's wife's relatives, he reminded himself.

Janak shook his head and picked up the scissors, and put them down again. He did not feel like starting on a new suit today. In fact, he did not feel like doing any work, which was strange. Janak touched his forehead. Perhaps he was falling sick. He thought for a moment and then decided to get some fresh air.

The street was pungent with the smell of garlic, which the farmers had just brought in after the harvest. Janak saw that Balu's door was still shut. Maybe he had read the truck sign and decided not to come out today. Here was a man with no worries, except about the late arrival of trucks in Giripul. Balu had achieved supreme peace on earth. He never did any work on his land and after his childless wife died, he had just built this shed and tucked himself in.

Everyone in Giripul took turns to leave food for him and gave him a set of clothes once a year. Balu only ate choice leftovers; he did not like flour, potatoes or food cooked in too much oil. He drank only cow's milk. 'Buffalo's milk will make you look and think like a buffalo,' he said. He bathed in the river everyday, even in winter, washing his three sets of clothes once a week. Sometimes during the rains, when his clothes did not dry, he wore his bedsheet and stayed indoors. He loved no one, hated no one, had no quarrels and no fears or responsibilities.

Janak had a cup of tea at Lala's shop and almost sat to watch a group of farmers playing cards when he remembered he had to stitch two more suits. He walked back to the shop reluctantly and sat once more at the sewing machine. As he began putting a new thread on the bobbin he thought about Balu's life. The life of a beggar was not bad. At least he did not have to work all day like Janak did. But a beggar had to give up many things.

Moreover, it needed will power and great strength of mind. Janak was not sure he had the courage to become a beggar. He also had to consider his family. What would his son say when people asked him what his father did? What would happen when he died? Would the priest who came to do his shraadh puja chant, 'We pray for this departed soul who lived a rich and full life on this earth as a beggar'? No. That did not sound right.

Janak sighed and turned the handle of his sewing machine slowly and then a little faster. The headman's third wife's blouse, which was hanging behind the window, suddenly fluttered down to the floor. Janak gave a start and clutched the handle of his sewing machine. The stitches pulled and jammed as he felt a surge of fear. What should he do about her dreams? He had pushed it all to the back of his mind since dealing with his spying mother-in-law and her parakeet was more urgent, but the blouse's sudden appearance jolted him. It was a bad omen.

The third wife stood before him smiling coyly, her eyes rimmed with kohl. She parted her mouth to show him her tiny, white teeth. She was wearing a shimmering pink satin blouse, but he could see that it had not been stitched by him. The hook sat unevenly, creating a bumpy ridge. A bad tailor had made this blouse for her. She swayed a little above his sewing machine and then floated towards him. She kept coming closer, till her face almost touched his. He could smell the jasmine oil in her hair.

'Why tailorji? What are you thinking?' she said in a deep, manly voice. It was the headman's voice. Janak shivered with fear and put his hands over his face. When he looked again, the third wife had vanished, but a faint scent of jasmine hung in the shop. Janak picked up the blouse from the floor. Yes, it was trying to tell him something. Something he could not understand.

He had only told Shankar about the dream, but Shankar had not offered any advice. It was not fair. Why had she confessed to him and not to someone else, like her father or brother? Maybe she had and they had ignored her like most men ignored their women folk's chatter. Only fools paid attention to their wives, or men like Bengali Baba, who made a living by listening to women's nonsense.

But the truth was, Janak could not help listen to them. He tried to shut his ears, but they said things men would never think of saying, their heads were full of strange and wonderful thoughts and they knew many more words than men did. They talked in circles, jumping from one topic to the next like grasshoppers, sometimes weaving in and out of stories so swiftly you had to really listen or you would miss the strands.

His head whirled with the images they conjured and he found it so fascinating, he sat frozen like a hare before a fox, listening to their endless chatter. He did not want to, but he could not resist. He wished his wife would talk to him like this because he could have sat and listened to her for hours, but she hardly ever spoke to him except to scold him.

So Janak decided he would learn to just listen to the women who came to his shop with one ear and ignore their words like other men did. Life would be manageable then, and much less complicated. But he knew in his heart he could never turn a woman away when she came to his shop, clutching a piece of cloth and her hopes. She would sit on the bench and after he had taken her measurements, she would begin telling him about her problems. Sometimes it was simple, like a toothache or a fight with her husband. Sometimes it was silly, like how her mother-in-law had stolen her knitting wool and given it to her daughter. She talked and he listened while he cut the cloth or turned the handle of his sewing machine. Some women just sat and twisted bits of thread around their fingers and watched him work, and then went away smiling, as if he had told them something really wonderful. But the third wife was the first woman who had come to him with such a terrible confession.

Why should he worry about the third wife's dream? Was he a policeman or a priest? No, he was the tailor of Giripul and his job was to sew clothes.

But what if the headman really got his head chopped off? Would the sin fall on Janak's head? The gods would certainly blame him, since he had failed to protect the headman's head. When Janak shut his eyes the headman's face appeared, and he knew he had to do something. After all, he had been chosen and he must do his duty to save the headman though what he was supposed to do, he had no idea.

'Janak ... Oye, Janak!' he looked out the window and saw Shankar and Lala waiting for him. They wanted to play cards. The headman was there too. But Janak could not face him today. Now, every time Janak saw the headman, he imagined him without his head; a stiff collar, a muffler and then nothing. He pretended not to hear them. They could find someone else to play cards with.

Janak picked up the third wife's blouse and noticed he had forgotten to sew one hook. That must be a bad sign, because never before had such a thing happened! Hooks and buttons were his speciality. The women always said the hooks never came undone even when they were cutting grass or chasing goats on the hillside. He double-stitched each one, making sure the thread was overlaid properly. In fact, women from faraway villages came to him with their blouses mainly because of his expertise in sewing hooks.

With trembling fingers Janak searched for a hook in the tin box full of buttons, old spools, pencil stubs, keys, bobbins, pins, coins and hooks. He found a new hook and began to sew it on. His fingers, which usually moved swiftly with a needle and thread, now moved clumsily.

Thank god he had done the hook's eye yesterday. He would not have managed to do it today, with such a distracted mind. The eyes would have come out uneven and the hook would not sit smoothly. It would form a tiny pimple on the blouse, and though some women would not notice it in their eagerness to wear their new blouse, it would irritate him each time he saw it. He would glare at the scar on the cloth and the women would giggle coyly, thinking he was staring at their breasts.

The satin blouse gleamed in his hands and suddenly it began to look like the veil of a shaitan's wife. He shut his eyes and saw in his mind's eye his tiny shop, filled to the brim with yards of pink satin silk swirling around his head, trying to strangle him. Maybe his head was going to be lopped off along with the headman's. Janak groaned. His wife often predicted the untimely deaths of various people, but since they were usually from her village, he never really listened. He would have to pay more attention to her when she got into her next dark mood.

From now on he would have to be alert all the time. Anything could happen. Suddenly Giripul felt like a dangerous place, its streets cracked with giant crevices he could fall through. He shut his eyes tightly and sensed that something bad was coming his way.

The door creaked and suddenly a heavy hand fell on his shoulder. Janak stifled a cry. The needle pierced his skin and he looked up to see the headman's cheerful face staring down at him, a trickle of paan juice running down his lips like fresh blood.

'Arre, bhai. Why are you looking like a scared rabbit? Are our women giving you too much trouble? Put that blouse down, it won't run away, though that salwar might.' The headman roared with laughter, slapping his massive thighs. His two bodyguards laughed along dutifully, slapping their thighs even louder. The tiny shop shook with their raucous laughter and thigh slapping, as Janak stood up, clutching the blouse.

'Listen, my friend, I have a task for you,' the headman told Janak. He turned to his bodyguards. 'Hey, you two, get out!'

The bodyguards ran out at once, their broad crocodile smiles still stuck on their faces.

'See this,' whispered the headman, pulling out a piece of pink silk clumsily from his pocket like a novice magician.

Gods in heaven, help me. More pink satin silk, Janak thought fearfully as he stared at the cloth. Now he was certain Giripul was going to be shaken by something really terrible. Maybe an earthquake or floods or a swarm of locusts. So much pink satin in the village could only bring disaster.

'I want you to make a salwar kameez with this,' said the headman, caressing the satin with his big hairy hands, which were big enough to wring a chicken's neck with a single twist. 'Put all those trimmings on it, you know, the kind young girls like these days. Every button, ribbon, gold and silver lace and frill you have in your trunk. It should look like no other suit you have made. But brother, this is only between you and me.' He put his finger on his lips and narrowed his eyes.

'But what size? I mean, for whom – not you?' Janak asked warily, touching the soft, shimmering cloth.

He knew some men liked to dress up in women's clothes, but he had never met anyone like that before. Shankar had an uncle who wore his wife's salwar, draped her dupatta over his head and chased her around the house, but somehow he could not imagine their village headman, a strong virile man with a moustache the entire village envied, doing such a thing.

'For me? You are a joker. Here are the measurements,' he said, pulling out a crumpled piece of paper. 'But brother, this is man to man. Promise me you will not tell my wife. If she gets to know she will kill me.' He ran a finger across his throat with a simpering, paan-stained smile.

She will, my friend, she will, whispered a voice in Janak's head and his heart jumped as he took the cloth from the headman's hands. He would not even have to change the thread in the machine. If he had come earlier, the third wife's blouse could have had matching sleeves, Janak thought as he watched the headman and his bodyguards stroll down the street and turn into Lala's tea shop. Tommy ran behind them.

The men in the tea shop greeted the headman with a loud cheer, as though they had not seen him for a long time, and made room for him on the bench. Lala shouted at the tea boys to hurry with the tea cups as he poured a cascade of fresh milk into a pan of boiling water, dark with tea leaves. He threw in some green cardamom which he kept only for important customers.

The sunlight glistened on the rocks and the pine trees cast a cool, fragrant shade on the roof tops. There was a muffled gunshot from far away in the forest, which made Tommy bark and then whimper as the headman gave him a playful kick. The wild apricot tree shed a few flowers as the late afternoon bus rumbled in, coughing and rattling, its musical horn blaring.

Janak looked around his little shop, where the sunlight was making patterns on the wall. He put the cover on the sewing machine, whispered a few soft words to it like he did everyday and then picked up the pink silk-satin cloth and held it to his face. It reeked of sandalwood and stale marigolds and he suddenly felt as if he were at a funeral.

'I must do something to stop this dream killing. The gods are trying to tell me something, or maybe the shaitan is,' he said loudly to himself and ran out into the street, still holding the pink silk in his hands.

Balu the beggar had received his third cup of tea from Lala and now sat quietly in his tin shed. The bus had been delayed this morning because of a landslide and the first truck had come in late as well, so he did not know till noon how his day would turn out. The truck's fender sign had announced it to be a *'Beware of evil foes'* day, so he decided to stay in his shed, tucked in bed. He had no foes, but why risk it? After all, an old enemy might turn up on the afternoon bus, attack him and then catch the evening bus back to Simla. No one would find out until his body started to rot. Only Tommy would sniff out his dead body, but who would listen to his barks? Balu wriggled his toes under the old blanket he had wrapped around two layers of flour sacks to make a bed. He loved lying in his snug bed, listening to the hail dancing on his tin roof. A faint smell of flour and spices from the sacks tickled his nose when he woke up in the morning and at night it made him dream of his late wife's fluffy hot chapattis.

He had three razais now, thanks to the wedding group that had dropped a bedding roll from the evening bus last month. He had also found a shaving mirror, a bottle of hair oil and a bar of soap in their luggage. If you kept your eyes open you could pick up a rich hoard from the streets. People were careless these days. They dropped watches, combs, handkerchiefs, spectacles, books, underwear, wallets, photographs and letters, all the time. Some of these things were useful, but most of them were of no use to him, like the ladies' handbag he had found on the road the other day. It was made of shiny red plastic and filled with tiny coloured jars, sticks of kajal, hairclips, a dried-up rose, cough drops, torn letters, bits of lace and one pen. What use could these things be to anyone? Why carry them from place to place? He had kept the pen and thrown the bag away, but later that day he saw Raja's wife walking down the street with the same bag, looking very pleased. Balu realized that everything in this world was created to give joy to someone, though it might appear useless to others.

Once he had picked up a packet of condoms, which were no use to him; they never had been, since God had made his wife barren. But she had been a good soul even if she could not give him a son. He had no need for a son now. He did not need anything apart from one meal a day, and the people of Giripul fed him – after all, he was the only beggar in the village.

Balu heard a shuffling outside his door and lifted his head to listen. He could see a line of sunlight through the tiny crack in the door, which was tied with a rope to keep the stray dogs out, though Tommy kept guard outside his door at night. During the day Tommy sat outside Janak's shop watching the women being measured, his tongue hanging out. He often edged his way into the shop and sat close to the women, his paw on their legs. He must have been a lecherous man in his former life and that was why he had been born a dog in this one.

Balu peered through the chink and saw Janak walking past, his head bowed. He was holding a piece of shiny pink cloth in his hands. Maybe he was bringing it for him, though it was not the kind of cloth Balu would ever use. He only liked soft white cotton that had been washed many times, not this ugly shiny stuff. But he liked Janak and it would be nice to talk to him today since he could not go out. He faintly called out to him and suddenly changed his mind. He felt too tired to deal with anyone. People always had some problem or the other to discuss and today he did not feel like sharing their lives. He would just pray for a while and then go back to sleep.

Janak stopped and turned around. He thought he had heard a sound from Balu's shed and so he waited. Maybe Balu would call him in for a chat.

This could be a good omen. Balu very rarely spoke to anyone. But when he did, it was as if a helping hand had come down from heaven. Balu knew how to solve each and every problem a man could have in this world, and maybe in the next one too. Janak believed that Balu had special powers which very few people in Giripul knew about. He would tell Balu about the third wife's dream and Balu would tell him what to do.

Janak stood in front of the tin shed. He did not want to go in because Balu hated anyone coming into his tiny shed or touching his few belongings. You could only go in if he pushed the door open for you.

'I do not like the cloth, take it away,' Balu suddenly shouted from inside, making Janak startle. He dropped the satin on the ground.

'Bring me some soft, white cotton if you want, not this whore's satin,' he cried and Janak gasped. How did Balu know that the satin belonged to a bad woman? The headman could not have confessed to him about his other woman. Balu just knew. He could hear things that went on in your head. Sometimes, even before you had the thought, Balu would pluck it out of your head.

Janak felt calmer and told himself once more that he had come to the right man and then he sat down in front of the door, where the sunlight made a warm triangle. He would rest here for a while till Balu spoke to him again. What was the hurry? He had opened the shop, fed the pigeons, finished the third wife's blouse and also brought along a kurta to be hemmed.

Janak took out a reel of thread from his pocket, but it slipped from his hand and fell on the ground. As he bent to pick it up, he saw a line of ants carrying grains of sugar that Balu must have given them. Janak moved his feet aside to let them pass. Despite being weighed down by a grain of sugar, each ant stopped near the reel and examined it carefully before continuing on its way. Was there a message in this too, Janak wondered as he began to hem the kurta. The ants hurried past and soon they had carried all the grains of sugar to their home under the rock.

Balu the beggar once lived in a big house on top of the hill, where the terraced fields ended and the forest began. The house had been built by his grandfather with stones gathered from the river bed, limestone and crushed shale. The roof was made of special silver-tinged slates which had been carried down by mules from the top of the highest peak. The beams were made from old deodar trees which once grew on their own land. Balu's wife, who was famed for her beauty all over the Simla hills, kept a neat garden patch where pumpkins, peas, cauliflowers and beans grew in abundance, and it also had all kinds of new flowers that nobody in the village had ever seen. They said she had stolen the seeds from an English memsahib's garden in Simla. The flowers grew all year round and even in winter the garden had strange white ones, sparkling at night like magical flowers that could only grow in Indra's garden in heaven.

Then one July, when the planets decided to clash, it rained and thundered for six days, causing landslides which blocked the path of the river. The waters began to rise quickly, almost half way up to the road. The rocks on which the women used to beat their clothes disappeared underwater and the bridge with the tin goddess was almost submerged – only the top half of her silver crown showed. The priest had just managed to escape when the water began to rise above the steps of the temple. He said the river rushed in so quickly that he had no time to pick up the silver lamps that decorated the temple though many people in the village whispered that he had quietly packed them off to his wife's village.

On the sixth day the rains stopped and the sun came out. The river was still flowing high and muddy, but the road was no longer buried under water. When the villagers came out to pick up their belongings that had been thrown about by the flood, they saw to their amazement that Balu's house had slid down the hill and come to stand in Raja's father's land.

It was as if a giant hand scooped up the house and placed it firmly on Raja's father's land. The vegetable garden had slid down too, the pumpkins still clinging to the vine. But the flowers had all died in the rain, since they were the delicate English kind, not used to the Indian monsoon.

Now a long and bitter dispute arose about whose house it was and whose land. 'It's not my fault that the landslide brought my house down,' said Balu, then a strapping young man with neatly oiled hair and plump cheeks.

'And is it my fault that your house landed on my land? I was here long before you, sitting quietly, minding my own business. It was you who came down on my head,' argued Raja's father.

The dispute went on for twenty years. The village elders mulled over it, but no one knew how to resolve it. Raja's father decided to bring an official from the Simla land revenue office, but the official was bitten by a mad dog on the way and had to go to the big hospital in Kasauli for twenty-one injections in his stomach. He never came back.

No one wanted to go near the house any more because it kept sinking. One day a door would slide into the ground, the next day a window. Everyone stayed away as the soft earth swallowed the house slowly, except Balu's wife, who stood guard over the foundationless house, trying to save her dying plants.

She would gather her precious English flowers and bathe them in milk to revive them. And as the house sank further into the soft hillside, her mind began to wander and by the time the house disappeared into the earth she was totally senile, singing loudly to the house as if it were a baby she was putting to sleep.

When she died, Balu decided to became a beggar. Had he been a clever, cunning man, he would have donned saffron robes and turned into a sadhu since only a fine line divided the two professions. But Balu was quite content to live a simple beggar's life.

Balu shut the door with a clanging of cattle bells and went back to sleep. Tommy had walked away to the far end of the street where the other dogs were examining a dead hare. Though Tommy was a vegetarian dog he did not mind occasionally sharing fresh scraps of meat with the other village dogs, but he looked so guilty afterwards that Janak always pretended he had not seen him enjoying the meaty bone.

Should I wait or go, Janak wondered and put the hemmed kurta away. He turned his head to look at his little shop, bathed in the bright sunlight, the signboard flashing boldly. He felt a twinge of pride because he was sure people living on top of the mountain could see his shop. Raja's wife and her sister were waiting outside, clutching a bag filled with some new material. 'Not pink satin, I hope,' he muttered and stood up.

He would not bother Balu with the dream now. He would attend to these two women, and then finish cutting the headman's whore's satin suit. That would require all his attention because he was not used to cutting many satin suits. Then he would go home, have his lunch and sleep a while. All this thinking had tired him. The morning had just floated away. His head felt heavy and he needed his rest now. His mother-in-law never missed her siesta, and even Mithoo dozed in the afternoon. He hoped Rama had left some food for him and the house was in a peaceful mood.

As he walked home, Janak saw a group of cinnamon sparrows fighting over a bit of wool. They must need it for their nest. How difficult life was for these little creatures, yet they managed to survive. Maybe they had problems no human knew about. Sometimes the birds he fed outside his shop looked quite sullen and bad-tempered, like Rama on her bad-mood days.

Giripul was quiet in the afternoon. A few women worked in their fields, clearing dried roots and weeds from the newly-ploughed earth, while the others cut grass on the hillside, just beyond the bridge. The men sat

on sunlit verandahs and played cards quietly. The babies
and old women slept in darkened rooms. The older
children roamed the hillside with their goats and cows,
playing games with wooden sticks or just happily rolling
down the hill, tearing their clothes which had been neatly
and lovingly darned by their mothers.

A few old men sat drinking tea and sharing a hookah
in Lala's tea shop. They were waiting for the last bus to
arrive. They placed bets on various things that would or
would not happen. Not big things like floods, elections
or earthquakes, but little things, like how many women
would arrive on the bus? How many goats would be on
it? How many men with green caps would get off? Would
the driver have his radio on or off?

The betting got quite intense sometimes and
arguments broke out even before the bus arrived, and
Lala had to give them free cups of tea to calm them
down. They sat down again to wait for the bus and
when it arrived they quickly settled their bets with
no arguments.

None of the men had plans to go anywhere, they just
liked to see the evening bus, with its wailing horn and
flashing red and green lights, arrive and then leave in
a cloud of dust. It marked the end of the day for them
and they could go home feeling contented and tell their
wives, 'The last bus has gone.' They never mentioned the
betting because women didn't understand things like
that and would not see the point.

The afternoon slipped away beyond the peaks and as
dusk floated into Giripul, the hills turned grey and the

pine trees stood in a dark, crooked line. A thin silver moon rose in the sky, which was still blue, while a weary sun struggled to set behind the hills. Then it finally sank and the street sighed, twisted a little to greet the falling dusk and became silent. The old men waved goodbye to the last bus as it went past and then turned around to watch a lone man climb up the hill, stumbling and singing a drunken song.

'There goes the headman's brother-in-law, full of good liquor from Simla,' said Balu from his shed. Tommy gave a short bark, but did not get up from his warm, grassy bed.

Janak, disappointed that Balu had not called him in, went home but even there he was unable to rest all afternoon and instead lay in bed counting his mother-in-law's snores. At the hundred-and-fifth snore he got out of bed, put on his cap and slipped out of the house. His wife was in the shed, grunting loudly. Why was she there? This was not the time for her morning ablutions, but Janak did not want to worry about that now. There were so many other things to worry about, his wife's bowels could wait. The parakeet opened one eye and then shut it again. His father – or whoever the man was – smiled from the wall, the faded garland gleaming like a copper chain.

Janak had an intuition that the bird knew about the headman's whore's satin and the third wife's dream, but the bird was helpless and could only glare at him with beady eyes. Thank god he was only a bird, or he could create a lot of problems for Janak.

Later, at the shop, he worked listlessly, cutting the pink satin with unsteady hands. The slippery cloth seemed to move in the flickering light of his kerosene lantern and he could see the headman's other woman prancing around, draped in this very suit. His hands began to sweat and he could not bear to touch the cloth so he quickly put the satin away in a box under the table. He sat still for a while to calm his fluttering heart and then he began working on Lala's wife's suit instead. The cheap cotton cloth was cool and he felt soothed by its rough texture.

Here was a pure woman who wore only full-sleeved blouses made of homespun cotton. Her neckline was cut high and from the back her blouse came up to her tightly coiled knot of oiled hair and then went down to be tucked into her petticoat. She showed no flesh around her midriff unlike most of the women in the village who liked the world to see their curves even when they kept their heads modestly covered. Lala's wife, a religious lady, reminded him of his mother, but without the complaining voice.

She was a good woman, Lala's wife, but even then Lala often went to Drena, on the other side of the mountains, to meet his other wife who, they said, had breasts like melons, but would beat him with a broom before letting him into her bed.

Lala's Giripul wife's chest size was only thirty-two inches. God made women like that, the good ones had thirty-two inches and the wicked ones had a forty-inch chest. He was sure of that fact, except that the headman's whore was also thirty-two inches. There must have been a mistake. God was in such a hurry these days. He had to create so many people every moment. Janak had heard the other day on the radio that there were more than a hundred crore people living in India. Janak was not sure how much a crore was, but it sounded like a lot.

He would make the suit according to the measurements the headman had given him. Let it not fit, who cared. The headman might be dead soon and then who would his whore complain to? She would not come to Giripul to catch him and ask for a refund, or would she? Surely the headman would not give his name and address to her. If he had, she could take the afternoon bus and come here in three hours. Anyone could be anywhere at anytime in these modern, evil times.

Janak finished cutting a blouse which Raja's wife had brought in, hemmed another kurta and then when his eyes began to hurt in the flickering light of the lamp, he put the cover on the machine. On his way back he stopped once more at Balu's door, but he could not hear any sound. Tommy looked up at him and wagged his tail; he had been waiting outside the shed for a long time for some sound from within. Now Janak and Tommy sat together side by side. They did not want to disturb Balu. A comforting smell of damp fur rose from Tommy and mingled with the scent of pinewood fires.

Night fell swiftly on the hills and the houses and fields turned pitch black. Only the headman's and Lala's houses, which had electricity, shone in the darkness. A few women were watching television in the headman's house. Janak could hear gunshots echoing all over the hillside.

Janak suddenly decided he must talk to Balu. This was the right time to tell him about the third wife's dream. No one was about, all the women were safely indoors and even Lala's tea shop was empty. There was just a lone figure walking unsteadily up the hill path. But as soon as Janak cleared his throat and started to speak, Balu's voice rang out from inside the shed and stopped him.

> Fly away pigeon,
> May your wings burn in the sun.
> You cheating, lying one,
> You have stolen my heart.
>
> And then left me for another ...

He sang the verse once more and then pushed the door open just a tiny bit and said, 'Janak, you worry too much, son. You should not believe what women say. Their head is full of petty nonsense. Go home and sleep. We will see what tomorrow's truck says and act accordingly. Bring some jaggery flavoured with black pepper and ginger for me, with some freshly-roasted gram. Go rest now, son. All will be well.'

Janak felt a cool, invisible hand touch his forehead and he nodded his head to thank Balu silently and then got up to go home. Tommy shook himself, tucked his head into his paws and sighed.

Janak stood outside his house watching the hills. Bats were flying towards the orchards and in the dark he could see Giripul's girl thief run up the hill path silently to steal the plums. She seemed like a child but was an accomplished fruit thief. Not just fruit, pumpkins, potatoes and milk too. Janak had once seen her crawl into his cowshed and shimmer out with a pail of milk. He had tried to catch her, but she had already merged into the misty darkness. To this day no one in the village had managed to catch her, so he did not feel so bad, though Rama did scold him for it. Janak watched the girl for a while, till her tiny form disappeared into the darkness. The owls began to hoot and Janak went into the house. Maybe he should have called the Shadow Chaser to catch her. He would have been able to tell if she was a living creature and not a spirit from the forest.

Rama blamed Janak for not running fast enough to catch the girl thief. 'Can you not catch a chit of a girl? What kind of a man are you? Or is she one of your hussies? Does she let you feel her breasts too like all the others? Like two peas in a pod, they must be, the thieving slut,' she would shout as Janak stood quietly, looking at her angry rosebud mouth.

Rama was quite certain, and her mother thought the same, that half the women in Giripul were running after Janak. 'Mrs Tailor, Mrs Tailor,' they simpered when they came to the house, their eyes lusting after her husband. Lala's saintly high-neck-blouse wife, Raja's wife with her head always covered, and the worst was the headman's third wife. She was shameless and did not care what people thought of her, making many trips to the shop with scraps of cloth – satin, silk, terracotta, cotton, muslin and even khadi. Why did she need so many clothes stitched?

Rama watched her husband as he ate. He was not ugly, but he wasn't handsome either. He was not tall or very strong. In fact, he got breathless quite easily while climbing up and down the hillside and she would have to carry their son. He hardly spoke or joked or laughed loudly like virile men did, showing their teeth and the tip of their tongue. His teeth were tiny like those of a mouse and when he smiled, his mouth drooped. He had large sad eyes that always looked worried, a weak chin, no moustache and though his hair was thick and curly, he already had a few grey hairs. What was it that attracted all the village women to him then, she wondered, peering at him closely.

He was her husband. She had married him because her father chose him for her after consulting the priest who had consulted the planets, but even that did not make him special. He was a good provider, a kind man who did not beat her, but she had given him one son and they were quits. It would have been best if he were a bad husband who beat her and kept a second wife, or else a docile husband who lived as quietly as a mouse with her. Why did he have to be a village Krishna who wasn't even dark and handsome?

Her mother had never liked him much and on their wedding night she had told her, 'Be wary, girl. A tailor husband is a dangerous thing. Women like him, feel close to him because he touches them here and there.'

Perhaps she was right. After all, Lala or the grocer or the paan-wallah could not reach out and touch any woman's breasts, could they? They would be killed by the woman's husband, brother or father. But Janak could do as he liked with these women as long as he held a measuring tape in his hands.

'My mother wants to go to the temple in Shaya. You had better shut shop tomorrow and take us,' Rama said, putting a hot chapatti on Janak's plate along with a dollop of fresh butter.

'All right, we will take the morning bus,' Janak said as he bit into a green chilli. He was happy to get away for a day. He would leave the blouse at Raja's shop for the headman's wife and start working on the other woman's satin kameez now. But what if Rama asked him who it was for? She knew all the women in the village and would know at once that this was for an outsider. The cloth was expensive and if any of the village women had bought it, they would have boasted about it.

Maybe he would go to the shop early and try to finish the frills on the sleeves at least. That would be the safest thing to do. No one should know about the satin suit because the headman had asked him to keep it a secret. It was a pity because it was going to be the prettiest suit he had ever made. How many secrets could one man keep inside his head, anyway?

In just a few days his calm and peaceful life had been filled with new dangers. The third wife with her murder dream, the headman with his secret satin suit, and his mother-in-law and her evil parakeet. Janak refused the fifth chapatti Rama offered him, burped softly and went to the courtyard to wash his hands.

The moon rose high in the black sky, the mountains stood like a wall around Giripul, and one by one the lights in the headman's house went out. It was eight o'clock and everyone but Janak was fast asleep. He thought of the day, wasted with useless things. He had just managed to cut one suit and hem one kurta. But he felt as tired, as though he had stitched uniforms for an entire army.

Giripul glimmered quietly in the moonlight and the river coiled around it like a silver snake. The spotted owlets came out from their day shelters and began to hunt for prey. A family of mice played hide and seek in Lala's shop as they collected leftover rice and sugar from the floor. High on the topmost hill, the jackals began to gather, but for some strange reason, they were silent tonight.

Shyamala, the third wife, dreamt once more of murdering the headman, this time with the new kitchen knife she had bought at the Simla fair. The headman dreamt of his girlfriend, wearing a short frilled dress like a circus monkey's. Rama dreamt of the girl thief being measured naked by her husband. Balu dreamt of his dead wife as she sank with their house, holding a fluffy chapatti in her hand. Shankar dreamt that Lala had drowned in the Giri river, a huge fish tied around his neck. Tommy dreamt that he had caught a hare, and Janak, when he finally fell asleep, dreamt that he was wearing a pink satin suit and dancing with a headless headman.

'We will have to follow the headman, and his wife too,' said Shankar. 'We must cheat fate. You keep an eye on the wife and I will see where he goes. We must be alert. We must be careful that fate does not find out what we are up to or she will change her plans.'

Janak was amazed, this was the longest speech his friend had made in the twenty-odd years they had known each other.

'But Balu says we must wait for the truck to give us the right message,' Janak said in a low voice.

'Yes, yes, that too. But meanwhile, what is the harm in keeping an eye on them. I saw this in an English film, *The Dead Do Not Sing*. In Hindi it was titled *Jasoosi Ladki*,' said Shankar, his eyes glistening.

Janak stared at Shankar. He could not understand this sudden change in him. Ever since he had told him about the third wife's dream, Shankar had shaken off his old sleepy self.

At first he had just been quiet, nodding and mumbling, and now, like a long dead volcano erupting, he jumped up. His eyes looked sharp and his frail, clumsy body was on high alert.

'But the headman must not know you are following him,' Shankar continued, 'In the film, the murderer catches the man following him and strangles him with a telephone wire. Though we do not have telephones in Giripul, we must still be careful. Any wire will do the job.'

When Shankar saw Janak staring at him, he stopped, looking a bit sheepish. Then he looked out of the window and said, 'You know, I have always longed to solve a murder mystery, ever since I was a boy. I waited and waited for something like this to happen, but all I got was a fish fight with Lala every morning.'

'You never told me this. You never even told me you had seen this film,' said Janak, feeling very hurt by this secret his friend had kept all these years. He knew Shankar liked reading detective novels and often bought them second-hand from Raja's shop, but he had never suspected that a detective lay hidden inside him. It was strange how people could change overnight. Janak had heard of wise men going suddenly mad and hacking people's heads off with an axe. Or a docile wife suddenly running off with the village postman. Yes, people did change, but it was a bit frightening when it happened to your childhood friend.

As Shankar went on and on about how he was going to follow the headman, Janak started cleaning his sewing machine. It always helped calm his nerves. He was annoyed with Shankar's new enthusiasm. All he wanted was someone to listen to him and he had chosen Shankar because he knew he would just listen quietly and let him take the lead. But he had misjudged his friend.

'All these years and you never said a word,' said Janak irritably.

'Well, I never thought the occasion would arise. I have read so many murder mysteries, it all seems so easy. The problem is finding a murder near your house – you don't want to travel far, change buses and all. You want to come back home for your evening meal,' he said, cleaning his nails with the scissors he had picked up from the sewing machine box. His face held a new crafty look on it, like a ferret, which Janak did not like at all.

Janak took the scissors away.

'This one will happen at our doorstep if we do not do something. Anyway, why follow both. It is enough to keep an eye on one of them. The murder cannot take place unless both are in the same place at the same time,' said Janak, already tired of the murder that might not even happen.

'That is also right,' Shankar said, scratching his nose. 'But you watch the wife – if I do it, my wife will kill me.'

'What about my wife, she already thinks half the women of Giripul are after me!'

'Are they?' said Shankar, looking away.

'Are you mad? Where do I have the time? All day long cutting, stitching, hemming, cutting-stitching-hemming necks, arm-holes, long sleeves, half bodice, pleats, long slits, v-necks, round-necks, buttons at the back, hooks in the front. All I can think of is a good meal from an even-tempered wife and sound sleep in a quiet house, but now this murder business has fallen on my head.'

'Your head, all right,' said Shankar, nodding and casting his eyes around suspiciously, as if someone could be listening to them.

Janak felt like slapping him, then shaking him till his teeth rattled.

'Anyway, I am taking my wife and her mother to the temple by the ten o' clock bus. You keep an eye on the headman. I must finish cutting this satin now. This secret suit stitching has brought more problems to my sore head.'

'What secret suit?' asked Shankar. But Janak kept silent. He was not going to say another word. This new Shankar was not to be trusted.

4

A visit to the forest temple; Janak is warned; Rama and mother-in-law upset; Shankar makes a bit of extra money

The bus smoked and coughed as it climbed the narrow road. The passengers coughed and spat out of the window in sympathy.

'If you get sick in the bus, then sit by the hillside or else your head will be lopped off by an oncoming bus,' shouted the bus conductor. All around him there was talk of heads being lopped off, thought Janak as he settled into the back seat. His wife and his mother-in-law sat in front with all the other women passengers. The parakeet had come along too, much to Janak's irritation.

'Why not, Mithoo also wants to visit the temple. He is a god-fearing bird and he knows all 108 names of Durga and will nod when you utter them, which is more than you can do, damaadji,' maaji had said before she got on the bus. Now the bird was dozing in its cage, even as the bus jolted over rough winding roads. The forest grew dense with tall deodar trees, there were sudden splashes of green where villagers had cleared the forest and cultivated the land. The Giri river had turned east and disappeared long ago and now only a gurgling mountain stream travelled by their side. A flock of red-billed blue magpies flew across the sky, screeching, and once in a while they got a glimpse of wild rhododendron shrubs in full bloom.

Maaji began to sing a bhajan and the parakeet opened one eye to stare at her belligerently. For the first time Janak felt a surge of sympathy for the bird. Maybe he was not a bad sort. How he must suffer being with the old witch all the time. He would get the bird some seeds tomorrow. He looked quite thin, maybe she ate up all his food. And that mean look in his eyes was probably just hunger. What a greedy woman. She had the appetite of a pregnant elephant.

No, better think pure thoughts, Janak reminded himself. If only he knew the 108 names of Durga. It would help to pass the time and clear his head of these unkind thoughts.

He wished they had brought his son along. Then he could have pointed out things to him from the window. He would have enjoyed seeing the black-faced langurs, the flocks of blossom-headed parakeets and the small tree shrines along the road. But the little boy did not want to come with them and had cried so much that they had to leave him with Raja's wife. They saw him playing happily in her courtyard when they left the village. This boy will never look after me in my old age, thought Janak.

He stared out at the forest where Shankar and he often went looking for partridges when they were boys. Ever since he had told him about the murder dream, he could not keep track of his friend any more.

Now Shankar recited the dream back to him ten times a day, adding something new each time until the murder dream took on a new meaning. He just could not believe a man could change overnight like this. It must be a curse of the third wife's dream.

Was Janak too going to suddenly change into a new man like his friend Shankar had? After all, the third wife had spoken to him first and her words could put some kind of a spell on him. Now that was something new to worry about, Janak thought as he turned away from the window with a deep frown; Rama thinking the frown was directed at her mother, scowled back at him.

The bus dropped them off at the bottom of the hill and after a short rest at a tea stall, they began to climb the narrow path. Janak walked ahead, carrying Mithoo's cage, Rama followed, and then her mother, who stopped every few minutes to cry, 'Jai devta!' The parakeet screeched a reply that sounded like an angry abuse to Janak, but he decided it was better not to say anything to his wife. She seemed to be in a good mood and had even smiled at him once or twice. It was a hint of a smile, but a smile all right.

The priest at the Shaya temple was an old man who, people said, could drink a kilo of ghee in one gulp. If you took a good offering, he would do a special puja for you. Everyone in the village was talking about a rival priest who had come out of nowhere and set up camp under a tree higher up in the mountains where the forest was so dense that daylight never filtered through. He claimed he had seen a vision of goddess Kali there and right after that, the branches of an old deodar tree had entwined into what looked liked the lower parts of a woman. 'We should go there too,' said maaji. 'Though it is mainly where barren women go to pray for sons, there is no harm in asking for her blessings. She may send you a few more sons. A woman can never have enough sons,' she said.

The temple, its golden crown gleaming in the sunlight, was crowded and noisy. A wedding party had camped there all night and men were cooking over large open fires while the women chopped vegetables on slabs of stone. This was the only time the village men cooked – in god's courtyard. Two goats that were to be sacrificed that evening were tied to a tree and happily nibbled the tender grass. A few children played with a ball made of tightly-rolled rags while their mothers shouted at them to fold their hands in prayer. They scampered away to play on the slope behind the temple where they would not be seen. Loud film music blared from a radio.

Janak joined the queue of devotees at the door and when his mother-in-law finally hobbled up with the parakeet's cage, they began climbing the wooden stairs. It took a long time to get to the room on top where the deity was installed since the crowd kept stopping and bowing. Janak took the cage from the old woman and joined the men's queue. Mithoo was strangely quiet. Maybe he was praying to God to set him free.

'I am on a diet now, no sugar or ghee – the doctor has

ordered', said the priest sadly when maaji offered him a kilo of ghee. She had made it last night, cooking the butter on a slow fire till it turned golden yellow. The delicious aroma had filled the house. The priest looked at the jar of fragrant golden ghee with sad eyes and coughed. 'The doctor in Simla said I have high blood pressure, and sugar is high too, so I must eat only boiled food, like English people do. You know they live forever in foreign lands,' he said and began muttering a prayer, pausing after every line to rub his chest. He gave Janak some raw rice and sugar to each of them, and smeared a bit of vermilion on Rama's forehead with an absent-minded blessing when she touched his feet. He did not look at Mithoo at all, even when he screeched out one of the names of Durga.

Maaji came out of the temple, complaining angrily under her breath. 'Imagine a priest who eats boiled food. He will not last long, I tell you. The gods do not like boiled food and what the priest eats, they get to eat. They want laddoos, kheer, rich halwa with ghee and sugar, not this boiled rubbish. Our gods are not English people. I tell you, this man will go soon and he will have a lot to answer to the gods for cheating them of an offering of good, pure ghee.'

'I could have taken the ghee back, but he might curse us then. A Brahmin priest's curse works, even if he eat boiled food,' she whispered and then folded her hands and touched them to her forehead as they all walked down the stairs. At the door she rang the temple bell loudly as if to make up for her harsh words.

'Now let us go to that other priest. I hope he likes ghee, I have brought one more bottle.' Janak wondered who was paying for all this ghee, but he dare not say anything. Ghee, even made at home, costs a lot, he thought. Anyway, offerings to priests should not be questioned or they would not bring any merit, his mother used to say.

The path was slippery and wet and maaji clutched Rama's arm as they walked into the forest. Janak held Mithoo's cage. A flock of blossom-headed parakeets swooped down to cross their path, but Mithoo ignored them. They were exactly like him, he was a parakeet and so were they, wild and untamed, they might even be his cousins, but he just ignored them. Maybe birds did not have to be kind to relatives like humans had to be, thought Janak as he glared at his mother-in-law walking breathlessly ahead of him.

They were now walking through dense forest; the trees grew so close they could barely pass through. The ancient deodar trees were covered with creepers with heart-shaped leaves and drooping white flowers. They hung like festive garlands all along the path, but Janak knew they were poisonous. At every bend, there were giant ferns and thorny, wild berry shrubs that blocked their way.

The rival priest had set up camp in a small clearing in the forest and surrounded it with red flags. He sat in the middle of a pale green circle, his eyes shut in deep meditation, but Janak could see his fingers drumming his knee impatiently. A pit had been dug in the ground and a large cauldron of milk bubbled in it. Janak walked up closer, followed by the women, and saw that a tall, gangly boy with red hair was stirring it with a long brass spoon. The boy raised his head after each turn to fix the few people who stood in a circle around the priest, with a sad, slightly cross-eyed gaze.

The roots of the old deodar tree where the priest sat really did look like a woman's lower parts, but a scrawny, misshapen woman with twisted legs. Janak went closer to examine it. Mithoo let out a loud screech when he was set down near the tree shrine. The priest opened his eyes and glared at the bird. 'Take her away. The goddess does not like her.' At first, Janak thought he was pointing to his mother-in-law and his heart jumped with glee. Then he realized the priest was looking at Mithoo.

'It is a he, not a she,' mumbled Janak, bowing his head.

'Shut up, I tell you, it is her and not him!' shouted the priest, his eyes glowering under his ash-covered skin. His matted hair coiled angrily around his shoulders and the people moved back in fear. Janak noticed that he was wearing a hearing aid in one ear, which was also smeared with ash. Then with a loud clapping of hands the priest began to sing, and as he sang, a lamp set in the tree shrine flashed green and red lights.

'A miracle,' Rama whispered, but Janak could see that it was being operated by a battery hidden behind the tree.

The deodar's branches swept the ground and they could hear thunder in the distance. The priest wrapped his arms around the trunk and began to shout: 'Jai ... jai ma!' He stopped and pointed at Janak. 'You, come here!'

'I see grief, a strange woman will bring grief to you. Go. Take this bird away, I said go! Woman! Leave that ghee! Here, take this,' he said, throwing a handful of jaggery at Janak.

The crowd surged forward and everyone caught lumps of jaggery deftly with open palms. Janak quickly put a few coins on the ground, picked up Mithoo's cage and began to run down the hill. Rama held her mother's hand and they both walked down whispering to each other. He knew he was in trouble. How could this priest sitting alone in the forest know anything about the third wife's dream? Or was he talking about the headman's woman?

Drops of rain fell on his head, but he did not bother to put his cap on. The parakeet was silent throughout the bus journey home and so were his wife and mother-in-law. But all three of them kept looking at Janak suspiciously and he knew they would have plenty to say when they got home. Janak stared out of the window at the mountains till they got to Giripul, his stomach rumbling anxiously.

It was raining when he opened his shop the next morning. Shankar walked in while Janak was cleaning the table, placing the bits of cloth neatly in a pile. It was early and the pigeons had not yet arrived for their feed. They were still hovering above the shop, muttering to each other. The brown and white bird was not there this morning; Janak hoped she would fly in later. Large black clouds hung over the highest peak and Janak was sure the rain would last all day. Soon it would be time to plant the maize crop, and the rains would make the soil much softer. Now the ploughed fields would receive the seeds easily, give them better nourishment and the crop would be plentiful. The gods were being kind to Giripul.

Shankar waited for him to finish cleaning and then said loudly, 'You will not believe this.' He had wrapped an old black scarf around his neck and was wearing a new English-style woollen cap with a checked pattern. 'The headman has a woman – a young girl he keeps in Simla. She has narrow, slit eyes like those Nepali children. But she is not Nepali, she comes from China which is very far from Giripul, you know.' He paused, looked up to see Janak's reaction and then continued. 'He visits her every Tuesday after the village headmen's collective council meetings in Simla.' He lowered his voice and began whispering, pulling at his cap and shrugging his shoulders, all at the same time. 'Ask me how I know all this. Go on, ask, my friend.'

Janak stared at him, but did not ask him anything. Let him suffer a little. How had he found out so much, so quickly?

Janak could not concentrate on what Shankar was saying. The words swirled around him, but all he could think of was Rama's angry face. The terrible things she had said to him last night were still spinning inside his head. 'You letch! You terrible man, running after strange women! The priest in the forest could see through you at once. Only I have been blind. You shameless man, you, the father of a son, behaving like this! What, Ma? Yes ... you, skirt chaser!' she had screamed, her mother prompting from the kitchen. He had tried so hard to explain to her that he was innocent, but he could not find the right words. How could he tell her that the priest was talking about the headman's foreign woman in Simla. 'I am innocent. Rama ... Rama, believe me,' he had said over and over again, but she had thrown pillows, glasses and slippers at him. He stood there helplessly, but he could not tell her the truth. A man should never betray another man, especially not the village headman.

Shankar watched Janak's face carefully and waited patiently. Then he could no longer contain himself and burst out:

'I took the first bus to Simla, but pretended to fall ill at Ouchghat and then I wrapped my head in my wife's old shawl which I was smart enough to bring with me and quickly caught the other bus, the one with the headman in it, at the next stop. I got off behind the headman in Simla and followed him. First he went to a shop and bought some things, I could not see what he bought because I did not want to get too close to him, besides my eyes were covered with the shawl. In fact, I stumbled once or twice, but I had to keep my face hidden, you see, or he would have recognized me.

'When you follow someone you have to make sure he does not get to see your face. All is lost then. They see your face and they know who you are at once and then they know you are following them. They might confront you and ask you what you are up to. You have to think of an excuse really fast or the game is up. Yes, the trick is to keep your face hidden...'

'Yes, yes. Stop repeating everything like a parrot. Tell me what happened next,' Janak said, raising his voice.

Shankar, though pleased that Janak had finally asked him a question, did not like being rushed. He wanted to savour his story, draw it out as long as possible, so he swallowed once or twice as if his throat was dry. Having been a quiet, taciturn person all his life, he was not used to talking so much.

Janak tapped his fingers on the table impatiently, and then said, 'He keeps a woman there.'

Looking at Shankar's dejected face he asked, feeling a little sorry for his old friend, 'Tell me, did she see you?'

'No. I do not think so. Anyway she does not know who I am and so many people were going in and out of her shop,' said Shankar in a gloomy voice.

Then as he recalled the scene he regained his enthusiasm and continued. 'She cuts hair – imagine, the headman sleeping with a she-barber. Maybe she cuts and shampoos his hair for free. It said on the door *Haircut and Shampoo – Rs 40, oil head massage – extra*. It was written in English, but I could read it quite easily since the letters were big and bold.'

As Shankar babbled on about how he had sat outside the shop for hours, pretending to be a beggar and how he made enough money to cover his bus fare, Janak suddenly thought of the priest in the forest. 'A woman will bring grief,' he had said, but had he said it would be a woman with slit eyes? Janak tried to remember.

There would be no haircuts and no shampoos if the headman lost his head. The suit must be for her. Yes, but she would like some English style dress, not a suit. The headman was a villager who had no idea about these modern women. But then, who knew what a woman who had slit eyes and cut men's hair for a living would like?

'Is she pretty?' asked Janak, as he brought out the pink satin and slipped it under the sewing-machine needle. He felt less anxious now that the secret was out. He always knew the suit was for the headman's other woman, but after Shankar had brought real proof, the woman stood in front of his eyes now. He should have cut the neck really low like those bad women in Hindi films wore and made the kurta sleeveless so that she could show her naked arms. But then the headman would know that Janak knew this woman was a shameless hussy who wore low necks and kept her arms bare. If the headman found out that he knew, god knows what would happen. 'Shankar, go and see where the headman is now,' said Janak, not taking his eyes off the machine. Shankar shrugged and went out into the street, looking over his shoulder to make sure no one was following him.

The passing shower had washed the pine trees clean and they shone quietly in the sunlight. Janak looked out at the shrine carved into the rocky side of the hill, just beyond the bridge, and saw that someone had left a few laddoos near the steps. Strangely, the monkeys hadn't eaten them yet. He cut off a bit of thread from the satin kurta and held it up. The low-cut neck had a pretty lace frill, and he could see the space for the two tiny breasts peering out. The kurta was the first modern style, frilled one he had ever made, glittering with bits of sequins and gold beads he had added on. The finished salwar lay on the table, its legs spread out in a wanton pose. Janak could see the headman crumpling the satin with his big clumsy hands, tearing out the lace frills he had so painstakingly stitched. Outside on the pine tree, the ravens screeched loudly and an angry koel answered. Janak wondered if it would be a bad day. Then the walls of his shops began to tremble as the first truck rumbled into Giripul.

A shadow appeared on the wall. Balu was tapping on the shop window with his stick, Janak, startled to see him, jumped up from his chair. He had not seen him coming out of his shed.

'Oh my love, why do you hit me? Lower your dipper and overtake me,' Balu said with a smile. 'Today is a good day to strike out. Come, let us go and confront the pair. Dreaming shreaming – rubbish. She suspects him and he is guilty. Let them fight it out. Kill each other in this life if it is ordained. So be it. Did you bring my jaggery?'

Rama saw her mother peering out of the door. 'Ma, who is it?' she asked. The day was passing so slowly. The housework had been done, the evening meal cooked, her son had been fed and was now fast asleep. Her mother usually chatted with her all day, telling her stories of the various childbirths she had attended when she worked as a midwife, but today she seemed very quiet. 'Who is it? No bus comes at this time,' Rama asked her again.

'There they go, following the whore,' her mother said, pointing to the hill above their house. Rama jumped up, toppling the bowl of shelled peas, and ran to the door. Balu the beggar and her husband were walking up the hill. High above them she could see the third wife's orange dupatta floating in the breeze like a victory flag.

'All day long they follow her, like that dog, sniffing her scent. I told you not once but countless times, watch out for that man. I told your father, do not wed her to a tailor. But would he listen? No. Will any man listen to his wife? No. You could have married the constable's son, so what if he was squint-eyed. His father made thousand rupees a week in bribes only. At least that boy would be faithful, like all cross-eyed men are, and not go trailing behind the village whore in broad daylight.'

Rama watched the figures get smaller and smaller as they climbed higher up the steep hill path. The third wife, who could walk much faster than the men, had disappeared over the edge of the hill. Janak trailed behind Balu.

What a shameless man, following her like this for the entire village to see. But why had he taken Balu with him? Was he scared to meet her alone? What a sissy. But maybe he was innocent. Maybe he was going to measure something for her. After all, no one else in Giripul had a measuring tape. But why on top of the hill? There was nothing there except for a few wild raspberry shrubs.

Her mother was right, she must keep an eye on him. Even that priest in the forest had warned them. 'A strange woman will bring grief'. That stupid friend of his Shankar could help her. Yes, she would ask Shankar where he went and who he met. She would buy a lot of fish from him from now on, though she hated eating meat or fish, but for the sake of saving her husband from that evil woman, she would become a non-vegetarian. She would go at once to Shankar's house. There was no time to lose. 'If I find he is up to some mischief with the third wife. I will make sure the headman brings him grief,' Rama said loudly to her mother.

The headman looked up from his verandah and saw his wife's orange dupatta draped on a tree on top of the hill. He recognized it at once. He had just bought it for her from Simla and paid good money for it because the shopkeeper said it was special cotton made in China. He had haggled a bit and got two for the price of one. He had given Rosy the other one, but she didn't seem to like it much and threw it carelessly in the basket where she kept her dirty laundry.

What was his wife doing on top of the hill at this time of the day? She usually sat in the kitchen, cleaning the rice for the evening meal and listening to the radio.

He had bought her the radio a few months after their marriage. But now, he hated the film songs it played all day long and late into the night. All he wanted was some peace and quiet, but none of his three wives ever gave him a moment's peace. The first two jabbered away even in their sleep and bickered about the smallest things. When he married Shyamala, a shy young girl with high breasts, he thought she would bring him joy and peace at last, but she turned out to be the most talkative of them all. Like a parakeet she chattered to him about nothing at all and sulked if he did not pay attention to her silly prattle. He had slapped her a few times to shut her up, but then she started wailing and that sound was even worse.

Only his beloved Rosy kept her mouth shut except when she kissed him. He could not speak English, let alone Chinese, and she spoke no Hindi apart from a few broken sentences. Her silent, tiny mouth and narrow eyes brought him such joy and peace that he wished with all his heart he could make her his fourth wife.

But what would the people of Giripul say? They would be shocked to hear that the headman's wife is a woman from China. They did not even know where China was. He too did not know where China was. It must be hundreds of kilometres beyond the snow-capped mountains. He did not even know what caste she belonged to and who her father was. Barbers were low caste anyway, and he could not even drink water in their homes. Was her father a barber too?

How could he answer all the questions the village people would ask when he did not know anything about her? Rosy could never be his wife. At least, not in this life.

But did he want her as his wife in the next life? It might prove to be too complicated. He did not want to be born in China. Wherever it was, it seemed too far away. And he did not want to be born into the barber caste. He was a Himachali and that is what he wanted to remain.

He wanted to be born in Giripul in his next life too. Right here was where he wanted to be in all his future lives. No wife from China for him, ever.

The headman quickly looked up at the hills. He did not want any passing gods to listen to his thoughts. They sometimes granted stray wishes and then you had to suffer the consequences. He hoped they had heard everything he had thought about and not just the bits about China.

The orange dupatta had disappeared. He saw Janak and Balu going up the hill path and a sudden wave of rage rose in his heart. 'My wife! He is going to meet my wife! I will kill him with my bare hands. I will shoot him with my gun. I have a new licence from the DC. I can shoot him legally now!' The headman narrowed his eyes.

'But why has Balu gone with him? Balu never goes anywhere. What could they be doing following my wife? Maybe he is innocent, just doing some cutting or measuring. But why are they on the hilltop? Why do they have to do it secretly?' he muttered to himself, rubbing his forehead.

He came out on the street. The men in Lala's shop greeted him loudly, but he ignored them. Then he saw Shankar strolling outside Janak's shop. The headman shouted at him and Shankar stopped in his tracks.

'Oh no. Why is he calling me?' Shankar stopped, his heart racing with panic. Does he suspect me of following him? He will kill me for sure, thought Shankar and his knees began to tremble. 'I did not mean any ... just wanted to see Simla ... I did not ...' he mumbled and turned back to face the headman, his head bowed.

The headman frowned and said, 'What are you muttering? Listen, I want you to do some work for me.' He pulled Shankar into Janak's shop. Shankar quickly sat down on the floor.

'Listen, I want you to keep an eye on Janak. I just want to make sure he is not up to any hanky panky with the village women. The other day in Simla, a tailor's shop was set on fire because the men suspected him of pinching their wives' breasts. Janak is a decent man, I know, but still I do not want any trouble like that in Giripul. So here is a hundred rupees for you. I want you to keep an eye on him, tell me where he goes, who he meets.' The headman gave Shankar a friendly slap and went out into the street. Shankar began to laugh with relief, playfully gathering the bits of scrap cloth on the floor and throwing them in the air.

Tommy was outside the shop, pretending to guard it and gave a short bark when he saw Janak. He had gone to the other side of the village to chase a gang of monkeys, but had rushed back because he knew it was time for his afternoon meal. He looked at Janak with accusing eyes for being late. It was easy to make Janak feel guilty. Janak quickly put two thick rotis on his tin plate and pushed the door of the shop open.

Shankar was sitting on the floor, reading an old newspaper. His head was covered with bits of cloth. He narrowed his eyes and smiled his new smile at Janak, then pulled out two fifty-rupee notes from his pocket and laid them on the table. Janak looked at him with surprise.

'What is this? Where did you get all this money from?'

'Your wife gave me hundred rupees for one small fish.'

'But we never cook fish in our house. She hates the smell of meat, fish or eggs.'

'She gave it to me to keep an eye on you, tell her where you go, who you meet, which woman talks to you and for how long,' said Shankar, pulling out another crisp hundred-rupee note from his pocket with a smug smile. 'The headman gave me this to keep an eye on you, tell him where you go, which women you meet. I think he thinks you meet his wife secretly. You know, this business of keeping an eye on you is much better than catching fish. Easy money, no worry whether the fish will bite or not. Just stroll behind you all day and then collect the cash,' Shankar said, peering closely at Janak as if he was seeing him for the first time.

Janak sat down on his chair and took out the satin suit. He began doing a quick satin stitch around the neck line. Shankar watched him for a while and then said, 'There is no need to sulk. You can have half the money if you wish. It's only fair. If you were not here to be watched, they would not pay me,' he held out a fifty-rupee note.

'You have to give me a hundred, not fifty if you want to pay me half. Anyway, I don't want the money,' Janak said, pushing his hand away.

'Listen, I went with Balu to the hilltop to tell the headman's wife to call her husband and tell him about the dream. But she refused. "He will kill me before I can kill him," she said and ran away, leaving her dupatta. I had hemmed it for her only last week,' he said, holding up an orange dupatta.

'You should hide that at once. If your wife or the headman see it here, they will suspect you for sure. It is called evidence or being caught red-handed, or orange-handed in this case,' said Shankar, stuffing the notes back into his pocket. 'What shall I do? I am going mad. So much work is left, but I cannot stitch or cut any more with all these worries in my head. See how unsteady my right hand has become. I cannot even do a simple daisy stitch properly. I feel like running away somewhere where all these head-chopping nightmares and husband-and-wife killings will not follow me. I want to be left alone with my sewing machine.'

Just then, as if a passing god had heard him and sent a quick answer to his prayers, there appeared a small boy at his door with a letter.

'Must be bad news,' said Shankar and took the letter from the boy. He held it up against the light and then sniffed it.

Janak snatched it from him, tore it open and began reading it, running his finger down the paper. It was written in Hindi, but in a childish hand.

'Tailor masterji. Please come to the house at 9 a.m. tomorrow. Bring black and red thread.'

'Tell Bibiji I will be at Badi Kothi at nine for sure,' Janak told the boy and took out an apple from a bag and gave it to him. The boy bit into it at once and ran out into the street.

'What shall I report to the headman?' asked Shankar in an irritated voice. 'You cannot just go away at this important stage when anything can happen. The headman could be killed or he could kill his wife.'

'You tell him anything you want. I am going home. Or else my wife will kill me,' Janak said, folding the dupatta into a small square.

'Someone will die for sure, that too a violent death. Don't blame me then,' Shankar muttered, walking out of the door.

'I do not want it to be me,' said Janak softly, tucking the dupatta into a box filled with broken buttons and then putting the box in a trunk where he stored odd bits of cloth. No one would ever find it there. He looked around for a moment as if he would never see his little shop again and then went out. Tommy rose from the steps as the shutter came down and stretched. He wondered where he could go for his evening meal.

5 Leela dreams and travels back in time; Janak and Shankar go to Badi Kothi; Shankar nervous but impressed

Leela had inherited the house from her uncle, who had no children. As a child, she would love coming here with her parents for her summer holidays and would play alone for hours in the orchard. The peach, apple and plum trees were laden with tiny green fruit and she always felt sorry that she had to leave before they could ripen. Later, she came here with her husband for longer holidays, but they left before the monsoon when the fruit was changing from green to orange-red, because her husband hated the leeches that came with the rains. They seemed to scent him out whenever they went for a walk and stuck to his legs, gorging on his blood, but never attacking her.

Now she lived here all through the year, sometimes even braving the cold winter months. The old apple trees were gnarled with age and many of them had stopped giving fruit, because the winters were no longer as cold as they used to be and the apple trees needed a certain number of hours of freezing temperature to be able to produce fruit. After all, they were first brought to the Simla hills from the West.

There used to be peach trees, too, in the orchard, but she could not remember now where they were and whether they still gave any fruit. The monkeys probably ate them all. That is what the mali said and she could not walk around the orchard any more to check.

The house was the same as it was when she was a child – shabby and comfortable. The expensive silk carpets had faded, the curtains had gone stiff with age and the silver, dull and tarnished, winked quietly in the glass sideboard. Only the floor, made of deodar wood planks, still gleamed as if it had just been polished. She used to skate from one end of the room to the other in her socks when she was a child and her uncle often scolded her for ruining the floor. Now Leela was afraid she might slip and fall if she walked too fast. Not that she could walk fast any more, and the gleaming old floor always reminded her of that. As if it was saying to her, 'You decrepit old woman, see how well I have aged.'

Bhanu, her old servant, had died a year ago, but his wife, who was thirty years younger than him, was still here with her brood of grandchildren to look after her.

Leela didn't need a lot of looking after, but someone had always helped her along right from her childhood. She had been surrounded by strong men, efficient women and loyal servants. Her mother told her what to wear, her husband told her what to say or do, and her mother-in-law told her how to manage the house and the servants. They were all dead now, but she still heard them sometimes, telling her what to do or say or what to order for lunch. She felt comforted when they did that.

God had been kind to her always and now she had come to live here, in the house she loved the most, till she too died and joined all her loved ones wherever they were.

Everybody had gone, parents long ago, her husband just last year, her brother, a few months back.

Leela did not have any children – just as well, or they would be grumbling about who would look after her. She was content in this house with its cosy, melancholy air, creaking wooden floors and deodar fragrant beds.

For fifty years she had repeated to herself everyday that she did not have any children, that she was barren, her womb shrivelled and dried like an old seedpod, till she had come to believe it. The shadowy image of that gentle face, those grey eyes haunted her at night, but she refused to let him come into her real world. She looked at her husband, his family, her garden, her dogs and willed him to go away.

But now the weight of that one forgotten memory sat heavily on her. It was as if it was tied to her back and she had to carry it around with her. All those forgotten words lying safe in the dark corners of her mind rose up to touch her, refusing to stay hidden. Now that she was all alone in this world, waiting for the friendly hand of death to take her away, that beloved face came and laid his cheek on hers when she slept. She could hear his deep voice teasing her, calling her silly names, 'My chittery-buttery, my jasmilloo, my rasaguloo.'

He must be dead now. He was twenty years older than her and maybe she would meet him soon. They could laugh together again. Were the rules the same for proper behaviour after you died or could you freely choose who you wanted to love?

Leela often woke up with her heart beating in fear as if someone had heard her secret thoughts, peered into her dream and seen her with Robert, his arms around her.

Sometimes old friends came to visit her, but the silence of the hills frightened them and they did not stay long.

'Why don't you get a television,' they said and left promising to come back soon, but they never did. Distant relatives called once in a while, surprised to know she was still alive, complained about the bad line and put the phone down quickly. They were all hoping to inherit the house and the orchard and tried not to show their impatience.

She was happy when they left her alone, but she was bored with life. Content but bored. Though she could not walk around much, the years sat lightly on her, she hardly had any wrinkles on her face and her hands were as soft as a girl's. During the day, she never allowed herself to think of the past. There was just too much to think about. It was like going down a long tunnel which did not seem to have an end. It was easier to look closely at each morning. Just take four or five things in your palm and look at them. What to have for lunch, cauliflower or bhindi? Roti or rice? Which flower had opened its petals today in the garden? Should she wear a shawl or just a light cardigan would do?

If she blocked each day with simple, boring things then nothing could reach up from the past to drag her back. There was so much to regret, to forgive and to love. So much to cling to so that she would not forget as her mind slowly began to erase what it did not like from her past. She had forgotten his face many years ago, but his voice still rang in her ears at night. His laughter made her cry in her sleep.

Leela smiled and looked down at her hands. They were covered with pale brown spots and her wedding ring hung loosely on her finger. Something new would make her feel alive. She would plant a new rose and make new curtains for her bedroom. She would send, at once, for the tailor who lived in the village. He had come many years ago or maybe just last year, she was not sure, but it was when her husband and the dog were both alive, to stitch a coat for their dog. She had given him an old blanket, a very nice one made in Scotland, for him to cut up and she remembered how shocked he was that she wanted to cut such a soft blanket for the dog.

He had cut it very neatly so that half of the blanket could still be used for a child; she had planned to give it to the tailor, he was such a nice man with large, kind eyes like a spaniel, but her husband had shouted so much at him that he had run away without his payment or the rest of the blanket. She had sent the money with Rabi, Bhanu's great grandson, down to his shop, 'Pink Rose Ladies' Tailor'. How she had laughed when she heard the name of his shop, which the servants said was a hole in the wall. But he was a very good tailor and now he would do up her bedroom for the last time so that when the relatives came to see her, to finally pay their last respects to her body laid out in the bedroom, they would be impressed by the new curtains.

She had already told Bhanu's wife Kammo which saree she would wear and which photograph of hers to put on the table, draped with a garland of marigolds. Now, while she waited for the final day to arrive, she must do something to pass the time. A long life was a heavy burden to bear, but she must carry on regardless, making new curtains, planting marigold borders.

'This cloth is very good, old but strong, must be from English days. They made good, strong cloth those days,' said Janak without lifting his head. Bibiji sat before him and he could see her feet clad in white slippers. The skin, transparent with fine blue veins, was as white as her slippers and it seemed both were made of the same cobweb-like material. She hovered around him, watching him work and asking him strange questions every few minutes.

'How old was your mother when she got married?' 'How many women have had abortions in Giripul?'

Janak just shook his head, he had no answers to any of her questions. Even his mother did not know how old she was when she got married, so how would he know?

'What is an abortion?' he asked the cook's wife later when they were eating in the courtyard, the sun warm on their necks.

'Dropping babies. You know, when these rich ladies do not want babies they just go to the doctor, pay him a few thousand rupees and get rid of the baby. God will punish them when they die. He will ask them who gave them permission to do this and they will have no answer. God will then line up all the dead babies in front of them and they will have to ask for forgiveness from each one,' said the cook, shoving a fistful of rice into her mouth.

As she chewed, she narrowed her eyes and stared angrily at Janak as if he was responsible for the rich ladies dropping their unborn babies, so he never dared to ask her anything after that. Better to sit quietly and do my work, he decided. Rich people had their own mysterious ways and who was he to question them? They ate rice with a spoon and fork, blew their nose in bits of paper and slept like babies all day long. He did not want to think too much about their lives. Down in Giripul there were so many strange things going on; he could not start worrying about life in the Badi Kothi. The old master had died, poor man, but it made it much safer to work here, though his loud voice still seemed to echo in the house, making Janak nervous.

They ate well here, thick rotis, a heap of good rice, dal with a lashing of ghee, with endless cups of hot, sweet, milky tea during the day. They even gave him pink, sugar-coated biscuits and some strange bread which was dark brown. Maybe it had gone bad and they wanted to get rid of it. It tasted like sawdust so he threw it away when the cook was not looking.

The curtains would take at least two weeks to complete and he would come every other day. It would be good to get away from Giripul till all the killing dreams vanished and things came back to normal. He liked sitting here on the long verandah with its basket-like chairs, surrounded by green plants and unusual flowers. It was as if he had come to a foreign land where everything was strange and new, though all he had done was climb the hillside.

All morning bibiji walked around the house, her stick making a tapping sound on the wooden floor. Janak heard the sound echoing behind him as he worked and thought of the water finder who had come to Giripul when he was a boy. He too walked around the village tapping a stick like this, though it was an ordinary wooden stump and did not have a silver top like bibiji's stick. Tap, tap, tap, he went all over the village, followed by all the children and men of Giripul. Sometimes he would pause, lie down on the ground, put his ear on the ground and listen. He said the earth spoke to him, told him about her underground streams. Then he would get up, and shake his head and walk away muttering to himself.

He stayed for many days in Girpul, eating huge meals at the headman's father's house and telling them stories about places he had been to in the plains to find water. But he never found any water in Giripul and was finally ordered to leave.

The day after he left, the spring suddenly began to gush out from the rocks, and had never run dry since then. They had built a stone hut near the spring and topped it with a wooden snake's head, to ward off the evil eye. The women fetched water every afternoon from the spring and stored it in big pitchers at home. 'One day we will have water from taps like in the city,' the headman had boasted then, but no one believed him.

Water from a tap which could be turned on and off had seemed like a magician's trick in his childhood days, but now quite a few houses had taps, including Janak's, and what bliss it was to bathe under a stream of running water. You could wash your hair, put as much soap as you liked, knowing there was plenty of water to wash it off. When you bathed with a bucket of water, you had to measure each mug.

There was a hand pump which the government had installed with great fanfare near the bus stand. The local MP had come, broken a coconut on it and got his picture taken for the local newspaper. But none of the women liked the taste of the water from the hand pump and preferred to fill their pitchers at the spring.

'The hand pump water is fine, a bit salty but safe to drink. The women like to gather at the spring to gossip about their husbands,' said the headman. 'Even though I have had the hand pump installed with great difficulty, running to Simla fifty times to meet the Water Board Authorities and paying everyone hefty bribes, now only strangers and dogs drink water from it,' he grumbled, but confessed in private to Janak that the water from the hand pump gave him indigestion.

In the Badi Kothi, they had taps everywhere and water came from a black tank on the roof. There were separate rooms where you did your morning job. You had to sit, not squat, in a chair made of white china like a huge cup. Then when you finished you pulled a chain and water came gushing out. There were big white tubs which you could bathe in, though why you should like to sit in a tub, Janak could not understand. Wouldn't the water be dirty?

These rooms, the cook said, were called bathrooms, and they were so big that Janak could live here with his family – without his mother-in-law, of course. Each bathroom had a cupboard filled with bottles of soap, shampoo and other things like tiny sticks with bits of cotton to clean your ears. Janak wanted to take one of them back to show Rama, that would really impress her, but the cook told him not to touch anything.

There were carpets everywhere and rows of photographs of foreign men and women hung on the wall. He knew they were foreigners because they all had golden hair and pale faces like people who lived in the remote mountains high above Simla. They stood straight, looking at him seriously, and they all had a dog at their feet.

Maybe he should get a picture taken with Tommy and hang it in his house, Janak thought. But his wife would want to be in it and she would want her mother too. That would ruin the picture for sure. He would have one taken secretly of Tommy and his son and hang it in the shop. Let the women say what they wished, sometimes a man should get his way.

There was a photographer who came to Giripul, but he was quite expensive and people got a photograph taken only once in their lifetime, on their wedding day.

Only rich people or foreigners could take pictures like this, of unimportant occasions, posing with their dogs. Everything was different and wonderful here, like a child's world. He would bring Rama and their son here one day, but he would wait till her mother had left.

I wonder what these people think about us, Leela wondered. I wish, I had gone down to the village when I could walk properly and seen their houses, though DN – as her late husband was called by everyone – would never allow me. 'You will catch some disease or be bitten by a rabid dog there,' he would say, Leela thought, as she watched Janak turn the sewing machine handle slowly, with loving care. It was an old one she had bought from an English lady in Simla when she and her family were leaving India. She had bought their entire household, all their crockery, cutlery and linen, for a song. Poor lady, how she had cried, the dear old English woman. 'I loved being here. We were so happy. Three generations of my family were born in India. Now I have to go and live in Shropshire where it rains all the time. No servants, my poor dogs to be left behind,' she sobbed, wiping her nose with a tiny lace handkerchief.

Leela had held her hand and they had both cried quietly for a while. Then tea was brought in with some tiny cakes which she said were called fairy cakes. They felt much better after eating two each. She wrote down the recipe for Leela which was still lying in some drawer she was sure.

The same tea set was on the tray in front of her, the tea pot spout was slightly chipped, the milk jug had a hairline crack but did not leak, after all it was Crown Derby china, but there was no Bhanu any more to make fairy cakes. His wife, Kammo, could make paper-thin paranthas and spicy potatoes, which Leela loved eating even though they gave her terrible indigestion at night.

'What do people eat for breakfast in your village?' the old lady asked Janak. He had just told her, but she seemed to have forgotten. 'Oh, anything their wives give them. Roti, dal, parantha with left over sabji. Some people even have bread nowadays,' Janak replied, though he did not know anyone in the village who ate bread.

He did not like the way the old lady sneaked up on him suddenly. It made him miss a stitch. Usually he could hear the tapping, but today she was gliding along without her stick. The old master would at least shout to tell you he was coming. Next time he would bring Shankar with him to keep him company.

'I need a helper, bibiji. These curtains are getting too heavy for me to handle alone,' he said.

'All right, but I will only pay him half the day's wages.' Janak, who was not expecting any payment for Shankar, only his lunch and endless cups of tea, looked up at her surprised.

'Well, all right, you can have full payment for him, if he repairs my cushion covers,' said the old lady, slowly sitting down in her chair. In a few minutes, she was fast asleep. Her gentle snores filled the air and the hill barbet began to call from the end of the garden.

Janak's mother had worked till the day she had died. In fact, a few hours before she collapsed, she had made five jars of pickles with turnip, carrots and cauliflowers, grumbling as usual about Rama not doing enough around the house.

'Not a good match for you, son. Your father was missing and I could not find a good bride for you. What could a poor husband-less woman do? She was the first girl we saw. She brought such a meagre dowry, no scooter for you, no new clothes for my relatives, not even a new sewing machine. If you wed your daughter to a tailor, least you can do is send a new sewing machine. Misers.' Two hours later, she was dead. Maybe if she had just sat on a chair like bibiji, and not worked in the fields, milked the cows and done all the cooking, she might still be alive. Rama did try to help, but the old lady had always pushed her away saying, 'While there is breath in my body, my son will only eat what I cook with my own hands.'

She never rested for a moment and sighed loudly as she went about the house doing her chores. She would get up from the floor with a long moan and then rub her back with her hands, glaring at Janak accusingly all the time.

Janak tried hard, but he could not imagine his mother sitting on a chair. Her callused feet had silver toe rings because she was still a married lady and she kept them on even on her widow-sari days, but like all the other old women in the village, she never wore slippers, except when they went for a wedding or a funeral to the next village.

'I have always wanted to see the Badi Kothi – the only big house in Giripul. You know, my father used to say it is haunted by English ladies who dance naked,' said Shankar, shielding his eyes from the sun as they walked up the narrow, steep path. The trees swayed in the gentle breeze and drops of rain which had collected last night on the branches, fell on their heads. Though it was still early in the day, the sun was quite strong and warmed the back of their necks soothingly. Soon they would be on top of the hill from where they could see the snow-capped mountains beyond Simla. A swarm of bees buzzed near them and they quickly covered their ears with their palms.

'No, that is the ruined bungalow behind the headman's house. That is where the English ladies dance naked. And they are not naked, they just wear sleeveless dresses,' Janak said, ducking his head to allow the bees to float past. He considered himself an authority on sleeveless dresses ever since he had made the other woman's satin suit.

'That is like being naked. My father said he saw them in this house when he came once to cut the hedges with his father,' insisted Shankar.

'How can there be so many English ghosts staying here in our small village? Some must have gone home to their English land too. And what about our own ghosts?

They have more right to be here and cannot give up all the space to foreigner ghosts. They must live here amongst their own people. All the time you see English ghosts only. You tell me then, what happened to all our dead relatives?' shouted Janak because the breeze was carrying his voice away.

'I have never heard of any of my relatives becoming ghosts. They were all cremated properly with full rites, pundits were fed, given bedding and copper vessels, umbrellas and many boxes of pure ghee sweets,' replied Shankar breathlessly.

'You know, Shankar. I am sure the headman's third wife will haunt our village if she is put to death by her husband,' Janak said and stopped to look at his friend struggling behind him.

'No. I think the she-barber with slit eyes will make a better ghost for Giripul,' replied Shankar, holding his chest to catch his breath.

'Why must we always have an outcast ghost? I prefer the third wife any day,' Janak said, climbing faster. Let Shankar try and keep up with him, he thought. 'Trying to become a great detective when he can't even walk up the hill without stopping to hold his chest ten times,' he mumbled, giving his friend a look of contempt.

'You do, do you? Well, I must tell your wife that, my friend, and earn another fifty rupees,' Shankar said with a malicious grin.

Janak stopped and caught hold of Shankar's neck and shook him. Shankar began to howl and suddenly a huge langur, the leader of a gang, leapt down from a tree. Very quickly, six more jumped down from the higher branches of the pine tree and scampered away, their long, silvery tails forming loops along the path. When they reached a safe distance, they sat down and stared at Janak, their black faces shining like silk masks.

Janak stopped and looked up at the steep path winding its way up the hill. 'Can you hear something?' he asked.

'Yes. I think there is a leopard here. I can smell it,' said Shankar, raising his head to the sky and sniffing the air. The forest was strangely quiet and they could hear the wind rustling softly through the pine trees as if a woman in a starched sari was walking behind the trees. The langurs had disappeared deep into the forest. Janak and Shankar could see the Badi Kothi high up on the hill, its white glass windows winking at them, half hidden behind a wall of old deodar trees.

The leopard could be watching them from anywhere, thought Janak and felt a wave of fear rise in his stomach. 'Leopards do not harm grown men. They only lift cattle, dogs and children,' he said loudly to show he was not frightened.

'What if it thinks I am a child? I am so short,' whimpered Shankar. Suddenly he looked like the small, frightened boy Janak had known all through their childhood and he felt a surge of affection for his old friend. He had not changed, but was putting on an act for a short while. Once all this murder-dream business was settled, he would go back to being the sleepy, fishy-smelling Shankar.

'Stand on your toes and walk. Raise your head. Hurry.

Sing loudly, make a noise, clap your hands,' shouted Janak.

They began to walk uphill, Janak singing an old film song in a loud, broken voice, beating the shrubs with a pine branch, while Shankar minced along daintily on tip toes, clapping his hands nervously. The swarm of bees came back and circled them, and then disappeared into the forest once more.

On sunny days, the servants used to put their chairs out in the lower lawn under the apricot tree, but far away from the deodar trees. DN did not like being too close to the forest because he was afraid of the bears. They had never seen one, but once an old woman with a scar running down her face had come to cut grass in the orchard and Bhanu had brought her to them to inspect. She stood tall and straight in the sunlight, her scarred face raised to the sky like a poodle in a dog show. Bhanu turned her face to show them the deep scars that ran down her face like a dry river bed, from her eye to her neck.

'A she-bear did this to her when she was out cutting grass in the forest three summers ago,' he said and the woman nodded, looking at the biscuits on the tea tray. Leela wished the poor woman would go away. How terrible to be disfigured like this for life, but DN was fascinated by her scars and went closer to examine the woman's scar, who obliged him by lifting her head scarf and showing him the torn lobes of her ear.

'The bear tore her ears too?' asked DN.

'No, no. Her gold wedding earrings were too heavy and tore her ear lobes,' said Bhanu and scolded the woman in their language. She covered her ears, gave them a toothless grin and went back to the edge of the garden where she was quickly swallowed up by the grass. Leela told Bhanu to give her tea and biscuits, but Bhanu said she would only have tea and no biscuits since she did not know what they were.

From that day, DN never went beyond the flower beds and warned Leela to stay within the walled area. 'I have heard people in America put electric fences to keep off wild animals. I will inquire in Delhi if we can get them here,' he said eagerly.

His endless battles with monkeys, hares, jackals, foxes, pigeons, porcupines and the neighbours, all always ended in defeat, yet DN kept thinking of new ways to trap, maim, kill or punish his unseen enemies. It was like a hobby for him.

It was not that he was particularly interested in the fruits or the meagre revenue the orchard produce fetched, he just did not like any animals or humans getting the better of him. 'Bloody creatures,' he would say each morning as he strolled down to the garden after breakfast, with their dog Sheroo running ahead, and saw the latest damage the 'enemy' had inflicted – nibbled-up apples, tooth-marked peaches, gnawed apricots and headless pea stalks. 'Bloody bastards, bandits, thieves,' he would mutter, gnashing his teeth.

The village boys working on the orchard would look up with frightened faces and bow as they walked past him, wondering what they had done wrong to annoy the master. One day he shouted, 'sons of bitches' so loudly, when he saw an entire peach-laden branch that had been attacked by the monkeys and was lying broken on the ground, that all the women cutting grass on the hillside fled.

'DN, please control yourself, all this shouting is not good for your blood pressure,' Leela would say, but he would run out with his gun and fire in the air. She would say a quick prayer and never would he manage to hit even one living creature.

The only battle he won was against the mice. It was on a rare occasion when they had visitors, a couple from a neighbouring orchard along with an old lady, who was either a mother or a mother-in-law. Since Leela never saw them again after that eventful day, she never found out.

That morning they were sitting on the sofa in the drawing room. They had discussed the bad apple crop, the corrupt chief minister, the mild winter, the chance of hail and now were sitting silently, staring out of the window.

As the gentle autumn sunshine danced on the hydrangea shrubs, each flower became a different shade of mauve and blue. A pair of cinnamon sparrows crashed against the windows and DN shot them an angry look. Then he turned his glare on the neighbours, willing them to get up and leave. Suddenly the neighbour's wife jumped up from the sofa.

'I think I can hear … There is something …' she said breathlessly, her sari pallu falling down to expose her huge breasts popping out of her blouse. As everyone stared at her, they heard a squealing sound which gradually grew louder. DN immediately reached for his gun, which he always kept near him.

'No, no, don't shoot! It is mice ... wait! Call Bhanu! Bhanu!' Leela cried. Bhanu appeared at once holding a tray of samosas in his hand, but he froze at the door, mesmerized by the neighbour's wife's exposed breasts.

'Sahib!' he cried suddenly, thinking he was going to witness a crime of passion.

'Bhanu, mice in the sofa!' Leela exclaimed, but before Bhanu could move forward, DN had pushed the sofa and it had overturned. The neighbour, his wife and his mother or mother-in-law, all toppled over and at the same time, a dozen baby mice scampered out from the sofa's torn underbelly. DN let out a joyous war cry and stamped his foot on the ground, spilling tea all over the guests still huddled on the carpet.

He grabbed a flower vase, luckily not Leela's favourite Chinese one, and threw it at the scampering baby mice while Bhanu brought the tray down swiftly. With a few hard thumps, he managed to massacre the entire family of mice. A few that tried to run back into the safety of their home in the sofa underbelly, were dragged out by Sheroo and shaken to death. They did not notice when the neighbours had quietly slunk away. She never saw them again.

Leela was sure the mother mouse had escaped and set up a new family in the prayer room because she heard the same squealing a month later. She did not tell DN about it, and since he never went to the puja room, the mice were safe there, living happily on raw rice, mishri and rose petals.

A pair of red-billed blue magpies floated down from the walnut tree, their long tails fluttering behind them, and began pecking at the seedlings the mali had just planted. This would have driven DN insane and he would have hurled abuses at the birds. But the wily birds were great mimics and would have screeched back the same abuses at DN and flown away. Even though life was much more peaceful after he had passed on, she missed his booming voice when the long silence of the day seemed endless.

The tailor was completing the curtains quite fast, but she did not want him to finish too soon. What would she do if the curtains were ready and she was still here waiting to be called to the other side? It was too tiring to think of yet another project to pass the endless days, months and years. She could make matching cushion covers from the rest of the cloth, she thought.

Janak had warned Shankar not to be too curious and snoop around the house. He was not sure what this new Shankar would be up to. He might suddenly decide that the third wife's dream had brought them here or the headman's woman was going to show up in bibiji's verandah. That would really shock the old lady, Janak thought, a strange she-barber suddenly walking up the steps and demanding free tea and biscuits. But the old lady was a bit like a child and one never knew what she would do or say. Sometimes she laughed for no reason and then muttered to herself in a sad voice. She was a woman after all, and you can never tell with women – rich or poor, old or young. She might just sit down with the she-barber and have tea or ask her to cut her snowy-white hair.

It was just as well, DN died a few months before the day the leopard got locked in the bathroom. The shock and excitement would have certainly killed him if he had managed to survive his massive heart attack. Sheroo, a brave, fearless creature like all Himalayan sheep dogs, was out in the garden one evening when he sighted the leopard. It was a juvenile one, only out to inspect the area, not to do any harm, but Sheroo was trained by DN from a young age to attack any intruders. He still had not got used to DN's absence and kept searching the house for him, going into each room and sniffing the air. Every evening he sat at the gate, looking down the path, waiting for DN to return.

Then he spotted the leopard. This was a prize he could take for his master. He would catch it and lay it down at his master's feet and would be rewarded with a big 'shabash'.

Very slowly and cunningly Sheroo rounded up the leopard cub, who thought the dog was playing a game, till he was trapped inside the house. The cub began to snarl and show his baby teeth, but Sheroo knew he was winning and began to slap him with his paws. The leopard retreated, a bit frightened now, and before Sheroo could do anything, it ran into the guest bathroom that had recently been decorated with new tiles and fluffy pink bath mats. Just when the leopard was growling at his reflection in the mirror, Bhanu had the presence of mind to slam the door shut. Now no one wanted to open the door in case the cub attacked them.

'It may be a baby, but it has very sharp teeth. It can blind us with its claws because it is furious with us,' said Bhanu. 'Especially with you, since you were the one to lock it up. Animals never forget,' said his wife maliciously. Bhanu told her to shut up, but he too looked quite scared now.

Leela called the police at once – luckily the phone was working – but they refused to deal with it, saying it was the forest department's job.

'Madam, it is our job only if the animal has killed or maimed someone. No body, no injury, no task for us,' the inspector said. The forest department wanted to know what fruits she grew, whether the hail had damaged the crop, and offered her an interest free loan, free mushroom spawns but they too could not do anything about the leopard. 'You should get in touch with the wildlife authorities in Delhi. Sorry, we cannot help,' the man said kindly.

'But it will take two days for them to get here. What should we do till then?' Leela asked, now feeling very helpless without DN. He would have handled it all so well by shouting at everyone concerned till they did what he demanded.

'Madam, then call the circus man. They will give you good money for the animal,' they replied and disconnected the phone.

Finally Bhanu, who felt he was responsible for the leopard, sent for his cousin who was a hunter. His cousin came by the afternoon bus, carrying a home-made gun on his shoulders. He did not want to kill the leopard since it was a only a cub, so he threw a gunny sack over it and took it away to the servant's quarters. He fed it some scraps of roti with his own hands and the cub played with him quite happily.

Soon he became as tame as a puppy and lived in the servants' courtyard, eating dal and chapattis and playing with their children. But the chickens and the goats watched him nervously and Sheroo kept trying to attack him till one day he chased him into the forest and neither of them came back again. Leela was sure Sheroo was with DN now, both roaming happily in the forest, fighting all the four-legged or two-legged creatures that came their way.

'Why does he have to go to the Badi Kothi everyday? I am sure he has got some woman there,' said maaji, peering out of the window. Rama was sweeping the floor with a pine-needle broom. She crawled around on her haunches, reaching into corners, under the bed, and then briskly backed out. The fine dust rose, formed an arc in the sunlight and settled down again on her hair and on the floor.

'He gets good money there, maaji, and it is safer for him to be there, away from all these sluts with their scraps of cloth,' Rama said, sitting on the floor.

'How do you know he is not with some hussy at this very minute? Men are like dogs, searching for a willing woman everywhere. Sniff, sniff – is all they have to do to find one,' maaji said, throwing the rice husk to the sparrows who had gathered in the courtyard. They swooped down at once and then flew away, chattering angrily. They expected grains of rice, not empty husks.

'Ma, the only woman there is the old memsahib who was born when the angrez laat sahibs ruled us. Janak says she looks like a white ghost. Her hair, skin, teeth and clothes are pure white. She is wrapped in a white shawl made of the softest, most expensive wool, and she walks with a cane. She is a pious lady though he says she eats meat and eggs everyday. He can smell it on her,' said Rama, shaking her head in wonder.

Her mother turned around and glared at her.

'So he says. What is this smelling business? Why does he have to get so close to her? Eighty or eighteen, women are women. I do not trust that tailor husband of yours. That day when we went to the temple, the priest said something about a woman .... Have you asked him about it?'

'No, ma. I will ask him tonight, but you know how he is. He will just look at me like a scared rabbit. But you are right, I will force him to tell me the truth. There must be something going on. Why else would the priest sitting in the remote forest see it?' said Rama, gazing towards the hills.

Her mother clicked her tongue angrily and said, 'I think we should visit Baba Bengali, I hear he has set up camp near Giripul bridge. He can solve any problem, cruel mothers-in-law, barren women, second wife, dead wife, and non-performing husbands. Women come to him from faraway villages. He has special low rates for women if they come between three and four in the afternoon,' she said, putting a tiny sliver of betel nut in her mouth.

Rama did not reply, but her mother's words sank deep into her heart. Tailorji would not cheat on her. He loved her, she knew that. She saw it everyday in his eyes, even when she was mean to him. It was the women who flocked to him. But then, he did touch them all day long, she had seen him.

'Oh, tailorji, the neck is too low.' 'Oh, masterji, the waist is too tight,' the women would whine, twisting and turning their bodies in front of him and he would put his arms around them to adjust the neck or the waist. What was a man to do when such temptation was put before him? One day he would reach out and grab them for sure.

She would insist from now that all the women brought an old kurta or blouse for measurement. There would be no need then for him to put his arms around their breasts, waist and hips. She would throw that measuring tape away. For the real enemy was the measuring tape which he always wore around his neck, as if ready to attack any woman he saw.

No, he would not do that. He was a good, harmless man, who loved his wife and son, she convinced herself. Her tailor husband was only interested in his stupid sewing machine.

Rama gathered the dust in a pan and threw it in the backyard. Then she began to sweep the old leaves that had fallen in the courtyard, gathering them in a high pile behind the shed. The goat that lived in their backyard came forward and began nibbling on the dry leaves, but lost interest and moved away in search of something tastier. The rooster and his four hens waited for the goat to leave and then stepped forward gingerly to inspect the leaves. They scratched at a few in a desultory way, but they too did not find them worth eating. The hens pecked at the broom angrily as if it was to blame for the lack of food, but the rooster, sensing their belligerent mood, quickly retreated into the shed. Rama threw them a handful of grain, put some fresh grass in the cow's bin and then sat down on the stone slab under the tap to wash clothes.

She picked up Janak's shirt and carefully went through the pockets. It was always important to check a man's pockets, her mother said. That way you could keep track of what he was up to. So far she had only found scraps of paper with measurements written on them. There was never any name to say who these breasts, waists and hips belonged to. Maybe he knew their bodies so well he did not have to write their names down like 36' bust – Shyamala, 32' bust – Kamala, thought Rama and put the shirt down. Something had to be done. After all, even that forest sadhu had warned Janak about some strange woman. When urged by maaji, she had asked him what that was all about, he had just stared at her with those silly rabbit eyes of his.

What was the harm in going to meet Bengali Baba? It would cost another hundred rupees, but it was well worth the money. She would not pay Shankar any more. All the fish she had bought was rotting in the pile of rubbish and even the cats did not go near them. She had tried to eat a bit, after all, she had paid good money for it, but the smell was so overpowering that she threw up.

Yes, Bengali Baba was so much smarter than Shankar and his foul, smelly fish. Everyone talked about Bengali Baba. He was so famous and he could chase shadows too, besides helping unhappy women. Maybe a shadow had come upon her husband and was trying to grab him – a female shadow. Yes. It was much better to go to Bengali Baba who could take care of any problem from either this world or the next. Much better than that Shankar. He had not given her any information till now worth the five kilos of fish.

Once, long ago, when she could walk much faster up and down the hillside, Leela had found a dog's grave at the bottom of the garden. She was searching for strawberries that sometimes grew here during summer. The patch was covered with grass, but suddenly she found a plump, red strawberry winking up at her. It was the sweetest she had ever eaten. Someone must have planted them long ago and she could see quite a few amongst the weeds.

Just when she bent down to pluck one, her toe hit something and when she looked down, she saw it was a stone slab. She pushed the grass aside, stamping her feet in case some snake was resting there, and saw, to

her surprise, a dog's head carved on the stained marble.
Some words were engraved on the stone and though the
letters were badly eroded, she could still read them.

> Here lies Raja,
> Faithful friend and companion,
> I will never forget you.
> And one day Mary and Raja
> will walk together again,
> in the garden of heaven.

There was something else written in a flowery script,
it looked like a date, 1909 or 1900. She was not sure
since the stone was broken around the edges and half
the letters had chipped away. She wet the end of her sari
with some water and tried to rub the dirt off the stone,
but it was embedded in the marble.

'Raja must be a dog because the grave was too small
for an adult. Could be a child, but the name is not right,'
she mused while talking to DN later.

'Could be a dwarf,' he replied gruffly, not looking up
from his newspaper.

'Why would a dwarf come here so far,' she asked, a bit
hurt by his tone.

'He did not have to walk here, you know. He could
have easily come by the railway. What date did it say?
1909? They had built the railway line to Simla by 1908.
He could have travelled by train, got on a tonga to Giripul
and then walked up to meet this Mary woman by the
steep hill path because the motor road had not been
built then. Then probably died of exhaustion or cholera
because of the water. They died like flies in those days,

the English, not dwarves, though he could have been an English one. They live a hundred years sometimes, I read somewhere. And are quite bright and fit till the very end,' said DN and went back to his week-old newspaper.

Leela did not like the idea of it being a dwarf's grave. It was not that she had anything against them and if she ever met one she would talk to him nicely, but she wanted it to be a dog's grave – a beloved dog's last resting place. She was sure it was the English lady's pet dog who she loved like her own child. 'Maybe she too did not have any children like me,' muttered Leela, watching the mali clear the grass around the grave.

When the grass was cut and the pile of stones removed, they found a neatly laid out flower bed beside the grave. Gradually, as they cleared all the overgrown shrubs and cut down the creepers entwined around them, they discovered a bird bath and a broken stone bench.

That summer, the mali and the young boy who helped him cleared out the entire area and planted some new seedlings in the flower beds – hollyhocks, phlox and pansies. These were the flowers she remembered from her childhood and from the English lady's garden in Simla. She remembered baby's breath, tulips and daffodils too, but she could not find them now anywhere in Simla.

Leela came here every afternoon when the sun was high above the house and sat on the broken bench. It tilted a bit under her weight, she was quite plump then, but the clawed feet would sink into the earth and it became firm and solid. This is where Mary must have sat and thought about her life at home with her beloved dog sitting at her feet, imagined Leela. She must have thought of all those people so far away, who she would probably never see again. Later, she must have sat here and thought about her dead dog. The air around the bench was heavy with sadness, but Leela felt at peace here. It was a comforting sort of sadness that tugged at your heart gently, like an old familiar ache you had learnt to live with.

Next year, in spring, a clump of iris suddenly appeared and then a few lone dahlias showed their brightly-coloured heads. Many years later, the dahlias were all over the hillside. They needed no looking after, like stray dogs, and grew wild in every corner of her orchard.

Leela could not walk to Raja's grave any more and she was sure the mali never bothered to clear the grass there now. He was old too and only liked to sit in the sunny part of the garden, pulling up weeds from the lawn in a haphazard manner. Anyway, Mary must be with her Raja in heaven's garden and it was best her garden be allowed to be lost to nature once more.

Did they allow dogs in heaven? She was sure they did. Otherwise, where would all these good faithful friends go?

Rama's mother not happy with visit to Bengali Baba; Magician arrives in Giripul; Janak worried about many things

Rama sat with the other women under the shade of an old banyan tree. They were waiting for the Baba to wake up. He always had a little nap at this time, his assistant, a scrawny boy with bleary eyes said, and asked them to sit a little further away so that their chatter would not disturb Baba. Her mother had brought Mithoo along too, and he was now also dozing under the tree. The women tried to feed him, but he ignored them and turned his head, much to her mother's joy. 'He only eats from my hands,' she said smugly, but when she tried to give him a piece of guava, Mithoo tried to peck at her hand. Some of the younger women tittered, but were silenced by an angry look from the older women. The bleary-eyed assistant glared at them, putting his finger on his lips like a school teacher. They remembered once more why they were here and some of them began to cry, but very softly so that they would not wake up Baba.

Rama remembered when Bengali Baba had come to the village the first time to chase the shadow that had settled down in one corner of Lala's tea shop, where the sacks of flour were stored. It would show itself to the card players at dusk, giving them a fright, and soon they stopped coming to the tea shop. At first, Lala tried to smoke it out by burning pine branches and coconut husk. But when he failed and the shadow grew bigger and darker and began to follow the women when they went to do their ablutions at dawn, the village decided to call Bengali Baba in.

He arrived with great fanfare, led by a boy beating a drum. His red-and-blue robes gleamed and the cock feather he wore on his turban, fluttered in the breeze. He looked grand. The men ran out to touch his feet while the women folded their hands and bowed. He raised a benevolent hand and blessed them all. Even though he was not a holy man, everyone respected and feared him as much as they did the priest.

'I need a plump chicken, pure mustard oil, a lamp and one metre of red cloth,' he said as soon as he had finished his second cup of tea.

The headman gave the chicken, Lala sent a bottle of mustard oil, Raja gave a new lamp made of stainless steel, not brass, and there was some argument whether this would work. But Baba accepted it. Janak brought out the cloth which was a little less than one metre, but Baba accepted that too. Then they all had to give one katori of rice, lentil, parched rice, matches and any other thing they wished, as long as it was dry, and could go into Baba's assistant's big cloth bag.

Raja gave a packet of playing cards which Baba's assistant put in his shirt pocket. Everyone saw him doing it, but none dared to say anything. For three days Baba sat around Lala's shop, his head covered with the red cloth, drawing triangles and circles on the ground with white chalk. The lamp kept burning and many cups of sweet tea were served to all those who came to the shop. When they wanted to pay, Lala refused, saying it was in Baba's honour. This pleased everyone and they had another cup, but Lala made them pay for that second cup of tea which everyone later said was too weak and had too little sugar.

On the third day, the chicken was beheaded and the blood sprinkled on the streets. The dogs went mad licking it up, but the monkeys chattered angrily from the trees. They seemed afraid of Baba which just showed how powerful he was because monkeys feared no one except a tiger.

Then Baba cooked by himself a delicious prasad with the beheaded chicken, chanting all the time, and gave it out to everyone on leaf plates. They ate it happily, first the men and then the women and children, even the widows who were not supposed to eat meat, ate a small portion. 'It is Baba's prasad, blessed by the gods,' they said, in case, some one raised their eyebrows at them with disapproval.

At first nothing happened, then suddenly they all saw the shadow rise like a thin plume of smoke, hover for a few seconds over the headman's house and then float away into the sky. The old women began to cry, children clapped their hands and the men stood still. No one spoke for a while and then they bowed to Baba, one by one. After that day no one saw the shadow again, though Rama was not sure who had seen it in the first place. But they all knew it had come to Giripul and Baba had chased it away.

Rama had waited patiently for a long time to meet Baba. The other women too waited with her, some had brought their children with them, who played around in the mud. Why were they all here? Was there so much sorrow in this world, Rama thought as she watched the women around her. Each one must have a sad tale to tell, otherwise they would not have come to Bengali Baba. Suddenly Rama felt her own problem was petty and small. So what if the tailor had looked at other women, maybe even touched them a little bit here and there. She must learn to ignore all this and be happy with her lot in life. Her son, her little house with a patch of garden with such good soil. She must not listen to her mother. She must not be jealous of the third wife. As soon as she thought of the third wife, Rama's heart filled with rage. 'No, I will not ignore her and let her carry on with my husband,' Rama said, and the woman next to her gave a start. She must have cried out because just then, Baba appeared and called her to him.

Before she could say anything, he said, 'Smile, child. God has been kind to you. Throw away anger, bitterness. Smile. Life is a rose, inhale its sweet fragrance. Leave fifty rupees with the boy.' He turned to another woman who had fallen at his feet sobbing. 'Rose. Inhale the scent of life,' she heard him say to her.

As they walked back to the village, Rama's mother kept scolding her, 'You should have explained the entire thing to him.'

'But I tried. He did not give me a chance,' cried Rama, tired and dusty and irritable.

'Smile, all he said was smile, and took our money,' muttered her mother.

Rama thought for a long time about what Baba had said and though she could not really understand anything, she forced herself to smile. To her surprise, she felt a strange sense of peace and serenity flood over her. She continued to smile all the way home.

The magician set up his tent across the bridge, on the flat ground where the buses slowed down for the passengers to throw coins into the river shrine. His assistant, an albino boy, had put posters on all the trees and rocks that lined the road from Simla. Most of them had flown away or had been torn up by the monkeys, but quite a few remained to announce the arrival of S.C. Salilaa, the great magician of India.

The next day, the magician shifted his tent from the bridge to the haunted English house. 'The atmosphere is better here,' said the boy with pale eyes and white hair, to everyone at Lala's tea shop. They were not sure what 'atmosphere' meant, maybe it was some magic word, but everyone nodded because they did not want the boy to think they were ignorant villagers.

Then the boy presented a plastic rose which squirted water when you pressed it to the headman with a low bow. 'Sir, a gift from my master,' he said in English, but slowly so that they could all understand.

The headman was very pleased and declared that he would buy twenty tickets for the first show which was to be held the next evening at six. He also declared it a school holiday though there was no need, since the children would be home by four o'clock in any case. But a holiday gave the occasion some importance.

The next day, Giripul was in an excited state. The women chatted about the show at the spring when they went to fetch water, the old men forgot to watch the bus or place bets as they argued about who had seen the best magic show and how long ago. The children, thrilled with their unexpected holiday, ran around the red-and-yellow tent and then when the albino boy came out, they ran away thinking he was a ghost.

The tent flapped and swayed in the breeze, making Tommy and the other dogs nervous – they had never seen anything like this since the last time a magic show was held in Giripul, they had not yet been born.

Janak had been given two free tickets since he had done some repair work on the magician's robe – a simple job of stitching the silver and gold stars that had come undone. By afternoon, people from the villages on top of the mountains, as far as Drena, Shaya and Banauth began streaming into Giripul. The men sat in Lala's tea shop while the women gathered under the tree, their heads covered with their new dupattas. Some held torn posters in their hands which the wind had carried to their homes right on top of the hill.

The bright crimson poster had the magician's name written in bold letters and his face sparkled in yellow and red. His mouth was open with a big smile and his teeth were painted blue.

'That was a mistake by the printer, but it looks nice and scary,' the albino boy told Janak, when he brought the robe to be fixed.

Janak felt sorry for the boy who looked so thin and had large eyes filled with fear, yet tried to smile and be friendly. The magician called him 'Choomantar', but Janak was sure it was not his real name. How sad it was to be born like this and not even have a real name.

Janak's wife was not happy when she heard they only had two tickets. 'What about maaji? She would like to go and take Mithoo too. He can learn a few tricks from the magician's bird,' she said when they were having dinner.

'That bird is a very expensive one from a faraway foreign land, maybe China,' said Janak and he could see Rama was impressed that he could say China so effortlessly, but she tried not to show it.

'So what? Mithoo can see what he does. He is a clever bird,' she said with a faint flicker of a smile. Her mood was changing, he could see.

'All right, I will buy a ticket for your mother. Mithoo can come for free, I am sure,' whispered Janak. This was an important moment and he had to tread very, very carefully. The moon was a semicircle and her temper was gentle these days, but it could go either way if he did something wrong. Janak took her hand and kissed each finger gently. Her skin tasted of fresh coriander.

'Get away, maaji will see us and your food will get cold,' she said, slapping his wrist playfully, but there was a faint promise in her eyes. He swallowed his chapatti in one quick gulp. The house smiled down at him, the half moon shone and Giripul was heaven on earth tonight.

7

Shadow Chaser alias Bengali Baba reflects on his dual life; List of shadows described; Methods given

The first time he was hit, he was not sure what had happened. He had gone to keep the milk outside the kitchen and then suddenly, out of the dim light came a blow. His head was almost wrenched from his neck and he saw the fine black cracks in the stone as his head hit the ground. There was blood everywhere and he could hear someone screaming. It was not him.

'Take him away! Take this son of the devil away! He has polluted my kitchen!' screamed the voice and a copper glass flew at him. This time he saw it coming and ducked. He ran back blindly to the cowshed and lay down on the floor. The cows groaned restlessly and stamped their hooves in the wet straw. He tried to soothe them, but when he tried to get up, his head hurt and one eye remained shut. He wiped his face with some straw and crept into the dark corner where they could not find him. The rats moved around him stealthily, afraid he would steal their secret hoard of food. He cried a little but soon fell asleep, wondering what he had done wrong.

From that day on the beatings began. At any given time of day, the new woman would throw copper glasses or bowls at him, lash out at him with a stick or a broom. 'Tainting my house, why don't you die, you wretch! They should have strangled you at birth, you monster. Devil's child! Go to your dead mother and leave us in peace,' she would scream, even when he was hiding in the cowshed. There was no food left on the steps for him any more and he had to drink the cows' milk secretly at night.

He did not know who she was and why she had suddenly come to live in his father's hut. Why was she so angry with him? What had he done wrong? Everyone else had gone and only she, another woman and his father lived there. He knew now that he was a terrible person, not fit to live with the others. He must go away from them. But that would mean going out during the day, and he had never done that. He was afraid the village children would throw stones at him. The men might attack him. But he must go somewhere far away, so that his father could be happy.

Bengali Baba knew they would come today from the other side of the mountain to call him. The boy had started talking yesterday in his dead grandfather's voice and the cows had refused to give milk in the evening. There had been a murder most foul a hundred years ago and the soul still roamed the hills, trying to get its revenge. Only he, the great Bengali Baba, the most renowned shadow chaser, could cleanse the air. Everyone living in the villages around Simla and on the mountains beyond knew that.

He was not always so sure of his powers, which waxed and waned with the moon, but the people believed in him completely. In fact, it was quite a headache to have so many people dependent on one's skills, but what could one do? All these shadows lurking in the crevices and corners had to be chased away and the air had to be purified. The money they paid him did not matter. He was above such petty things, but extra cash didn't harm anyone. It kept his wife in a mellow mood.

Anyway, this was a good time to go on a journey to the higher hills. The boy had talked at the right time. If he had started talking in his late grandfather's voice last month, reminding the family of all their wrong-doings, it would have been very inconvenient for Bengali Baba. He had to make sure the boys had ploughed the fields properly, otherwise the corn would not grow well. The stalks would be fragile and the slightest wind would twist them. Now he had supervised the planting of the corn and the cow had safely delivered a calf – a female one, which meant the goddess was pleased with him and good things would come his way.

The goddess had given him four sturdy sons, but none of his boys were very bright. Though he himself never mentioned it, everyone said they had taken after his wife's family: short, stocky and stupid.

'Look at you, Baba, so tall and fair. You could easily pass for an Englishman in the dark,' all his followers would would say when they saw him walking with his sons.

'Alas, your sons, who do not have your noble features, may the gods give them long lives. But then, one cannot have everything in life. You get the monsoon rains on time, but then you get floods. You get a sweet-tempered wife, but a harridan of a mother-in-law. God gives you four sons, but just enough brains for one, and that has to be shared equally among the four of them,' they muttered over and over again, the same words Baba had spoken to them earlier.

Baba knew as long as he was alive there would be plenty to eat, but after him who knew. He had married them to girls from good, land-owning families. Healthy, wide-hipped girls who would breed well, and he could see they were much smarter than his sons, but they were women. What use were women to keep the lands in order and bring money into the house? Women were only good for begetting sons and keeping house. But he was happy God had made women, otherwise where would all his earnings come from?

Bengali Baba's career started gradually. First, he did a bit of faith healing only on weekends and then, as his circle of eager clients grew, he began working after office hours too. He had a good government job, in the water and electricity board in Simla, which entitled him to a two-bedroom house and a scooter allowance. But when his fame as a shadow chaser began to spread far and wide, he gave up his government job and carried on with the faith healing and shadow chasing.

Now, he divided his time equally between these two demanding professions. The first brought him more money since there were so many unhappy women in this world, especially around Simla. It must have something to do with the spring water or the amount of mica in the soil. Women came to him like flocks of parakeets to a sunflower field and he just sat still, dressed in white robes, not saffron, because he was not a holy man who had given up the joys of the world.

He had a wife, four stupid-but-strapping sons, one new scooter, which he could not drive any more since his robes got entangled in the front wheel, a colour TV, and had recently bought a fridge to be paid for in monthly instalments.

He never claimed to be a sadhu, yet the women flocked to him, seeking the special powers they believed he possessed. Most of them just came, saw him and went away quite satisfied, smiling, a gentle glow on their pretty faces, even though he had not said a word to them.

To the ones who wanted more from him, he gave simple advice like, 'Be happy with the little things in life,' or 'Think good thoughts of your enemy,' and the most popular one: 'Life is a rosebud, inhale its fragrance and count your blessings'. This one always brought tears to his eyes and made the women cry too.

He was sure it was the crying that really helped them; sobbing cleared the heart and the head all at once. The women cried with much joy, taking deep, noisy breaths to clear their lungs and then wiping their noses on their saris. Some banged their heads on trees and tore their hair. Some lifted their faces to the sky and howled like she-wolves and soon the air around the banyan tree became dark and heavy with their sobs. All the women loved a good cry, all but the barren ones. They hardly said anything. They didn't cry or look up, even when he called out their names, which their mothers or mothers-in-law had written down for him on slips of paper. They just shuffled their feet and looked anxiously at the trees beyond, as if someone was calling out to them from far away.

He could not do much for them except give them some gur prasad and pat their bowed heads when they touched his feet.

He was always amazed when some of them came back after a year, holding a squealing baby in their arms. God helped in mysterious ways. He was happy to help these women, but he always felt a bit guilty taking their money. Their trusting eyes haunted him at night. But he had to feed his family too. After all, food did not grow on trees, even for those who had special powers, and living well was so expensive these days. Moreover, his sons had huge appetites.

His other profession, that of a shadow chaser, was not easy, but it brought him great joy, and fame too. It never made him feel uneasy like the faith healing did. It was an ancient, noble profession and he was proud to be a shadow chaser, the only one in the entire area of the Simla hills. A few others had tried to come up to challenge him, but they soon disappeared back into the hills.

Shadow chasing was a gift given only to a few chosen men. Fate had looked all over the Simla hills and chosen him. It was usually after the rainy season that the shadows began appearing in the villages. Like humans, they were unique. Each one had some special feature. Some were feeble and did not do much harm except frighten the cows, which made them give less milk. These simple shadows just shimmered around the cattle shed, slid into the barns and then slipped out again. They were what he called shunnis, or low-grade shadows, and could be chased away with just one ritual – a simple one, in which two kilos of yoghurt and one kilo of besan were made into a spicy kadhi and fed to all who had seen the shadow. His fee for clearing shunnis was only 201 rupees along with the gift of a tiffin carrier full of kadhi and rice, which he took home for his wife.

Then there were other, denser shadows called dhunnis, that implanted themselves in the village homes and refused to leave until something serious was done. These were medium-grade shadows and did not do much harm either, except sour the milk or frighten the women into giving birth early or giving the children coughs and colds, but their continued presence in the house was irritating, like that of a house guest who would not leave. They made doors slam at night, stole little things like needle and thread, an odd slipper, pickles and matchboxes. Bengali Baba needed at least two days to clear them. That cost the householder 1001 rupees and one chicken – a freshly slaughtered jungle fowl worked best. They usually called him for dhunni shadows because shunnis often went away on their own after the rains.

Then, of course, there was the maha-dhunni – the supreme dark shadow, which was really a wandering spirit. This frightening presence was always seen on moonlit nights and the entire village was very keen to get rid of this important shadow as soon as they could. It roamed the lanes at night, floated into the houses, made children seriously ill and the cattle barren. It often ruined the crops or set the pine forest on fire.

This shadow was usually the spirit of a long dead relative who had not been cremated with proper rites and had lingered on. It refused to cross the river of death until something was done to appease it.

To get rid of this shadow was an art which not every shadow chaser was skilled at. Even the wise old men who had been practising it for decades, often failed to get rid of this king of all shadows. But Bengali Baba loved the challenge and concentrated very hard so that his mind, heart and soul engaged perfectly with the shadow, pursuing his prey.

The pursuit process took one whole week, sometimes even longer, if the shadow was a stubborn one with a strong grip on the household. Sometimes these lost souls settled in so comfortably in the village, they gave up all thoughts of passing over. He had to put in all his efforts to uproot them and send them on their way to the other world.

When he finished, every bone in his body ached and he felt drained, as if someone had sucked up all his energy, but chasing these giant shadows was what made him famous and ensured that people would talk about him long after he was dead. This was what was going to make him – Bengali Baba – immortal.

Though every shadow required individual attention, they all needed a divine combination of circles, stars and triangles. He drew these grids on the ground with rice powder, turmeric and vermilion to placate the planets. He had to draw patterns of eight or sixteen, depending on how much the shadow host was willing to spend. For every extra triangle, he charged hundred rupees more.

The next day he would get up at dawn, bathe and bleed a few jungle fowls to feed the spirit. You had to put them in a mellow mood before you could trap them. They were wily creatures since they belonged neither to the dead nor the living, hovering in between, trying to grab the best of both worlds. So he cajoled them, bullied them and gradually brought them out of their crevices and corners.

He chanted holy verses all day long, though he was not from a priestly caste and did not have any authority to conduct marriages or funerals. But shadow chasing could be practised by any caste. The Brahmin families, the most powerful people in the village, did not mind as long as he kept away from the temple and did not try to impinge on their earnings. The lower castes did not mind as long as he chased the shadows away. It was an unpleasant task, like cleaning drains, but someone had to do it – and not just anybody, someone with special powers and skill.

Sometimes the shadow host would bring out a sick cow or a child with a swollen neck and ask him to heal it too, as if he was offering a package deal, like the hotels in Simla. But Bengali Baba always refused. When he came to the house to chase shadows, that was all he was going to do. If you started doing other things, the shadows took advantage and bore into the cracks in the roof beams and became as difficult to get rid of as termites.

After scattering the feathers all over the house, he cooked the bird with chillies and garlic for prasad. This was not like the fruit and sweet prasad you got in the temple, this was a pungent curry with a heady aroma which flew into every nook and cranny of the house and forced the shadow out into the open. He always cooked it himself and did not allow any women to come near him. They always tainted things with their needs and sorrows. He did not want any sorrowing woman to dilute the curry with her tears.

Sometimes a goat had to be slaughtered if the shadow was a strong one, usually a lost male soul. This cost 400 rupees extra because a big male goat had to be brought all the way from the Simla bazaar since no one in the village would sell their goat to a shadow chaser. They did not mind giving one to the temple for a sacrifice ceremony because they knew the gods would be pleased. But in this case, they were not sure where the offering would go, and they did not want to risk it. What if it went to the wrong spirits and made matters worse? No one minded offering chickens and jungle fowls, but goats were difficult to get hold of.

But once he decided to get a goat, the villagers shared the cost and then everyone got a bit of meat prasad. The host and the shadow chaser always took the best pieces, but no one minded because they all knew it was their right. There was nothing better than a delicious goat curry made with ghee, garlic and chillies.

On the third day, he would walk around the village, sprinkling holy water which he had carried all the way from Ganga and stored safely in his house in large vessels, to be used only for such important occasions. After that he lit a fire with a bunch of fragrant wild herbs and barks which he carried into every corner of the house to smoke out the remaining bits of the shadow. Then he cooked another dish, but this time it was just milk and rice with bits of jaggery.

He never stopped chanting, even when he was chopping the chicken or cooking the rice. He loved the way people stared at him in amazement as he chanted meaningless words. He knew two holy verses and after he finished chanting them, he just made up the rest, and it all seemed to work like magic.

He had wanted to be a magician when he was young, but his father had forced him to take up a government job. After that, life just took over and there was no time for magic. He had no choice but to become Bengali Baba and soon he had even forgotten that his real name was Gangaprasad. But he was content now that this path had been chosen for him. You eventually become what God has planned for you, however much you try to be something else. Government jobs, marriage, buying and selling land, children, wives, cattle – everything and everyone could be swept away in a moment if the gods willed it. Anyone with a clever twist of mind could become a magician, but to be able to chase a mighty shadow and set free a soul not cremated with proper rites was far more difficult. It required a great mind.

He was more powerful than an ordinary magician and people respected him much more. No one ever bowed to magicians, they only got a round of applause, but when *he* swept into a village, they all folded their hands and touched his feet, all except the Brahmins, of course.

In every village he did a new act and it gave him great joy to think of new ways to get rid of the shadow. He usually thought out the plan while listening to the women telling him their tales of woe and in this way he could kill two birds with one stone.

Last week, he had cleansed a village near the forest of one small shadow. They said it was a strange looking thing, half boy, half shadow. Very few people in the village had seen him and those who had, said he looked like a living ghost. His skin was white, not like an English sahib's, but like milk gone sour, like a worm found under a stone. This boy shadow lived in a cowshed and only came out at night to look into people's homes. He never stole anything or harmed anyone, but people wanted him to leave. Actually, it was one woman who started it and then everyone wanted to get rid of him.

So he moved the cows out of the shed and then smoked it with copper shavings, neem, sulphur, mud and cow dung. But no one came out. Only the cows got agitated and the owner of the hut asked them all to leave, but the village people refused to go. Then two women came out of the smaller hut and began screaming at the owner. Bengali Baba decided to slip away while the argument was going on. They had paid him in advance, he always made sure of that. The villagers seemed annoyed that no shadow had been seen, but they assumed he had chased it away, and later gave him a chicken to show their gratitude.

The village had a dhunni too which had entrenched itself in the village spring. It jumped out at dusk to frighten the women when they went to fetch water. He had chanted for six days and nights before he finally saw the shadow gliding into the sky, leaving a trail of blurred white lines. The entire village could see it and all the men and women cried out loudly and clapped their hands with joy. He left with his fee – 5001 rupees – and knew the maize crop would be healthy, the cows would give plenty of milk, the rains would come on time and the village would be well and happy. At least till another shadow came wandering in.

Bengali Baba sighed and looked at the hills, which stretched all the way to the great English town of Simla. It no longer belonged to the English sarkar, but its soul still remained white. It was crowded, noisy and filled with tourists and sari shops, but if you looked carefully at the shadows lurking in the streets, you could see they belonged to the white sahibs and memsahibs who had lived here a hundred years ago.

They had loved their Simla so much, that they still floated about, reluctant to leave it. He remembered when he was a child and was not allowed to walk on the Mall

Road. His father told him the policeman standing near
the gates would beat them with a big stick if they took
even one step on the Mall.

How he longed to saunter down the Mall like the
sahibs, wearing a solar topi, cane in hand, looking at
the shops selling strange, expensive things. But only the
English sahibs and their memsahibs and children were
allowed to walk on the Mall. He had to stay on the Lower
Mall, in the noisy, smoke-filled bazaar, and eat in the dark
tea shops with other people from his village.

Above him he could see English ladies eating ice-cream,
taking dainty licks like kittens. How pretty they looked.

They had never called him to chase any shadows
in Simla because it had become a big town with many
government offices. And everyone knew that the
government did not believe in shadow chasing.

Until last week he had been busy digging, ploughing
and planting. All the villagers on the hillside were busy
in their fields. Nobody wanted to waste these golden
days of summer. The rains had held off, the sunshine was
steady, and now, at last, the corn had been safely sown.
The prayers to the harvest gods were done and they
were all free to pay attention to other important things
like spirits and shadows. He must now get ready to cross
the river and climb up to Giripul, where the shadow, the
first one of the season, lurked.

He was surprised that no one threw stones at him or
shouted abuses at him outside the village. They seemed

to not notice him, as if he had become invisible to people after hiding all his life from their cruel eyes. No one tried to stop him. Even the dogs did not bother to bark as he walked past them. But he was frightened by all the strange new things around him and made himself small by crouching like a turtle he had once seen, and tried to blend into the grey dawn.

He crawled and stumbled down the hill, taking the shady hidden path that only shepherds knew about. He had seen them going this way every morning, when he stood on the roof of the cowshed, talking to the mountains. At first he could not lift his face towards the light and cast his eyes down all the time. Then, as he walked, he began to look around and the light did not bother him much. He was fascinated by how the shadows played on the rocks and the way the plants that grew in the crevices changed from light to dark green as he went past. Everything looked bigger and brighter under the open sky.

A tiny hope flickered inside him that his father would run after him, call him back, but when he looked back, the path was always empty. He shook his head to get rid of the thought. Why should his father, who had not even spoken to him all these years, follow him? A gang of monkeys watched him suspiciously. When he hissed at them, they leapt down in surprise and scampered away. The stream sang along and soon he began to feel a little less afraid of being seen.

He reached the end of the path, which opened into a valley, crossed the stream and then climbed the next hill. He did not know where he was going, but he knew he had to go as far as he could so they could not find him. He knew now for sure that his father would not follow him, but the others might. Who would do all the work, now that he had left? He hoped the cows would not be sad that he was not there to talk to them or stroke their backs.

He walked till it was dark and then he crept into a cave in the hill and slept. He woke up at dawn when he heard voices, and even though he was afraid, he went out. He was dizzy with hunger. The goatherds did not seem at all surprised to see a thin, pale boy come out of the cave and offered him some fresh milk and dried chapattis, as if he were a relative or a long-lost friend. Their handsome, shaggy-haired gaddi dogs came rushing up to him and when he moved back in fear, they sat in front of him, wagging their tails.

For the next few days he followed the goatherds, helping them carry their kids and getting food in return. Once they crossed the mica hills and came to a valley full of green meadows, the goatherds pointed to the main road and told him he could find work there on the road building sites.

A crowd of villagers waiting at the bus stop stared at him when he crossed the bridge, but when the bus arrived, they forgot about him and began rushing about, shouting and throwing their bags onto the roof of the bus. He stood uncertainly on the road, watching the shops. They were full of bright, colourful food he had never seen before. The breeze swirled the dust around his head and as he rubbed his eyes, two men playing cards in a tea shop threw a few coins at his feet, and then a boy came out and gave him a chapatti, taking care not to touch him. When he reached for the food, he saw that his hands were covered with mud and silvery mica dust from the hillside. They did not look white any more.

He soon found out that if he sat outside a temple, someone would throw a few coins or leave some food for him. He wondered why they did, till he saw a line of beggars outside the temple. But when he tried to sit with them, they threw stones at him and one lame beggar, hobbling on a crutch, chased him to the end of the village.

So he began walking again. He avoided the villages and took the stony path where the cattle grazed. At night he crept closer to the villages where he could find a safe place to sleep. There was always someone to give him a few scraps to eat. After climbing and descending the mountain paths for many days, he began to feel weak with hunger. Just when he thought he could not take another step, his swollen and bloody feet would fall away from his body, he saw a town just at the foot of the hill. Though he was afraid, he forced himself to walk down to the road where he could see buses moving and people milling about in a busy market. As he went into the crowd, no one looked at him, until he went too close. Then they shouted, 'Get away, son of an owl, move off!' but the noise and the chaos around him was so great that it did not matter any more. He would be safe here since everyone was shouting, pushing and grabbing at everyone else.

One day when he was roaming near the bus stop, looking for any discarded food on the road, he saw a boy following him. The boy was looking hungrily at his half eaten chapatti so he gave it to him, throwing it at him, just like people threw food at him.

'You think I am a dog? You, son of a witch! How dare you?' shouted the boy, shaking his fist.

'I wanted you to eat it,' he said, surprised at how easy it was to talk to someone. Until now he had only talked to the cows and goats and sometimes to the mountains. It felt good to talk to a person who could talk back, even if angrily.

'Then give it properly. Like this ...' said the boy. He picked up the chapatti, wiped the dust off with his fingers and offered it to him. When he tried to take it, the boy quickly rolled it and popped it into his own mouth and laughed.

They began walking around together. For the first time in his life, there was someone he could walk with. The boy said to call him Baboo, but he hardly spoke to him, except to bark orders. 'Come here, pale-skin,' or 'Walk faster, you worm'. Baboo did not like him standing too close to him and told him to always walk a few steps behind. They both began to beg near the temple. The other beggars grumbled, but did not chase them away since they were afraid of Baboo and his foul abuses. Baboo showed him how to whine in a high-pitched nasal tone, roll his eyes and make his hands tremble as he stretched them out to beg. They hung around the temple all day long, Baboo calling out to people in a sing-song voice, 'Give, give this poor boy something. The gods will bless you, your children will flourish.' People stopped to stare at him and some gave him one-rupee or two-rupee coins, sometimes even more when he shut his eyes and pretended to be blind. Sometimes the women gave him a banana or a stale samosa, which he was happy to eat, but Baboo only wanted money. He would take all the coins and run off to buy food, pleading with the tea shop owner to throw in something extra. They found a safe place under a water tank where the stray dogs would not bother them and ate to their heart's content. Then Baboo would smoke a bidi while he sat a safe distance away, calling out to the ravens on the pine tree, mimicking their raucous tones. The pale boy had never been happier in all the nine years of his life.

Then one day, all of a sudden, Baboo said he was going to Simla, a big city where all the rich people came for holidays and threw money on the streets.

Baboo did not ask him to come along so he just sat still and crouched. He felt a strange ache in his heart like he had felt when he turned around and found the hill path empty. He took a deep breath and began to hum softly as if he was listening to the stream. It eased the pain. 'You can come if you want to,' said Baboo, chewing a bit of string. 'But don't walk too close to me ... understand? I don't want people to think you are my brother or something ... a freak like you'.

The noise in Simla made him dizzy and he had to cover his ears. The motorcars, the tongas, the stream of people rushing about like ants – it was frightening. But soon he found that here in this noisy confusing city, people did not care about him at all. He went about anywhere and no one even glanced at him. He saw another person, a grown man who looked like him, but when he tried to talk to him, the man gave him a sharp kick in his shins and shuffled away.

Baboo had given him a name now. He called him Kaloo and thought it was very funny. The other boys at the railway station where they now lived, called him various names like Chotu, Dondu and Gadhe, and he answered to them cheerfully. They gave him a corner to sleep in and he had his own blanket and plate. A man the boys called Mamoo, came to check him out and then after poking him with a stick as if he was a dog, he said, 'I think I will sell him to the circus. They pay good money for freaks.' He lived in fear from that day on, but the man did not say anything again. He just came to collect money from the boys, slapped a few of them for not earning enough and then went way. He always jabbed him with a stick before he left and when he cried out in pain, Mamoo roared with laughter. 'Look at him squirming like a lizard. Son of a devil.'

All day, he and the boys worked as coolies in the Lower Bazaar, fetching and carrying for the shopkeepers. Sometimes they did chores for Mamoo, collecting strange packages from underground hovels during the early hours of the morning. At night, when the shops closed and the station was quiet, they sat around a bonfire drinking rice wine. He did not drink or smoke like the other boys, so now they called him Sadhu.

A real sadhu baba lived nearby and he often went and sat outside his tent, which was tied with a rope to a mulberry tree. In summer, the tree was laden with fruit and birds of many colours came and sat on its branches. In a tiny patch by the railway yard, the sadhu grew ginger and tulsi. He would make all kinds of medicines from plants and herbs that grew on the hill outside Simla and sell them in tiny glass bottles. He sometimes took the boy along to gather the plants, making him climb the trees to cut leaves from various creepers. They sorted out the leaves and roots and then tied them into bunches to dry them. Soon he could recognize each plant and knew their names, but the sadhu would not show him how to make the medicinal oils. 'You will take my livelihood away, though I am not sure people will trust a boy with skin disease,' he said. He was not unkind to him and gave him good things to eat, like apples and sometimes a lump of sweet jaggery. He also gave him some brown powder and haldi to eat everyday. 'It will turn your unbaked skin brown like ours in just ten days, you watch.' Everyday when he woke up he looked at his hands to see if his skin had changed colour, though in his heart he knew it never would. Mamoo was right; he was a freak and would always remain one. That was why his father had not come to look for him.

8

Janak blissfully flying over mountains; Rama content; Shankar turns sleuth

Janak reached over the butter-smeared chapatti, took Rama's face in his hands and kissed her loudly, knocking over a glass of water. The steel glass rolled across the kitchen floor, making a loud clanking sound, and finally rolled down the steps into the courtyard. Rama giggled but did not move away. 'Shush,' she said, 'Maaji will hear you.'

'So what? Let her. What does she know about kissing? This is a modern trick and only young men like me know it. Your father, may he rest in heaven, must never have done all this,' he said, feeling recklessly happy. Rama's eyes sparkled and her teeth shone like tiny pearls. How beautiful she was. The stones on the kitchen floor, the pots and pans, the old stove, all looked so bright and lively, and even the walls were smiling. The entire house trembled with joy as the smoke from the kitchen fire floated through it. It had a warm, sweet scent as if they were burning sandalwood and not just dried pine twigs.

It was as if he was sitting in Indra's garden in heaven, Janak thought, and began tickling his wife. She giggled and hid her face in her hands. He tickled her again. Rama laughed loudly. This tickling trick seemed to be working. Janak watched her breasts peeping out of her blouse as she shook with laughter. Why had he cut the neck line so low, he thought suddenly. Forget the blouse, worry about it later, this is bliss, he told himself, closing his eyes. He had imagined this moment many a time, and now he felt quite dizzy.

Maybe he was changing too, like Shankar, and becoming a strong, fearless man who could make women giggle and tremble with joy. He could perhaps even grow a moustache now, like the headman, and walk down the street with his chest puffed out. His teeth would become stronger and whiter, his eyes would acquire a bold light like the headman's eyes did, when he looked at women.

The thought of the headman dampened his joyous spirits somewhat, but he cheered up when Rama began hitting him coyly with her long plait. The moonlight stroked their faces and made their eyes gleam with its soft silvery touch.

The easterly wind, making its way from Simla towards the higher mountains, decided to linger in Giripul for a while, whispering softly outside Janak's window. The deodar trees shook their heavy branches languidly to greet the wind, inhaled its cool fragrance, and then settled down to caress the earth once more.

Janak felt his entire body being lifted up into the sky. This was what happiness meant. It was not difficult to achieve it. You did not have to be rich or powerful or have strong teeth and a rich moustache. All you needed was the love of a good woman. Rama was his wife and a good woman, despite her short temper.

He could see the houses in Giripul getting smaller and smaller as he floated above the snow-capped mountains. The great Himalayan range lay below him and he felt as though he could have reached out and picked up a handful of snow. He could take it back for Rama and she would be surprised and pleased, or maybe she would be irritated with him for bringing snow into her spotless kitchen.

Sometimes he felt like taking her in his arms and kissing her till her black mood melted away. But that would be shocking. His dead mother would tremble in heaven and his son would grow up insane if he ever saw them embracing. The village might get to hear of it and then everyone would point a finger at them. Kissing one's wife was only for ones who lived in big houses in big cities. There they could behave in any way they wanted. Kiss their wives, hold hands, go to see films alone with them. No one would say anything at all. On his rare visits to Simla to buy thread and machine oil, he had seen newly-married couples strolling hand in hand, laughing and talking happily. If he did that here in Giripul, the villagers would look at them with horror and Rama would start crying with shame. She might even go home to her mother and never come back. To this day she called him 'Tailorji' and never by his name. She never held his hand or touched him at all. Their son had been born after a furtive fumbling in the dark, with his mother snoring in the next room. He had cried out Rama's name in one unguarded moment and she had looked at him with irritation and asked sharply, 'What do you want? Keep your voice down. You will wake up maaji.'

The spotted owlets felt the wind's gentle touch on their wings, but did not move in case their prey saw them and scuttled away. It was still early in the night and they did not want to go without a meal. The houses of Giripul huddled closer in the moonlight, as though in need of each other's warmth, forming a tight circle against the wind, that blew from the mountains. It was not the harsh and cruel winter wind, yet it had a sting to it.

Above the courtyard wall, where Mithoo dozed in his cage, the Giripul shadow lurked not sure about where to go. The wind touched it gently and then passed through its silver layers, making it shimmer and dance. It sighed as it floated in and out of the closed doors of the houses, unable to make up its mind about where to settle down.

For a while, it just stood still, looking at the people asleep in their beds. It touched their faces, put its cool hands on their foreheads and saw their dreams. If they were complicated and interesting, showing bloodshed or passionate love, it hovered and watched, but if they were dreaming about their goats and debts, it moved on. It strolled for a while on the roofs of the houses and then it got restless and flew up into the sky, its silvery form melting into the darkness. It would not settle here tonight. There was nothing in Giripul that it could attach itself to as yet.

Tommy did not hear anything but he sniffed a faint unfamiliar scent in the air and wondered what it was.

Mona the fruit thief who was searching for ripe plums in the headman's garden suddenly began to shiver and ran home, afraid for the first time in her young life. Many others felt a mild flutter in the air and thought a thunder storm was brewing. Balu too heard the wind sigh and woke up. Who could be strolling about at this time of the night, he thought, snuggling deeper into his flour sack quilt. Was it a shadow, a dog, or a thief? he wondered and then, without really caring, he fell asleep once more.

Janak, happy and tired after his wandering in the sky, had fallen into a deep sleep, his arms wrapped around Rama. He woke with a start when he heard the windows rattle. He raised his head and listened for a few moments. It must be the house changing its mood. It had been quiet for long and he knew its mellow mood would not last. I hope it doesn't affect Rama, Janak thought, gazing at his wife's face. The moonlight made her skin glow like a burnished silver plate, but with soft edges. She had a tiny dimple on her chin and Janak leaned forward to kiss it gently. 'God forgive me for loving her so much,' he whispered.

Rama muttered something in her sleep and Janak thought it sounded like 'chest 34 inches, waist ...' but he was not sure. Then Tommy began to bark and Janak, cursing under his breath, got up from bed. The jackals must be gathering near the bridge tonight and that always made Tommy and the village dogs nervous. He threw a shawl over his shoulders and went out. The sky was dark but a streak of grey and pink danced behind the highest peak. It would not be dawn for a while, but Janak was wide awake.

Tommy was now joined by other dogs and they all barked loudly till someone from the headman's house opened a window and threw a bucket of water on them. The dogs yelped and ran away. 'Yes. They must have seen a jackal,' Janak mumbled to himself, yawning and stretching his arms above his head.

He stood outside the house and looked up at the hills. The forest seemed to sway in the grey-blue light, as if the old deodar trees were changing their places. Janak wondered where his father was. Was he there in the dark shadows, watching them all the time like a leopard, or was he sitting peacefully in heaven, being fed hot chapattis with butter by his wife.

Deep in his heart, Janak felt that his father was still alive and would remain alive even after Janak passed on. His missing spirit seemed eternal, like the old trees in the forest which had been there forever and would be standing there long after they were all dead and gone.

His father was the youngest of seven brothers, his mother had told him one day when she was feeling less belligerent towards her lost husband. She was dressed in white that day and that always made her calmer.

'Your father and his older brothers were drunkards and did no work, except to brew rice and jaggery wine. Their poor mother, father and sisters worked in the fields all day, cutting grass, collecting firewood and looking after the cattle. The brothers played cards under a big boulder near the ravine, drank rice wine and came home in the evening only to eat.

'Sometimes they got so drunk they just slept under

the boulder. Everyone in the village felt sorry for your grandfather. "Imagine being blessed with seven sons but each one a drunkard. God's ways are strange," they said to the old man, but what could he do? The brothers brewed their own liquor and all the men in the village bought rice and jaggery wine from them, so they always had plenty of money. Of course, they never gave any money to their parents. The old man, father of seven sons, was sad, poor and helpless.

'But God was watching. Waiting and watching. In the year of the great flood in our village, fate decided to strike the bad brothers dead one by one. Not an ordinary, comfortable death in their own bed, mind you. Fate made sure they were all given special deaths.

'The brothers met their terrible end, as they well deserved, by falling into a deep ravine near their house as they came home after their drinking session. Fate did not round them up in a bunch and throw them into the khud together. No, she sent them down, one by one. After the fourth brother fell to his death, they got scared and started drinking at home, but one night, the fifth one went out to relieve himself and toppled into the khud with his pajama cord undone, and broke his neck.

'The sixth brother got hysterical when he heard and jumped headlong into the khud to rescue him, but he landed on a boulder and broke his neck too.

'It was then that your father, the last of the seven brothers, God rest his soul if he is dead and keep him safe if he is alive, swore never to drink again. He kept his word and not a drop touched his lips, at least when he was within my sight. What he does now in heaven or on this earth is not my business. What I cannot see with my own two eyes, I cannot reprimand,' his late mother would always say to end this ghastly tale.

Maybe it was that tremendous vow that made my father run away from his family, from the hills with their treacherous ravines. He could be somewhere in the plains, safely enjoying his daily drink on flat land, no dangerous pits to swallow him, or maybe he lived in a tall deodar tree, his feet never touching the earth.

Janak had promised his mother he would never drink, but sometimes he drank a glass or two of home-brewed jaggery wine with Shankar and Raja. There was no khud near their house, only the Giri river, and he could swim quite well, unless he fell down head first and hit a rock.

Janak went back quietly to his room and got into bed. Rama did not stir as he pulled the blanket closer. He tried to go back to sleep, but his head was spinning with thoughts. Not worrying thoughts, but just important questions he stored in his head and brought out to examine at night.

He shut his eyes. Death can strike one anywhere and at any time and making vows just means putting one's life in shackles, he thought. He did feel a twinge of guilt every time he picked up a glass of rice-brew, but after a few sips of the warm, sweet wine, his mother's face blurred and then vanished totally. Sometimes he saw his father or an old man who could be his father, but he too vanished by the time the glass was empty.

Janak tried to sleep, but he could only doze fitfully. The whistling thrush began calling even when the sky was still dark. It came and sat right next to his window and sang and sang till he could no longer bear it. He quietly got out of bed and throw his shawl over Rama, who was sleeping with her hand curled under her head like a baby.

The sky was turning light pink now above the hills, where the forest began. A few cinnamon sparrows started chirping in the shrubs nearby. Tommy had run away with the other dogs to explore the garbage dump where they had heard the jackals at night. Janak could smell the first wood fires from the village homes and he began to feel hungry. The women of these early rising houses must be making breakfast for their men now, boiling milk, kneading dough.

Some lucky men's wives might have made fresh butter last night and would now be placing it in small, perfect rounds on top of the hot chapattis and handing it to their husbands.

Janak wished his mother were still alive and making tea for him. A wife who rose at dawn and made fresh butter, was too much to wish for in this life, thought Janak and sighed as he went in to wake up his wife.

'Kill the bastards! Shoot them!' Leela heard her late husband's voice and woke up with a start. The pigeons were outside her window, muttering and cooing to each other in loud, affectionate tones. It was still dark outside she could tell, even though the curtains were drawn, just the way her late husband had liked them to be. Not a chink of light could shine through or else he would be awake at dawn, pulling and tugging at the curtains.

The pigeons woke them up, in any case, making him jump out of bed shouting, 'Kill them, bloody birds, shitting everywhere. Shoot them. Where is my gun?' And then he would start thumping on the windows.

'Get out, get out, you bastards, you stinking vermin!' The servants heard him but never came out. They treated it merely as a wake up call. They knew it was a daily battle with the piegons which their master always lost, so they quietly sipped their morning tea in the kitchen till it was time to set out the bed-tea tray, with a pot of tea, four peeled almonds and four Marie biscuits, and bring it up to them.

By then the pigeons had flown away to the neighbouring fields in search of grain and fruit, unaware of the abuses that DN had hurled at them. He too quickly forgot the pigeons as the day progressed, because there were so many other battles waiting to be fought.

A constant favourite was the one with the neighbours whose land bordered their orchard. The present owner's father had offered the piece of land to Leela's uncle in exchange for a fridge, but he had refused.

'What do I need more land for, I have enough for my need and have no sons to pass it on to,' Leela's uncle had said.

A few years later, the neighbour's son, a carpenter, had come back to the village after making a lot of money in the city and had built a large, ugly, pink-and-green house with a high roof and picture windows which looked right into their garden. It was the grandest house in that area and many people from the neighbouring villages came up to admire the big glass windows, something they had never seen before.

At first, when Leela's uncle was still alive and they only came up for the summer, DN was only mildly irritated by the neighbours and just glared at them as they went about cutting grass. But gradually, as they began spending more time his resentment grew.

'Why do they stare at us all the time, bloody peasants? I can't stand the sight of them. Giving themselves airs and building grand houses. They stink of cow dung. I can smell it even here. Why don't they live in their cowshed?' he would mutter, as they sat down to breakfast under the curious gazes of the neighbours.

Sometimes the children would come right up to the fence and stand on their toes and stare, their curious eyes as round as saucers. They never spoke, just fixed their eyes on the breakfast table and watched unblinkingly, as DN ate his toast. One morning, Uncle was dozing in his chair while DN sat, as usual, hidden behind his week-old newspaper, Leela offered the children, who were sitting near a rock and staring at them, some fruit, but they broke into giggles and hid behind the rock.

DN heard them and got up with a shout, waving his newspaper at them like a threatening weapon.

'Go away, get out!' he shouted. 'Filthy urchins.'

Uncle, who was quite hard of hearing, woke up confused and said, 'What? What was that? Yes, yes, I can't stand this brown bread either, but Leela insists we have it. Nothing like soft white bread, I say. So nice and easy to chew and swallow, but who listens to me? I am an old man and no one cares for me. Brown bread, boiled veggies, what a life, I tell you,' he mumbled over and over into his napkin.

'I said, sir, I do not like the way these villagers sit and stare at us!' DN shouted, waving his newspaper about angrily, knocking over the milk jug. Bhanu came out of the shadows, wiped it with a napkin, and disappeared. None of the servants liked to be there at the breakfast table and kept slinking away to the kitchen.

'Yes, the village is far away,' said Uncle. 'In my days it was quite near. I do not know how it has moved so far. Well, strange things happen here ... I would like some soft mashed potatoes with butter for lunch, Leela,' he said and tucked his napkin under his chin and dozed off once more.

'Why can't we order them to move away from here, bloody village idiots?' DN continued to mutter in a low voice so that Uncle would not wake up from his post-breakfast slumber.

'No... no... Bhanu cannot go anywhere. I need him,' said Uncle, waking up again with a start, 'Only he knows how to clean my dentures nicely.'

'Bhanu is not going anywhere. DN does not like the villagers sitting there, near the fence. Uncle, look there,' pointed Leela.

But when the old man turned around to look at the neighbours' children, they scampered away, bowing to him as they left.

'Nice, pretty children, so polite,' the old man said. 'I want mashed potatoes, Leela, with peas. And lots of butter, I do not care what the doctor says. It is time I went anyway, and I want to go a happy, well-fed man.'

When the uncle died and she inherited the house, DN immediately built a high wall dividing their land from the neighbours', but they retaliated by building a second floor. Now they sat in their verandah and stared down at DN having breakfast. Almost everyday for the last five years of his life, he had made many devious plans to get even with the neighbours. After the breakfast battle, when his rage would be at its peak, he would retire to the study and plan his attack on the unsuspecting neighbours.

He wrote furious letters to the police, the local authorities, the chief minister, even the prime minister, complaining about his neighbours.

He accused them of stealing his fruit, his water, his dog, his petrol, even his clothes from the drying line. Fortunately, no one took any notice of his false accusations, except one government officer from the Simla Public Road Works Department who, oddly enough, accused DN of being a communist, which enraged him even more.

The neighbours never retaliated except to stare at him in relentless fascination as he sat down at his breakfast table every morning. Even when they spread fresh manure on their fields out of necessity and not any malicious intent, it made DN tear his hair with rage. He even walked down one day, insisting Leela go with him, to their closest neighbour Raja Ranjit Singh and asked him to come and shoot partridges on their land. 'We need gunshots. It will scare those wretched peasants away,' he said to the dapper man, who seemed quite amused, but his wife Rati was not amused at all and politely, but firmly declined DN's invitation.

'Why don't we move our breakfast table to the other side of the garden,' Leela suggested one day when DN had a mild flutter in his chest after exploding angrily at breakfast – the neighbours had bought a new radio which they were playing loudly in their verandah.

'Over my dead body,' he had shouted, shaking a fist at

the line of curious faces peering at them over the boundary wall while a religious song blared on their radio.

It did eventually come to that. She moved the table two weeks after he died and now she had breakfast in the far side of the garden, under the old walnut tree, though she often walked to the other side and peered over the fence. There was never anyone there. The neighbours seemed to have lost interest in their house – now a beat-up, unoccupied building – once the object of their fascination, DN, had gone. She wished the children would come out and stare at her once again. It would have been nice to have some company.

Last night, Robert had come to see her. She made room for him on her bed, complaining that he was hogging most of the quilt. They quarrelled like an old married couple and she woke up smiling till she realized she was alone in the big four-poster bed. Could she ever have married him? He was free and so was she. But he was an English officer, quite senior, her father had said, and she was only eighteen then – an Indian girl brought up strictly, taught at home by lady tutors, though she was allowed more freedom by her father than other girls of her age. Her mother refused to go to parties with her father, who was a government official and had to attend many functions. So Leela went everywhere with him. There were endless tea parties at the Viceregal Lodge, official dinners at the Resident's house and many other such functions where she often got very bored. Her mother was not very happy about this. 'It will give the girl wrong ideas,' she said, but her father said, 'Rubbish,' and took her everywhere.

It was strange that she had met Robert at all, because in those days the British and Indians did not mix much except at official functions. The English had their dinner parties, picnics and tea parties and the Indians had theirs. Robert moved about in circles far removed from hers, yet god had seen to it that they met. Two people from different worlds had been tied together by a thread of love that no one could ever know about. 'An Indian girl can never fall in love with an Englishman nor can an Englishwoman ever think of marrying an Indian,' she had read somewhere long ago.

Everything had changed now. She often got letters from friends announcing their children's marriage to an English girl or boy. If she had been born fifty years later, Robert could have married her. They did not know what the future would bring then. In those days, even talking to him was seen as a bold gesture by both the English matrons and the Indian men. A young Indian girl, smiling and chatting to an unmarried English gentleman below seventy years. They would have fainted with horror if they had known about her love for Robert and they would have died of shock if they had learnt about his love for her.

It was an early summer's morning when she first saw him. The garden at the British commander-in-chief's house was filled with flowers – pansies, petunias, stock, and some others she did not recognize – the peach trees were shining with newly-sprouted green leaves. A hill barbet called from somewhere behind the shrubs and when she turned to look for it, she saw him. He was smoking a cigarette and talking to her father. His hair, curly and soft, was cut very short, like a young boy's. He looked at her with surprise when she came and stood near them, stubbing his cigarette so quickly that he singed the tablecloth. An odour of burning cotton rose in the air as her father introduced them, waving a hand absentmindedly, 'My daughter, Leela. She is studying to be a lawyer, though she spends all her time playing with her dogs instead of studying.'

'Robert Marvel, pleased to meet you.'

He smiled as he took her hand in his. She suddenly felt very shy and confused. She flushed and quickly withdrew her hand. Robert continued to look at her and then laughed for no reason. 'That was a hill barbet calling,' he said, his grey eyes half closed as if the morning sun was too strong for him.

'You winked at me. It was outrageous. What if the viceroy had seen us?' she told him later.

'I did no such thing, my darling. You blushed so prettily that I could not help laughing. I suddenly wanted to kiss you. Imagine what the good ladies of the Simla Garden Committee would have to say then?'

'They would all faint, the poor dears, and would be lying on the lawn like dead ducks,' she replied and he laughed and touched her cheek gently. They could not meet often, but when they did, they talked and talked and it seemed as if they had known each other for years. She could talk to him about anything and he never got bored or irritable. He told her all about his childhood in Ireland and then the terrible days at the boarding school in Scotland. His mother had died when he was very young and he had been brought up by his maiden aunt. His wife had died a few months after he had come to India and was buried in Simla.

'She taught me to look at everything in the garden, made me learn the name of every shrub, tree and flower. I wanted to become a botanist, but my father's entire family had served in India, so I was put on a ship and sent here to meet you ... ' he said but he did not smile. They looked at each other and knew they would never see each other after he left India.

But they pretended that one day she would come to Wiltshire where he lived with his five dogs. 'You shall wear a golden sari and ride out in a horse and carriage with me. Everyone in our village will bow to you and whisper, "Look at the beautiful Indian princess our squire has brought home."'

'Yes, along with a monkey, an elephant and a sadhu doing a rope trick. That is all you British can think about,' Leela said and pulled his hair.

They went for long walks each time he came to visit her father. Since they both worked in the department of civil supplies to the British government, they had plenty to discuss. But it was difficult to find time alone. Either her father would join them when they went out into the garden or some junior officer would accompany Robert on his visit. But they did manage to escape, and her uncle, who was a bit deaf even then, was of great help. He had a vintage car Robert was very fond of driving. So the three of them would go for drives around Simla and soon her uncle would fall asleep and Robert and she would have half an hour to be alone.

Robert taught her the names of all the birds in Simla, pointing out each one they sighted as they drove. 'Keep your eyes on the wheel, sir,' her uncle would grumble before he dozed off. Now, each bird reminded her of Robert –

Cinnamon sparrows, meadow buntings, blue chats, verditer flycatchers, red-billed blue magpies, and their favourite, the whistling thrush. It was just as well she could no longer walk around the garden, though she would sometimes hear them call and her heart would ache with longing for her old friend.

If only they had met now, in these times, when anyone could love anyone, when being English or Indian did not matter, even gender did not matter.

He wrote to her every month for many years after he left India, even though she stopped replying after three years. What was the use? It was better to bury those golden days deep in her heart and only focus on her present life. DN was her husband and he needed all her attention for the rest of her life. She could never love him, but he was a good man, a kind husband despite his fiery temper, and she cared for him till the day he died.

Now, at the very end of her life, she could allow herself the luxury of bringing those precious days out, twenty-three of them, and relive them in the darkness of her lonely sleepless nights.

Janak came home in the afternoon to rest for a while. He was feeling sleepy since he had hardly slept all night. The house scowled at him as soon as he entered and he knew something was wrong. The door slammed into his hand and almost cut his fingers off. He heard someone crying and quickly rushed to the kitchen. Rama was sitting by the fire, kneading dough and sobbing. His son and Rama's mother did not seem to be at home, but Mithoo was in his cage watching Rama as she wept. Tears streamed down her face and fell into the copper bowl of water for the dough. Her hands were sticky with flour.

'What is the matter?' Janak quickly sat down beside her and began stroking her head. How beautiful she looked when she cried, her eyes moist with tears, the tip of her nose pale pink. Her rosebud mouth trembled as she bit her lips and sobbed. 'Oh, my heart, please do not cry,' he said, bringing her hand up to his face.

'Why should I not cry, you tell me? Why should I not cry when I am insulted by a stranger?' she said and threw the bowl of water at him. 'Am I a woman of the street or your wife?' she said and stood up. Her hair, loose and unplaited, streamed down her back.

Janak stared at her. She was Durga in her ferocious image, she was Kali about to slay the demons. 'What happened? Who insulted you?' he asked, not daring to go near her.

'You ask me, you who are supposed to protect me till you die? You who swore on the sacred fire to protect me from every danger? Now you stand here in my kitchen and ask me who insulted me?' she screamed. Janak did not know what to say or do. Should he wait till her anger was spent and she told him what had happened or should he try and find out somehow who had insulted her? He stood frozen by the door, unable to make up his mind. After crying for a while and calling him all kinds of names, Rama wiped her tears with the end of her sari pallu and sat down again, glaring at him. Janak held his breath. He knew she would explain now.

'I was cutting grass in the hills this morning. I went with Raja's wife but I climbed higher, where the grass grows in thicker clumps. She stayed back because her knee was hurting. She always has some complaint or the other. I cut the grass and was making my bundles when I heard someone whistle. At first I thought it was a bird – you know, the black one that wakes us up at dawn?' She pointed to the window. Janak nodded eagerly to show he was paying attention to her every word. 'Then a pine cone came flying at me from somewhere. I looked up and saw him.'

Janak leaned forward. 'Saw who? Who was there?'

'Keep quiet and listen to me. It was a strange man. A city man in a red shirt. He whistled at me again and then said ...' Rama began to cry again, beating her forehead with her palm.

Janak tried to touch her, but she pushed him away.

'He said, "Come, my little munia, I will take you home,"' Rama sobbed.

Janak did not know what to say. It was a terrible thing to happen to a woman. A strange man whistling and calling her his 'little munia'. But what was done, was done. There was nothing to do but forget about it. 'Now, stop crying. Nothing is the matter. You are my beautiful wife. Just wipe your face and come and sit with me. Come, come here,' he said and clicked his tongue in sympathy, not realizing what was coming.

'You click your tongue at me as if I am a goat with a thorn in my backside! You are my husband and all you can do is this?' she roared and threw the ball of dough at him. It hit his face and fell on his lap with a loud plop. His son had just come into the kitchen to see what was happening. He clapped his little hands and laughed.

'What should I do?' asked Janak, picking bits of dough off his face.

'You seek revenge like all real men would. Your wife has been insulted and now you must seek out this man and kill him,' shouted Rama and her mother suddenly appeared at the door and said, 'Yes, yes. Kill the man.'

'Kill him? I do not even know him,' Janak stuttered, a shocked look on his dough-smeared face.

'Did Bheem argue with Draupadi when she asked him to avenge her honour? Did he mumble helplessly, "Who is Duryodhana and how can I find him?" No, he did not. He swore to kill Duryodhana and drink his blood!' said maaji, waving her hands. Rama nodded and flashed him an angry look.

'But I am not Bheem. I am Janak, ladies' tailor,' he said, wringing his hands. 'I cannot drink anyone's blood. Let bygones be bygones, my sweet.'

'Do not call me your sweet in front of my mother. I will not speak to you till you find this wretched man and kill him. You can find him easily – no one in the village has a red shirt.'

Janak turned to leave. His son waved and Rama scowled.

He had to do something, at least pretend to take some action, otherwise Rama would never speak to him again. And that would be the end of the world for him. Janak stood at the door nervously wringing his hands, wondering what to do. This was a new problem fate had sent him. Just when he had stopped worrying about the third wife's dream, this crisis had dropped from the sky right into his own home.

'Go. Do not stand here like a timid girl. And do not ask that jackass Shankar to help you. He is a bigger fool than you are.'

As Janak dragged his feet out of the house, the windows began to rattle and hiss and the door handle jabbed his hand. Behind him he heard Rama shout, 'He had a mole on his left cheek and big hairy ears. His nose is crooked and broken.'

A crowd of bus passengers had gathered in Lala's tea shop and Janak saw Shankar sitting at one of the tables, trying to sell a bag of small fish he had caught that morning. He waved his hand at him, but Shankar did not see him. Janak walked up to his table and sat down. A boy brought him a cup of masala tea and Janak sipped it thoughtfully. The afternoon bus arrived in a cloud of smoke and dust and the passengers ran out to find seats.

'Why so morose, my friend?' asked Shankar, counting his money. He had made a good sale. The fish were tiny and full of bones, but the man he had sold the fish to did not know that. He would only find out in the evening when he sat down to eat it and it would be too late.

Janak quickly explained to Shankar what had happened.

'How dare he? How dare he insult one of our women? We must seek him out,' he shouted and Lala came out to see what was going on. He too began shouting as soon as he heard what had happened and before he knew it, Janak was standing on a table and declaring that he would seek revenge.

'I will kill him with my bare hands!' he heard himself say in a strange, unfamiliar voice and everyone slapped him on the back.

'What a brave man. Our tailor is going to be a hero.'

Soon the entire village knew about the insult and Janak's vow and they jumped into the fray. Everyone had seen the man with the red shirt, but no one knew who he was or where he was from. Raja said he looked like his wife's cousin brother who had run away to Mumbai to become a movie star. Channa barber said he looked like one of his old customers who lived in Simla but his hair was thicker. 'My man wore a red shirt too, but he was quite bald. Yet he came to get his hair trimmed every month,' he said.

Everyone in Lala's tea shop was very excited now. They all talked at the same time, swearing they would help Janak seek revenge. But after several cups of tea, their tempers cooled down and they began discussing something of greater interest – the magic show. Janak, exhausted by this show of bravery which was very unusual for him, slumped in a chair and listened to the others. He began regretting all that he had said earlier. In fact, now he could hardly remember what he had said. He hoped it wasn't something too brave.

The next day the magic show began an hour late because the kerosene lamps hired from Grand Tent House in Simla had been kept near the hand pump by mistake and got drenched with water. Janak heard someone in the crowd say that some monkeys, irritated by their smell, had peed on them. The lamps, lit after much coaxing, now stood in a corner, casting a strange, grey-blue smoke on the stage and added to the mysterious, gloomy atmosphere. The lamps also gave out a powerful monkey-urine odour which made the people sitting near them sneeze violently, but no one minded. They were in an excited state and the sneezing just added to their joyous frenzy.

Janak sat in the front row on a plastic chair, also hired from Grand Tent House, feeling a bit awkward but important. It was not often they sat on chairs like this – all in a neat row: the headman, Lala, Shankar, Raja, and the village school teacher, Shamu. They looked at each other shyly as if they had just met and not known each other all their lives. Janak tried to sit back, but he felt a sudden dizzy spell and sat up straight again. He had a chair in his shop but it was an old broken one and he preferred to sit on the floor. These proper chairs were made of aluminium, had bright red plastic seats, and made a faint squeaking sound when you sat down or got up, as if you had farted.

The last chair in the front row was occupied by a stranger dressed in city clothes. Janak, assuming him to be a friend of the magician's, greeted him with a polite namaste, but the man just scowled back. Janak looked away, feeling a bit hurt. The man was dressed in a shiny black nylon shirt, readymade and expensive, Janak could tell. There floated from him a strong, spicy scent like lemons, cloves and roses, and Janak noticed how comfortable he looked sitting on the chair, his legs crossed effortlessly.

He looked like a man who was used to sitting on chairs all the time, not just on special occasions. He looked like he smoked all the time too, cupping his hand over the cigarette to light it. His hands were heavy and thick like a wrestler's, and he kept looking at his gold wristwatch as if waiting for someone. Janak wanted very much to have a closer look at the gleaming watch which had a complicated face with many signs, but the stranger looked like a very bad-tempered man. He had hair growing like clumps of grass on his ears.

That was a sure sign of a fierce temper. His mother's maternal uncle, who used to throw cups and saucers at his wife, had hairy ears like that. Janak felt a bit afraid of the stranger, so he stared at the stage instead of the watch. Anyway, what would he do with such a costly watch? You could only wear a flashy watch like that when you went visiting your relatives or went to Simla on some important work. It was the kind of watch that would surely get stolen. He did not need a watch like that, though it would have been nice just to see what exactly it did and tell other people he had once seen a watch like that.

The makeshift stage was still draped with a black cloth and all the children kept peering behind it. The stranger suddenly got up and shouted at them and they scampered away, but when Janak looked down the row later, he had disappeared. Though Janak had not organized the magic show, he felt a bit insulted by this. It was not nice to waste a ticket. Someone else could have sat on his chair. It was not everyday they got a chance to sit in the front row like important people from the city.

Some men did not appreciate their good luck in life. An empty seat in a crowded show was a gift from the gods and one should not spurn it like this.

The women and the children sat on the floor on durris – also hired from Simla along with a big music box which trembled each time the notes hit a high pitch, and then shuddered into silence again. The women sitting near the box covered their ears with their hands and laughed each time this happened.

Despite the loud music, they were all chattering happily because it was not often they came out on a night like this. Some of them had even put on their best saris and salwar suits, ones usually reserved for wedding feasts. Janak did not turn around to see where his wife was because that would look unseemly with all the older women around, but he felt happy knowing she was somewhere in the crowd not too far from him. His mother-in-law was here too, but the parakeet had been left at home and that was a sign of how mellow Rama's mood was. He hoped the magic show would make her forget their quarrel and she would not ask him again to avenge her honour. He tried not to think about his boasting at Lala's tea shop. Please God, keep her like this. I will stitch you a set of new clothes and bring them to the temple,' Janak hummed under his breath to ease the anxious thoughts still swirling in his head but then, all of a sudden, he got a cramp in his left leg. His left eyelid began to throb as well.

What was this now? Was it a bad omen? Did the gods not want a set of new clothes? Had someone cast an evil eye on him? Janak's head reeled with fearful thoughts. 'No. No. Calm down. All is well. All is at peace. Rama is in a good mood, despite our little quarrel, the house is in a good mood, the mother-in-law's temper is quiet and the headman is still alive,' he said over and over again, rubbing his eye and stamping his left leg to stop the pins and needles creeping up and down his leg like ants. Then, just as he was beginning to feel better, an eerie, shrill cry jolted him out of his seat. The magic show had begun.

It was at that moment that Janak suddenly realized who the man was. He was the same man who had teased Rama. How stupid of him not to realize it earlier. He had not seen the man's nose, but he was sure it was crooked. Evil men like him who teased other men's wives always had a crooked nose. He would go out and look for him. If he had a broken nose and a mole on his cheek, then he was the man.

Janak was about to get up from his chair, but he stopped. If it was the same man, the ruffian from the city who had teased his wife, then what would he do? How could he just walk up to him and say, 'I will kill you, you have teased my wife.' But he had vowed to do so in front of Lala and Shankar and the whole village. Maybe the man would say he was sorry and they could both have a cup of tea at Lala's shop. After all, how do you kill a man just like that? First they would have to have a fight. No. First they would exchange angry words, then have a fight, and then Janak would kill him. But what if the man killed him? He looked very dangerous. Why had he chosen Rama to tease? There were so many other pretty women in the village, plumper than Rama, fairer than Rama. 'What shall I do?' Janak said, not realizing he had spoken out aloud. But the music was blaring now and no one heard him. 'Rama will never forgive me if I do not do something,' he whispered. He would be disgraced and whatever little hope there was of Rama returning his love would be lost forever and ever. No. He could never allow that to happen. He would get up right now. He would confront the evil man and be killed if the gods wished it. He would avenge his wife's honour, right after the first act of the magic show was over. He stared at the stage blankly as he rubbed his hands over his stomach to quieten it. Now he knew why his left eye had been throbbing.

The magician, his face painted with streaks of red and white, screamed like a banshee again and then jumped on the stage, his glittering cape flying behind him like black wings. Janak forgot everything for a moment as he admired the cape, pleased to see that all the silver stars he had stitched on were firmly in place, all fifteen of them. His sewing machine never let him down, nor demanded anything from him. Loud, discordant music began to play once more from the music box and the albino boy, now dressed like an English boy in a blue suit and hat, brought in a table covered with a red cloth.

The magician bowed once more and then the tricks began to roll out quickly. Brightly coloured silk handkerchiefs rippled and tumbled, white doves flew out of a box and turned into mice, one rabbit leapt out from a basket and then disappeared into the magician's hat, playing cards fell in an arc and went back neatly, into a pile untouched by hand, water poured from an empty glass like a tiny waterfall and the magician drank it all up. He coughed a few times as if he was going to be sick and just when everyone was laughing a bit nervously in case he really threw up on their best clothes, he breathed a long quivering flame out of his mouth. The tent was filled with blue smoke that smelled like tobacco. A few people began to sneeze. Everyone gasped and clapped and some babies began to cry, but their mothers quickly clamped them to their breasts to quieten them.

Now the music box began blaring out an English marching tune and the magician brought out a black and white board and made the albino boy stand against it. He whistled a few times and then began throwing knives at the board, one by one. They flew at the board, narrowly missing the albino boy who stood absolutely still, his back touching the board, looking like a frail, sad ghost as the knives formed a jagged outline around his body.

A short break and a religious song later, during which some children got up and started to dance on the empty stage, the act they were all waiting for began.

A boy, not the albino, but a tall, hawk-nosed one, dressed in a black and gold costume, rolled out a long wooden box on stage. The music box fell silent. Everyone sat up to stare at the magician, who was now dressed in a new, scarlet robe.

'I am going to cut a body in half. Who is the brave man who will come up on stage to face my saw?' the magician shouted, rolling his kohl-rimmed eyes.

Everyone clapped excitedly and waited for the headman to get up. It was his privilege to be cut in half since he was the most important man in Giripul.

Janak stared at him, his stomach tight with fear once more. Maybe this was why his left eye had been throbbing, for this and the earlier worry. So many terrible things waiting to happen. Was this going to be the moment of truth? Was the headman going to be cut in half and not beheaded like the dream had predicted? Had the third wife planned this? Had she paid the magician to plot this event? Women could never let things be. Just because Rama had been insulted, he too would have to go out now to be killed by some strange man with a crooked nose and a mole on his cheek. Was it the left or right cheek, he thought as panic began to rise. He and the headman would die together.

No, that was not possible. The third wife could not

have met the magician. She never left the village and everyone would at once know if she got on the bus to go to Simla. No women from Giripul had ever travelled by bus alone. Women were never supposed to go anywhere alone, everyone knew that. Moreover, the third wife could never have planned such a complicated murder. It needed brains, and God had not been generous to her when it came to putting brains in her pretty head. A lovely face, thick black hair and gorgeous breasts she had, but no brains. His beloved Rama was much more intelligent and if she had gone to school, she could have been a teacher. That was all that intelligent women could do, become teachers in a village school. Women could never become doctors, lawyers or police inspectors, however clever they may be. That was the rule. Their men had to protect them, that was the rule too. He was now going to have to fight a strange man, maybe get killed, because of the stupid rule.

The magician called out again, his smiling face tired and strained now. Some of the red and white face paint had begun to run down his throat and looked like blood, as though someone had stabbed him. Oh! No. No. I must not think like this. No throats will be cut. We are all safe and watching a magic show and as soon as it finishes I will go out and seek the man who whistled at my wife and called her a munia, Janak told himself sternly and tried to breathe slowly, but his heart kept pounding as if something terrible was about to happen. The pins and needles in his leg had gone, but his left eye began throbbing again. He looked for Shankar, but could not see him.

The crowd was calling out the headman's name. Not his real name, which was Hari Om – very few people knew it, and anyway, it would be disrespectful to call him by his name – so they shouted 'Mukhiya' lustily, enjoying the noise they were making. The women did not shout, but nodded and smiled.

But the headman shook his head and pushed Raja on the stage instead. Raja walked up to the steps, grinning nervously, pulling at his green trousers. The magician pulled him up, slapped his back with a wicked smile and then with one wave of his silver stick, he opened the wooden box. Raja smiled at the audience sheepishly, scratched his head and got into the box. At first they could see his legs twitching about, but then the magician's boy held them down firmly. The music box shuddered into life once more and drums began to roll. Then there was silence, expect for a baby whimpering as he suckled at his mother's breast.

10

Murder; Tommy finds the body; Raja sawed in half; Janak in grave trouble

Later, everyone recalled that the ravens had been calling that night on the hills and that was a very bad omen. Of course, people remembered many strange things that they had seen before the murder. A white dove with black marks on its left wing, a two-headed snake floating in the stream, an owl hooting during the day and many other such bad omens. Everyday someone would come up with a new bad omen they had seen on that fateful night and others would say at once that they had seen it too.

It was Tommy who found the body. After the pouring-water-from-the-invisible-glass act and the fire-breathing act, he went out to see if there was any food left for him outside Balu's shed. There was nothing in his bowl and Balu was snoring inside. He was the only one in the village who did not want to see the magic show. 'Enough magic shows have happened in my life. God shows his magic to me every time he makes the sun and the moon rise, every time a child is born and spring arrives after

winter,' he announced and stayed in his shed. The truck
legend had said '*Evil-eyed one, stay away from my beloved*',
which meant it would be a bad day.

From the top of the street, Tommy saw the girl thief
slide into the magician's tent, not where the show was
being held but the smaller one where he lived and where
all his trunks were stored. He wanted to bark, but as
usual his throat went dry. Anyway, she was too far away
to hear him. Sometimes he wondered if the girl was real
or just a shadow, but then when Rama shouted at Janak
for not catching her, he knew she was human. Feeling
helpless, he ran down the street and that was when he
saw the light streaming out on the street.

Someone was lying on the steps outside Janak's shop.
Tommy, curious about who it could be at this odd hour,
ran up to inspect. It was a man, but he lay very still,
like a corpse. It was very odd. Tommy sniffed the air.
He was a stranger and a strange new smell of spices
and lemons came from him, like freshly made chutney.
Tommy began to bark and all the other dogs ran up to
join him. They had to do more than just bark, Tommy
thought. After a few minutes, he ran back at top speed
to the magic-show tent to fetch Janak.

The music box was dancing frantically as the drums
rolled louder and louder. The wooden box on stage
shook agitatedly as Raja twisted and turned inside. The
magician held up his saw, danced about on the stage,
brandishing it in the light as if he was Ravan in a Ramlila
show. He pretended he was going to jump off the stage
to attack the audience and Janak could not help jumping

back. Everyone laughed and he felt very foolish and hoped Rama had not seen his cowardly behaviour.

A wailing trumpet sound now played from the music box and the magician rolled his eyes as if he was going into a trance. He whirled about a few times with his arms spread out like people who were in a trance in front of the devta did sometimes, and then with a roar he leapt on the box.

Janak was glad he was not in it. Poor Raja must have wet his pants by now. But even if he did, no one would be able to see anything, he would have to hide the wet patch on his pants when he came out of the wooden box. Janak felt sorry for his friend.

It was wrong of the headman to push Raja on stage. He should have braved this sawing-the-body act himself. After all, he was the headman of Giripul. He had to be the leader in every situation, and this magic show was an important situation to deal with – a historic occasion for Giripul. The headman should have been sawed in half on stage in front of the entire village, not poor Raja. He turned to look at the headman but he was not in his seat. How strange – why should he leave at such an exciting moment of the show? Did he have to go out and take revenge on someone too? How fortunate if that villain had whistled at the third wife too, thought Janak. These whistling type of men always whistle at every woman they see. Then the headman would have to fight the man and avenge both their honours with one good blow to the man's jaw. The headman could break that man's crooked and broken nose even more. Janak silently began praying,

God, please make it happen and I will never ask you for anything else for at least one month.

He frowned and stared at the stage, wishing the act would get over soon and they could all go home. At the same time he wished it would go one forever and he would not have to go out to seek his enemy. He wanted Raja safely back in his seat, grinning as usual. He'd had enough of this magic show. Life was full of fearful suspense as it was, who needed more fears, more unexpected things, more chopping up of bodies? Soon he too would have to kill or be killed. Maybe the matter could be settled with just a few abuses. Maybe the man had not called Rama, but some other woman, his little munia. Maybe he was just whistling because it was a nice summer morning which makes you feel like whistling and Rama just came along at that moment.

Janak shut his eyes and let the cool breeze touch his face as he climbed up the hilly path. Soon he was standing right on top of the mountain where the clouds played. Wild flowers covered every inch of the ground, larks sang as they rose high in the air, and Janak began to whistle. All around him, birds began to sing their sweet, cheerful songs to keep him company. He could see Rama far away, cutting grass. He felt happy and carefree, like a young boy, and began whistling louder and louder. Suddenly, he heard a scream and opened his eyes. The magician had began his greatest act of the evening. Raja was getting ready to be sawed in half. Janak rubbed his eyes and gaped at the stage.

The magician was screaming loudly in a high-pitched

voice as he sawed the box and then suddenly there was a loud crash as Teera, Lala's new cook, leapt on the stage. 'Stop! Stop! You cannot do this to this poor man. He is innocent,' he shouted, trying to grab the magician's saw. 'Let him go. I will kill you with this saw. You murderer!' he screamed. The magician tried to push him away, but Teera was too strong for him and both of them fell on the stage. Raja, stuck in the box, stared helplessly, his eyes round with fear, and his feet shook up and down as if they were trying to run. Janak jumped out of his chair and people began shouting, 'Teera, Teera ... come back!' Lala rushed to the stage and tried to pull Teera away from the magician, but he looked a bit unsteady on his feet and kept falling himself. The children, thinking this was part of the magic show, began to clap loudly and whistle. Janak wanted to go up on the stage, but he felt afraid. What if Teera attacked him with the saw?

'Enough! Stop it you two!' shouted the headman in such a booming voice that Teera, startled, let go of the magician, who quickly got up. He dusted his robe, picked up the saw and smiled at the audience.

'Thank you. Thank you,' he said and bowed as the headman dragged Teera and Lala off the stage.

After a short pause, the sawing of the body began again. The magician, chanting in a shrill voice, drew his saw over the box. Raja shut his eyes and everyone was mesmerized once more. Even the babies were not whimpering any more.

Janak tried to concentrate on what was happening on the stage, but far away on the street he could hear dogs barking loudly. They seemed to be going mad. Janak hoped a leopard had not come into the village. Well, the cattle were all home safely and all the children were here, so there was nothing to worry about.

Janak wondered where the poor albino boy was. How sad it was to be so different from other people. Whatever you did or said would be taken in a different light and even your most innocent gestures would be taken amiss by people. Maybe if you blinked your eyes when your eyelashes were white, people thought you were angry and shouted back at you. It was like being stuck in an alien land where no one could understand you at all.

Janak had just spoken a few words to the boy, yet he felt a closeness to him. His only fault was that his skin was not the same colour as everyone else's. What if he went to a foreign land where everybody was white? No, even there they would look at him in disgust because he was not one of them. It was like the hatred between a crow and a pigeon. They were both birds but neither would allow another's chick to hatch in its nest. He had seen them peck another's chick to death.

Janak, lost in his thoughts, felt a sudden tug at his feet. He gave a start, thinking it was the man with the broken nose, but saw it was only Tommy. He tried to make him sit down, but Tommy kept tugging at his shawl, barking loudly. Everyone around him began to mutter angrily and hissed at Tommy to shut him up. The magician, now sawing with a great fanfare of drums and trumpets, stopped and looked down angrily at them. Janak tried to push Tommy away; he had never behaved like this before. But he growled and then began howling, as if in pain.

'Make this mongrel go away or I will stop the show. Too many disturbances here. I am warning you, or I will turn him into a rabbit,' shouted the magician and some people in the crowd got up to see what was happening. Everyone was staring at him. Janak got up, his face red with embarrassment, and followed Tommy as he ran out. Why was he behaving like this? Was loyal, dependable Tommy going to become unpredictable like everyone else?

As soon as he came out of the tent, he saw Shankar standing against a tree. 'There you are, peeing again. You fool, you are going to miss the best part of the show and so will I. I don't know why this dog is behaving like this. Something is the matter with him. He seems to be trying to tell me something. Listen, Shankar, come with me.' It would be safe to take Shankar along in case the whistling man was lurking somewhere near by. It was quite dark now and the narrow street looked menacing.

Shankar shouted, 'Wait, I am about to finish.' But Tommy would not stop barking and Shankar could not stop mid stream. So they left him grumbling loudly. As Janak ran behind Tommy, he remembered his mother saying men were like fountains, always sprouting water.

By the time they climbed up the hill path and got to the street, Shankar had caught up with them, breathless and looking around furtively though there was no one about.

'I know something is wrong. My right eyelid has been throbbing all day,' he said, rubbing his eyes. Janak wanted to tell him about his left eyelid, but kept quiet. It would seem he was trying to copy Shankar. He hated the way Shankar always beat him at everything. Even when they were boys, he always had the worst bee sting, the biggest boil and the deepest cut on his knee. When they threw rocks down the hillside, his always went further and he could reach the topmost branch of a tree much before Janak, even though he was so short. Thank god he had remained shorter than him.

Tommy, now barking even louder, ran to Janak's shop and suddenly stopped near the steps, whimpering in a strange way. Janak's heart suddenly began to beat loudly and his ear buzzed as if a bee had got stuck in it. Something terrible was going to happen. He opened his eyes wide. There was someone lying on the steps. He ran ahead of Shankar, trembling with fear. The man's eyes were open, staring at him accusingly. The broken nose looked more crooked in the moonlight and the mole gleamed on the left cheek.

'Oh my god, dead! He is dead! The man I said I would kill, is dead already ... Oh god ...' mumbled Janak, staring at him with horror and disbelief. Should he shake the man to see if he was really dead? No, No. He was not going to touch him. He was dead all right ... That glassy look in his eyes. Janak tried to go closer to see if the man was breathing, but his legs refused to move. This was a nightmare and he would wake up soon. He would get up and find Rama beside him. He must open his eyes and all would be well. Janak suddenly felt he could not breathe and clutched his chest and groaned. A dead body lay at his feet. A real dead body of the very man he had vowed to kill.

Shankar came and stood by him. 'What? ... How? ... My god. This man looks dead,' he gasped. 'But I ... We can check. We can hold a feather under his nose and see if he sneezes.' He began searching the ground for a feather. 'A dead body ... in our village,' he kept saying over and over again. 'You can never find a feather when you need one. There, ah! I can see one.'

Janak stood frozen with terror and watched as Shankar waved a tiny feather under the man's nose.

'Dead, totally dead,' said Shankar and moved back, shaking his head, and then began cleaning his own ears with the end of the feather.

'The same man, the man I said I would kill,' whispered Janak.

'Oh, no! You are in big trouble. They will hang you. You said in front of the entire village you will kill this man and here he is, lying on your doorstep, nice and dead. But I know you have not killed him, you would never do such a thing. You do not have the guts, my friend,' said Shankar, giving him a sympathetic pat on the back.

'We must move him. Shankar, we must take him somewhere else at once. If they find him here, I will go to jail. Oh Devi, help me.' he said, almost choking.

They stood for a few minutes, watching the man. Janak felt his heart thumping in his chest as if it was going to burst. He tried to take long, slow breaths and counted till ten. Then Shankar calmly jumped over the dead body and pulled down an old sack hanging on the wall. 'Here, wrap his head and then we will drag him,' he said briskly.

'Where shall we go? Where shall we put him? Oh god! Why have you done this to me? I have been such a devoted servant to you!' cried Janak, tugging at the sack, tears streaming down his face.

'Shut up and lift him. Look, there is someone coming. Hurry up. Let us put him in Channa barber's shop,' whispered Shankar.

They quickly lifted the body, swinging him like a sack of flour, and half carried, half dragged him to the barber's shop next door. 'Let's put him in the chair, so that everyone will think he just died while having a haircut,' said Shankar, and Janak stared at his friend in awe. How clever his old friend was. They propped him up in the chair. Janak thought for a moment and then quickly mixed some shaving soap and lathered the dead man's face. 'No one will recognize him now.' He was amazed at how calm he was feeling suddenly. His fears had vanished as soon as he put the dead man in the barber's chair. It was as if he had become a cold, calculating murderer, erasing the signs of the crime he had committed. He knew, if he stayed calm, no one could catch him. Shankar stared at him in surprise and said with grudging admiration, 'That was clever of you, but I was going to do the same thing.' Both looked at each other silently. They were partners in crime now.

They heard a voice and jumped.

'What are you two doing? You are missing Raja being cut in half. What a show,' said Lala, coming towards them.

'I just came out to get a little ... you know, a little drop of cough medicine,' he said, winking at them. Then he stopped. 'Arre! Who could be getting a shave at this time of the night? Moreover, Channa barber is at the magic show. I am sure I saw him standing at the back,' said Lala, now walking closer to them. Shankar pushed Janak forward and they quickly barred the door to the barber's shop.

'Come, Lala, give us a drop of your cough medicine. I tell you, we need it,' said Shankar loudly.

'But who is this man? Look, he seems to be sleeping,' said Lala, trying to push Shankar away to get a better look.

'Maybe he is a bus passenger waiting for a quick shave,' said Shankar, washing his hands at the handpump. 'The dogs do not seem to like him though. See, how they are all whimpering.'

'The last bus went two hours ago, you idiot,' said Lala.

'Maybe Channa barber forgot about him. Put the lather on and forgot about him. You know how barbers always do that. They put the white cloth around your neck, lather your face and then go off to cut someone else's hair or keep talking to each other. You are trapped in the chair and cannot get away. Come on, give us a sip of the cough medicine and then let's go back, we might catch the last bit of the magic show. He will put Raja back now or we will have two bits of our old friend to live with. Come, let's go,' Shankar said, pulling Lala's hand.

For once Janak was happy that his friend was in his garrulous mood and had saved him from awkward questions. He was in real danger now and must try and be strong. 'Stay calm and breathe evenly,' he muttered to himself. How had this terrible thing happen? Who had killed this stranger? Was it another angry husband out to get revenge? This evil stranger must have whistled at various women during his visit to Giripul.

'Come, Janak, let us go,' shouted Shankar and Janak was about to turn too when Lala suddeny gave a shout, 'You know the man ... he looks dead.'

'No, No... He is just relaxing. You know how sleepy you feel after Channa gives you a head massage. Come, let us go!' Shankar shouted, but Lala would not move.

'But his eyes are wide open. Look ... there is blood on the towel.'

'No, no. Those are just paan stains. This man looks like a great paan eater to me,' said Janak, suddenly finding his voice. Lala now pushed them aside and rushed towards the chair.

'Lala, wait,' Shankar shouted. Janak felt his heart dropping into his stomach as panic rushed into his head again. 'Don't touch him ...' Janak whispered, his throat dry with fear, but Lala had already put his hand on the dead man's shoulder and the body rolled off the chair.

'Oh god! Shiva in heaven! Protect us! Oh Durga devi, save us!' cried Janak, covering his face with his hands. It was as if he was seeing the dead body for the first time. Now he would never get away. They would catch him and put him in jail. Rama would be a criminal's wife. His son would be a criminal's son. He felt his earlier fearlessness drain away as the ground beneath him swayed. Everything was spinning around him, the dead body, the barber's chair the entire street. He was going to faint and then he heard a loud crash behind him and turned around, trembling in fear. Lala had fainted and fallen on the floor and Tommy was whimpering and licking his face.

Shyamala could not believe her eyes. The body was actually going to be cut in half by the huge saw. One minute ago, Raja, whose shop she often went to buy lipstick, talcum powder and brassieres, was sitting in his chair grinning his silly grin and the next minute he was getting ready to be cut into two equal halves. In her dream she had often seen her husband's head being chopped off by her very own hands, but this was something else. It was real and happening in front of her eyes.

Maybe she should tell the magician about her dream. That Janak tailor had done nothing to help her except sending his idiotic, fish-smelling friend Shankar to trail her. Now every time she left the house she had to make sure he was not following her. Anyway, it was quite difficult to follow anyone secretly in Giripul since there was only one narrow street and everyone could look out of their window and see who was following whom. In fact, most people kept a constant lookout from their verandah to see who was going where, not only in Giripul but in the neighbouring villages too.

The saw was making such a terrible sound. It was like the headman's snores. She had to often prod him on his stomach when he snored like that. But she had to be careful because if he woke up, he pounced on her, muttering something in English. It sounded like 'Darrrling ... darrrling!'

Oh dear goddess, protect us. Raja, the only shopkeeper of Giripul, was now going to be divided in two halves. His head stuck out from one end of the box and his feet from the other. What was really scary was that his smile was still pasted on his face. Shyamala covered her face with her hands, but peered through the gaps between her fingers.

She would never chop her husband's head off, however often she dreamt about it. It would be terrible; moreover, she could never do it neatly like this. It was sure to become very messy and her clothes would be ruined forever. They said blood stains never came off, however much soap you used.

Anyway, he was a good husband, why should she get rid of him, just because of a stupid dream? It was no fun to be a widow. She would have to throw away all her pink and red suits, her heavy gold bangles which her mother had got made for her at the new jewellers' shop in Simla and the pretty golden sandals the headman had bought for her just the other day when he went to Simla. He always got her something nice from Simla, unlike other husbands in Giripul.

Rama said Janak never gave her anything at all, not even a bit of cloth, though he had a trunk full of leftover cloth. Raja's wife said he had only given her an old watch he found on the road once. Shankar's wife said she would never take anything even if he gave it to her because it would smell of fish.

No, her headman was a good husband. She could never chop his head off. Husbands were not easy to find once they went. She would just dream this bad dream till it vanished and nothing bad would ever happen in her waking life. But just to be safe, she would go to the temple in Shaya, tie a red cloth and place one rupee and twenty-five paise at the devta's feet along with a coconut. He would make sure she never lopped off her husband's head.

It had been silly of her to confess to the tailor. What could he do, a helpless man like him? He was a very good tailor who could stitch a blouse with just 75 centimetres of cloth, but a mild, soft man, unlike her husband. How proud and handsome he looked, sitting in the front row on a chair with his heavy arms crossed over his manly chest. Shyamala's heart filled with love and she bowed her head like a shy bride. Yes, he was a strong man – the headman of Giripul. He could do anything, but just to be on the safe side, she would go and visit Bengali Baba early tomorrow morning.

Rama looked away from the stage and saw her husband get up and leave the tent. What was he up to now? Why could he never sit still? This was going to be the best part of the show. He had been behaving really oddly these days, so shifty and nervous. Her mother said it was another woman, but she could not believe it. Who could it be?

Shyamala, the headman's wife was sitting right next to her, her face covered with her hands, silly woman. It was just a magic show. Raja was not going to die, unless there was an accident.

Her mother had told her once that in their village, a man had tried to do a rope trick on the hill and was strangled by the rope. They had to cremate him right there and then, with the rope around him.

No, Janak was not in love with any other woman, she was sure. He might not be very strong or very intelligent, but he was faithful. Her mother might say all kinds of things about him, but he loved only her and never stopped looking at her with lovesick eyes like a newborn calf. It was embarrassing, his love for her. She was afraid the village people would find out and they would become the laughing stock not just in Giripul, but all over the Simla hills. Whoever heard of a man dying of love like this for his wife. Love was for city people and movie stars. The gods too fell in love and did all kinds of things for their beloved. But love in Giripul was unheard of, and she was not going to be its first victim.

His odd behaviour really irritated her. He looked so worried all the time, like a pregnant mouse searching for a home. Even when he walked he kept looking over his shoulder as if someone was going to attack him. He often watched her at night when he thought she was asleep and his face looked so sad and forlorn. He had still not found the city man who had whistled at her and called her munia. What kind of a husband let his wife be insulted like this? The headman would have found the rascal and killed him by now.

She wished Janak would show some manly courage sometimes, shout at her and slap her now and then, just to show he was her lord and master. Why could he not be normal like other men, or like the headman. Now that was a real man. She wished her parents had found her someone like him, tall, strong, with gleaming white teeth and a rich moustache. How handsome he looked, sitting on a chair in the first row. She was sure she would make him a better wife than Shyamala. All she did was get new suits stitched and then parade in them up and down the hillside for the crows and goats to admire.

If she was the headman's wife, she would behave with quiet dignity, not too friendly with everyone who came to visit them, yet smiling and listening to their complaints. She would match the headman perfectly, and together they would rule like the king and queen of Giripul. But why think such thoughts when she was married to Janak and would be his wife till she died.

The sound of the saw was getting on her nerves. She wished the magician would speed up this sawing-of-Raja act and the magic show would end so that they could go home. She could feel a headache coming on and wished she had brought her favourite scarf to tie around her head. But her mother was enjoying the show and the poor thing hardly ever went anywhere, so she, better sit it out for her sake.

Bengali Baba had told her to smile and count her

breath when she felt irritated. Rama began to count as the saw moved up and down and stretched her mouth into a painful smile. Bengali Baba, the great Shadow Chaser, was always right. She began to feel better at once and clapped her hands with all the others as the sawing act unfolded on the stage.

11

Janak anxious and afraid; Lala drunk and boastful; Shankar alert; A long night with dead body

Janak stood absolutely still for what seemed like a long time staring at the dead man. He breathed slowly and began chanting, 'Om Namah Shivaye Bhagwate Vasudevaye.' His mother had told him this sacred Sanskrit chant would chase away any evil shadow lurking around him. As long as he kept chanting, the dead man's spirit could not harm him. Lala was still lying on the floor, but his eyes were open.

'Look, a dead man. A dead body in Channa barber's chair. Quick, run, we have to fetch the headman … Help me get up. Murder has happened right here – Oh devta! Murder in our Giripul!' he suddenly cried and fell back on the floor. Shankar looked at Janak, winked and then said loudly, 'Oh my god. How did this happen? Janak, look a dead man! A dead stranger who no one in Giripul has ever seen. How did he come here!'

The white and red lather was now forming a pool around Lala as he lay on the ground and it looked as if there were two dead bodies lying on the floor. It was getting crowded here in the tiny barber's shop with dead men all over the place, like some hospital ward. Janak was trying very hard to stand still. He knew Shankar was trying to save him by pretending they had never seen the body before. Anyway, there was no place on the floor, what with Lala and the dead man already stretched full length in the tiny shop. His head began to swim. He needed air. 'I must not faint,' he said loudly and hung on to Shankar's shoulder.

'Yes ... Come, Lala. We must hurry. We must run and fetch the headman. I must not be afraid,' Janak said over and over till he began to feel a little calmer. He took a deep breath and rushed out of the shop, almost tripping over Lala who was now sitting up, rubbing his head.

Shankar hissed at him angrily, but Lala ignored him and kept staring at the dead man. He wouldn't budge, so Shankar decided to leave him with the body. As Janak ran towards the magic show tent, he could see the police taking him away in handcuffs and hear Rama wailing. He could not run any more. His heart began to thump loudly, sounding like the magician's drums. The man he had vowed to kill was dead. Rama had got her revenge, but her husband might soon be dead too. Dead by hanging.

Janak felt the rope, heavy and rough, around his neck. It had a strange smell of dried blood and grass, as if some poor animal had been dragged to death with this rope. His neck was beginning to itch now and he tried to tear the rope away, but his hands could not find it. He could not breathe as the rope tightened around his neck. He was choking now. His body was squirming and twisting as he tried to pull the rope off. Rama's face swam before his eyes. She had covered her head with a white dupatta. Why so soon? He was not yet dead, he thought as he fell into a dark hole. Tommy was barking far away and Rama gradually moved out of his vision. She did not even say goodbye.

'Murder, murder!' he heard someone shout and he opened his eyes.

'Murder, murder in our very own Giripul! Oh! May the gods protect us,' shouted Shankar. Janak slowly walked up to the tent rubbing his neck and coughing. His legs could barely support him. He would have to confess everything. But what had he done? He had only talked about killing the man. It wasn't his fault that the man was now dead. This was the first time he had ever threatened to kill someone. How cruel fate was to do this to him. 'Oh Rama! What have you done? You have sent me to hell!' he cried. His head was spinning and he could barely remember the way back to the tent. He went the wrong way twice.

Now he stood at the entrance of the tent, unsure of what to do. He decided to call the headman, but he seemed to have lost his voice. He went up to the front row, but the headman was not in his seat. 'What to do now?' Janak muttered and began to tremble. 'Om Namah Shivaye Bhagwate Vasudevaye,' he whispered, mopping the sweat that poured down his forehead. The rope felt tighter around his neck.

The magician was chanting some strange foreign sounding words and dancing around the box with the saw in his hand. He would place the saw on Raja's head, move it up and down, and then jump back to admire his stroke. Raja grinned foolishly, his head lolling out from the box as if he had already been beheaded. Janak looked at the women sitting on the ground and saw the third wife agape as she stared at the stage. He went to her and whispered, 'Where is the headman?' the words barely coming out of his throat. She just waved him away.

'Sit down, Janak, sit down,' the women shouted. Janak thought he would fall as a wave of nausea hit him. He rushed out of the tent to get sick on the grass. Tommy came and stood quietly by his side. Behind him the music box thundered and the sawing of the body finally began with great fanfare.

'Look, talking to her in front of all the women of Giripul. He has brought you shame, daughter, shame,' Rama's mother hissed, not taking her eyes off the stage.

'You should never forgive him. We will go back to my house.'

No, why should they go? Her house was too small, with only one room and a kitchen which was outside. They would be uncomfortable there. They would stay on in Giripul and throw him out. Yes, throw him out on the street. But then her daughter would become a half widow like her dead mother-in-law.

What if Janak moved in with the third wife, when he was thrown out by them? She looked at Shyamala with venom in her heart. It was all her fault. Shameless hussy, she had ruined her daughter's life. Bengali Baba had not helped at all, just took fifty rupees, and told Rama to smile. Wretched man. She thought once again with anger.

The saw finally stopped moving and the drums fell silent. Raja's body had been cut into two and now they stood before them, two totally separate boxes. One held his head, and the other his legs.

What an amazing and frightening thing, Rama thought as she stared at the boxes, her hand placed on her heart. No blood, no cries of pain. This magician was truly great. She hoped her son, sitting in her lap, had learned something from him and would grow up to be a great magician too and not a tailor like his father.

After a stunned silence, everyone began clapping. The two halves of Raja's body slowly began moving towards each other. The music box played a popular romantic song which they all knew.

> Come to me, my heart,
> Come to me swiftly, my heart,
> On this delicious moonlit night.

Rama stared at the boxes; she could feel the skin on her arms prickling with excitement. How were the boxes moving? The magician stood at a distance. He stood quietly, stroking his chin as if in deep thought, at the far end of the stage.

Slowly, inch by inch, the two boxes moved like two lovers dancing. When one moved forward, the other moved back and they circled the stage. Everyone watched in total silence except for a few nervous giggles from the young girls.

Then, with a loud noise, the boxes bumped into each other and the magician stepped forward at once. He bowed to them and then turned around, stretching his arms wide to cover both the boxes with his cape. Then he chanted loudly, swaying from side to side, and the drums began to play softly. For a few minutes all they saw were the stars on the black velvet of the magician's cape. Rama counted there were fifteen of them. Janak had told her he had stitched them with a chain stitch. She felt a sudden surge of affection for her husband. She would never let another woman steal him from her. But where was he? He had missed the best part of the show. He could never do anything right. She was sure he would never find the man who had insulted her. He could do nothing but stare at her like a lost calf.

The drum beats began to thunder loudly again and the magician moved aside with a flurry of his cape. There, on the stage stood Raja grinning broadly, his body the same, thin and awkward, his green trousers a bit crumpled, his feet bare.

She forgot about Janak and clapped loudly with the crowd. It was the circle of life and death dancing in front of their eyes. This magician could do anything with his magic, cut a man in half and then make him whole. Maybe she should have been married to him. She would make such a perfect magician's wife; she would make all the arrangements, be helpful on stage, but always take care to stay one step behind her husband. She would let him have all the fame and glory.

Men always wanted that. She never said a sharp word to Janak in front of other people, but he knew when she was angry with him. There was no need for words, a look was enough.

Shyamala uncovered her face and clapped loudly. What a great show! What a clever man this magician was, surely he could find the answer to her strange dream.

Maybe she could do a magic show in which she chopped off her husband's head and then put it back again. She would love to talk to the magician. Maybe she could ask Janak, she thought, but when she turned around she could not see him anywhere.

Rama's mother shook her head in wonder. If only life was like magic, then all would be well in the world. Her poor husband, who had drowned in a well, would rise up to be back with her. She would be a happily married woman again, respected by all and not living on charity. If only magic could bring all the dead people in her life back again. Her father who had died in the war in a faraway land would come back to the village, her mother who had died giving birth to her tenth child would be with her again. Her grandparents, all the old uncles and aunts would return home, though that might create problems because where would they all live?

Maybe the magic could bring back only those who were needed by her and would leave the others wherever they were now, happily dead. The magician was marching on the stage to the drum beat and the women in the crowd looked at each other, their eyes gleaming in wonder, and clapped as the magician stopped and bowed.

12

Janak struggles with more anxious thoughts; Shankar thrilled with murder; Police are called

'We must stay here with the dead body,' said Janak. He did not want to, but he knew it was the right thing to do.

'I will stay here with you, but let's keep Tommy with us, just in case,' said Shankar.

'Just in case what? You think the dead man's ghost will jump up and grab your throat?' asked Lala.

'Don't make jokes. This is very serious. A dead man lying in Channa barber's chair ...' said Janak in a low voice. Lala gave him a sharp look and then took a long sip from his bottle.

They had sat up all night, Shankar, Lala and Janak.

Janak knew they had to guard the body, though what was there to guard now, he did not know. Who would steal him? Tommy stayed with them, which made Janak feel safer, but he still could not bring himself to look at the body. He looked at the dark hills instead, and wondered why his wife had given him a strange, knowing smile when he had told her to go home with her mother and that he would come later.

Luckily, the crowd, unaware of what had happened, had gone home from the magic show, happily talking about all the tricks they had seen. Raja, cheered by the crowd like a hero, strutted about for a while, but when they told him about the dead body in the barber's chair, he turned around at once and ran home.

They sat quietly for a while, watching the stars. Janak walked out to the street and sat near the water tank so that he would not have to be so close to the body slumped on the chair, but Shankar kept describing it in great detail. 'Looks like a healthy fellow, not very tall, but a strong man. Looks like he has been doing push-ups, or he could be a wrestler. Big biceps, but his head looks too big for a wrestler, they have to have small heads so that when their opponents catch hold of their necks, they can wriggle out,' he prattled on, showing them various wrestling positions, till Janak shouted at him.

'You must respect the dead and not chatter on like this as if we are at a fun fair. Think of his feelings.'

Shankar snorted and said, 'Dead men do not have feelings. Think about what you are saying, Janak, my friend. When you are dead, your feelings, your anger, your honour, your hatred, your shame and your joys – everything dies with you.'

'How do you know? Have you been dead? Please tell me how many times you have sat with your throat slit, blood dripping on the floor?' said Janak in a sharp voice. Lala sniggered as he opened the new bottle of rum he had brought from the tea shop. He wiped the rim with his sleeve and offered the bottle to Janak, but Janak shook his head. His heart was full of sadness and he turned his face away so that Lala could not see his tears.

How terrible it must be to lie dead in a strange place with strangers drinking rum and talking nonsense.

Just an hour or two ago, he had wanted to fight this man just to please Rama, but now that he was dead he felt sorry for him.

Janak looked up at the dark sky and said a quick prayer. He hoped God would give him a dignified death. He must start praying for it every night. It was never too early because who knew when who'd be called to cross the river of death. His turn might come very soon if the man is identified by the police.

'I do not think his throat is slit. I think he has been stabbed in his neck. Look. Can you see the big red gash here?' said Lala, going close to the body. Though he was outside on the street, Janak's felt his stomach turn.

'Listen, stay away from the man. The police will not like it. How have you suddenly become so brave? You fainted as soon as you saw him,' Janak shouted as he turned away to look at the street.

Lala grinned sheepishly and replied. 'I fainted because it was my first dead body. You know how frightening everything is when you experience it for the first time. I will never faint again. Bring me any number of dead bodies, I dare you,' he said, nudging Shankar.

Janak stared at the sky. It was cloudy but a few stars hung above the peaks, glittering brightly. His mother used to say that stars were people who had died a noble death. This man lying in Channa barber's shop, would never become a star in the sky. Shankar came and stood close to him. 'You better have a good story ready in case the police come for you.'

It was well past midnight. Lala, who had fallen asleep, suddenly woke up and in a slurred voice began to narrate stories of all the dead people he had seen in his life. Some he had seen first hand while others he had heard about. 'My first dead man was that nice Englishman who came to Giripul, married Raja's grandmother and then fell down the khud. I was only four then and my father carried me on his shoulders to the river to see the body. He looked so peaceful and happy as he lay in the water like a fair, golden-haired god.'

'Who? Your father?' asked Shankar.

'No. The dead Englishman, stupid. My father had black hair till he was sixty. After that, I saw a man dying right in front of my eyes in our classroom at school,' said Lala, taking a long swig from the bottle. Shankar sat up at once, a belligerent look on his face.

'What? When was that? I never saw anything and I was in the same class as you. Janak, did you see any such thing?' asked Shankar, standing before Lala with his hands on his hips as if he was a policeman.

Lala ignored him and carried on.

'The man, a school inspector, died right after he had finished giving us a lecture on morals and hygiene.'

Shankar shook his head and muttered, 'I never saw that. Are you sure it happened in our school?' he asked in a challenging tone. 'I never even heard about it.'

'Well, you must have been absent that day, you were always ill or catching fish or something,' said Lala and before Shankar could retaliate, he went on to his next dead body. 'I was at my wife's house, at her sister's wedding. The groom's party had arrived, they were about to exchange garlands when suddenly they turned the groom's horse around and went back. At first everyone thought the bride's father had not given the promised dowry, but later we heard that the groom's ninety-nine-year-old grandmother who had been carried in a palki to the wedding, had died. Apparently she had eaten all the sweets that were meant for the bride's party – all five kilos of laddoo and kajoo barfi. What a sweet death,' said Lala and laughed.

Shankar gave him a sullen look. He was sure Lala was telling lies and he was going to check about the school inspector's death by asking other men in the village.

Janak walked further away from all the chatter. He was worried about what would happen in the morning. What would they do?

When he had finished half the bottle of rum and sung a religious song to ward off the evil eye, Lala had the clever idea of asking his friend who worked at the Fagu telephone exchange to phone the Simla police station. Janak offered at once to go to the man's house, which was in the Kotli village, on the other side of the river.

'Shall I come too?' Shankar asked.

'No, you stay here and guard the body,' Lala told him. Shankar frowned and then sat down.

'Okay, but let Tommy stay with me. Anyway it will soon be dawn,' he said, looking around nervously.

As they walked down the path to the bridge, Lala began telling him about the dead body he had seen in village Kotli but Janak put his finger on his lips and Lala taken aback, kept quiet. Janak could hear the owls hooting above them. Though it was a warm night, the crickets were silent. Maybe they were mourning the death of the stranger.

Though it was still early dawn and the sky, a dark purple, the telephone operator's wife was awake, brewing tea in the kitchen. She quickly covered her face when they knocked on the door and when they came in, she pointed to the durree on the floor. After a few minutes she brought them two cups of steaming ginger tea and went to wake up the operator.

'Listen, Monu's father, two men from Giripul have come to meet you,' they heard her repeat softly a few times. How lucky the telephone operator was to have such a gentle wife, who brewed tea at dawn and woke him up so gently.

When the telephone operator finally woke up at his wife's cajoling and was told what had happened, he was not at all shocked. He clapped his hands and said, 'Jai, jai devi. The man's time had come. May the goddess preserve us all from Yama's eye. Woman, hurry up and fetch more tea for Lalaji and tailormasterji. Put cardamom in it. It is not everyday important people come to the house at dawn.'

'Jai ho. Jai ho. Jai ho,' he shouted over and over again, his voice cutting through the silent dawn.

As they sat drinking tea with him, Lala talked about the dead body, describing everything in great detail as if it was his own body. Then he repeated his earlier talk about the various dead bodies he had seen till now, making the list longer this time.

The telephone operator, who had been listening with rapt attention, started talking about his own father's dead body and how difficult it had been to cremate it because the wood was damp, and Janak began to feel sick in his belly. He nudged Lala to get up, but the telephone operator's wife brought pakoras and more tea and Lala refused to move.

Finally, after they had eaten and talked a bit more about the new bus service and the low market price of potatoes this season, the operator yawned and promised to call the police as soon as he got to the Fagu telephone exchange.

'After all, this is what telephones are for – to announce death, birth and other important events in life. People, especially women, nowadays use it for idle chatter. I tell them, "Cut the nonsense and give the important news only." You know, we must get at least one telephone installed in Giripul for this kind of emergency. Tell the headman to apply for a connection,' he said and shouted for more tea and two telephone application forms.

Lala said later that the operator took a long time to get through to the police because the line was down. Then he got several wrong numbers, but he gave them the news of the murder anyway so now everyone in the surrounding villages as well as in Simla knew about the Giripul murder.

13

Mayhem and murder in Giripul;
Crowds gather; Police arrives;
Dead body removed in van;
Third wife's dream vanishes

The monkeys knew about the dead body long before anyone else and they chattered excitedly on the hillside, picking lice off each others' backs. The ravens sensed it too and sat brooding silently on the pine tree right above the barber's shop.

'Murder! Murder in the barber's shop!' shouted the children as the morning light streamed into the houses. The dogs ran around barking hysterically as Giripul woke up to turmoil. People rushed out of their houses even before having their first cups of tea, and started telling each other what they had been doing when they heard about the dead body in Channa barber's shop.

Everyone was talking loudly and no one was listening.

'I was doing my puja when Raja told me and I almost fainted.'

'I was out by the stream when Shankar came running.' I was preparing breakfast when my mother-in-law heard from the headman's wife. Raja's wife had told her,' they said in excited voices. They all shook their heads and looked at each other in disbelief. 'Murder, murder, murder,' the wind hissed to the trees on top of the hill.

More and more people arrived as the news spread and soon it was difficult to go near the barber's shop. Shankar took charge as minor scuffles broke out in the crowd since people pushed each other to get a closer look at the dead body.

The women stood at a distance and information was relayed to them by their children, who had managed to sneak into the shop for a close look.

Finally, the headman arrived and the crowd parted to allow him to go inside the shop. He stood there rubbing his chin, looking at the dead man, but did not say anything. Then he began biting his nails. Janak, despite being nervous and distraught himself, noticed that the headman was very agitated and upset, but why? The headman never behaved like this and moreover, he did not know this man, so why should he feel so distraught at his death? Maybe dead people made him nervous and frightened. Even a headman had his weakness. He was relieved to see the headman and hoped he would take charge. He could just stand by now and let fate decide what she wanted to do. He was innocent, but only Shankar and the gods in heaven knew that.

'I cannot believe it. A murder right here in our village. I think it is the first time since the British left India. My grandfather told me they had seen a dead man in the forest once, killed by a bear, but you could not call that a murder,' said the oldest man in Giripul. Balu seemed to know what had happened because he called out to them once, asking them if the dead person was a man or woman, but did not come out of his shed when they told him it was a man – a stranger who looked like a wrestler, Shankar added, hoping Balu would ask for more details, but there was silence from the shed.

As the day wore on, people began arriving from other villages. Shankar had already gone around telling the bus passengers what had happened. 'Imagine, I was there yesterday getting a shave and a haircut, I had a head massage too – you know, it is included in the price. And then yesterday I discover a dead body in the same chair – the very same chair,' Janak heard him say to Raja. What a gifted liar his friend was. He too now began to believe that the body had been found in Channa barber's shop.

By nine 'o' clock, about fifty people had gathered around the shop, chatting in loud voices and asking questions to which Shankar happily replied. He was not pleased when Lala offered to give a guided tour of how he had come down the street from the magic show tent, led by Tommy, and how they had found the body. 'You should also tell them how you fainted and fell on the ground,' hissed Shankar, but Lala, his face glowing with excitement, ignored him.

Gradually, by noon, a small fair came up on the street. Raja quickly set up a stall to sell roasted peanuts, a gypsy with a dancing bear appeared out of nowhere, and Lala's shop was filled with new customers. He ordered the servant boys to bring out the big kettle which was usually kept for wedding feast. An aroma of freshly-fried samosas and pakoras floated down the street as more and more people arrived from distant villages. Quite a few bus passengers decided to break their journey and linger in Giripul for a while. It was not often that they could be in a place where a murder had happened and when they went home by the later bus, they could tell the story to everyone in their village.

Old people walked up slowly with their walking sticks, while women were dragged by their children who wanted to see the dead body. A new bride, her face covered with a red dupatta, came with her husband's family which people thought was a bit bold.

Suddenly there was an uproar and the dogs started to bark as a white police van with a flashing red light arrived in a cloud of dust. They could see two policemen sitting in the front seat. A cheer went up as the crowd rushed forward to surround the van and even the afternoon bus halted longer to let its passengers have a good look. But the policemen, one plump and henna haired and his junior a thin, hawk-nosed man, were kept waiting in their police van by a group of ferociously barking Giripul dogs, led by Tommy.

They refused to come out even after being repeatedly told that the dogs were harmless and were only enjoying all the excitement the murder had brought to Giripul.

'It is the first time anything like this has happened here, sir,' said Lala, bowing.

'Barking dogs never bite,' said Raja, 'It says so in my son's English book'. But despite all the persuasion the policemen stayed in the van.

Several cups of tea were sent to them on a tray from

Lala's shop along with some freshly-made biscuits which they liked a lot. After half an hour the dogs got bored and moved on and just then the headman arrived to welcome them ceremoniously with folded palms to Giripul. The policemen finally got out, stretched their legs and then walked to the barber's shop.

A hushed silence fell on the street. Only the headman was asked to come forward and the rest of the crowd was ordered to stand back by the junior policeman. Shankar tried to push forward, but the policeman glared at him and held up his stick. Everyone, even the children, watched quietly as the body was examined by the senior policeman, who lifted the bloodstained sheet and poked the body with his stick. Janak caught a brief glimpse of one hairy ear before it disappeared under a black plastic sheet the younger policeman brought out from the van and carelessly threw over the body. The mole, he could not see. He should have checked when he was putting the soap on the dead man's face, but his mind had gone blank then.

The senior policeman whispered something to his junior, who repeatedly nodded his head and then shouted, 'We need some strong men to get this body into the van. It has to go to Simla for post-mortem.' The crowd which had been eagerly pressing forward to see what was going on immediately fell back when they heard the announcement.

None of them knew what a post-mortem was and they did not wait to find out. All the men, women and children quickly turned around and began walking back to their homes. Soon only the headman, Lala and Janak remained. Raja and Shankar had vanished too.

'We have to help. This body is ours after all,' whispered Lala. Janak was not sure he wanted to claim any kinship with the body. After all, he might go to jail because of it. But before he could move back, he was pushed forward by Lala and found himself staring into the dead man's face as the black sheet slipped. It seemed to be smiling up at him with joy as if he was an old friend who he had seen after an absence of many years. One of his eyes was open, the other one shut in a friendly wink. All his scowling arrogance had vanished and he looked quite humble. A mole gleamed on his cheek.

'Here, you hold this,' said the junior policeman, giving him one end of the plastic sheet and then throwing Lala the other end. The policemen caught the other two ends and shouted, 'One, two, three,' in English. They heaved the body up and swung it into the van. But the younger policeman had forgotten to open the door and they narrowly missed hitting the van's shut door. The body began to roll sideways, but before it could fall out of the sheet, the senior policeman swung him back with a triumphant cry of, 'Oi, oi, shabash!' The body swung to and fro in the rippling black sheet. 'Well done, well done, very good boys,' he added in English like a schoolmaster pleased with his pupils. 'Once more now. One, two, three.' And the bundle landed on the back seat of the van.

The headman, who had stood back so far, gave the bundled up body a friendly, ceremonial pat as if bidding him farewell and then began to laugh in an odd way.

Like a woman about to have a fit. Janak stared at him in amazement.

A few women who had trickled back to watch began to wail now as if they were professional mourners called in for a proper funeral ceremony. Balu opened his shed door and came out to watch, and for some strange reason the headman had rushed down the hillside, still laughing hysterically.

Once the body was tucked into the back seat of the van, the senior policeman sat in front. He took out a small black comb from his pocket, adjusted the rearview mirror and began combing his hair. Then, after wiping his hands with a red handkerchief, he pulled out a notebook. The junior policeman stood outside and kept an eye out for the dogs.

'Who found the body?' the senior constable barked. When Tommy was brought forward by Janak, he quickly shrank back. Janak took a deep breath to calm himself. One false move and the noose would be around his neck.

'Okay. Okay, take him away. Has anyone seen this dead man before?' he asked, scratching his chin with his pen. Janak felt his heart jump, but he looked down at his feet and kept quiet.

You see so many people in your life everyday, but that does not mean you know who they are, what they do or why they have been murdered, he thought, trying to quieten his guilt.

The crowd had quietly come back again, now that the body was safely packed in the van, but no one said anything. The headman returned too, he was quiet now, but kept biting his nails. Raja suddenly jumped forward, bowed to the policemen and said, 'Sirji, he is my wife's cousin.' The crowd gave a collective gasp. The junior policeman looked at him, frowned, and then asked him to give his and his father's name and address.

Raja shrugged his shoulders, rubbed his collar and began shouting out his name in a shrill voice. It took him a few moments to remember his dead father's name and he had to be prompted by an old man in the crowd. While the name writing was going on laboriously, since the old man was very deaf and not quite sure who was dead, they heard a sudden commotion, and Raja's wife came running out on the street, her face covered.

The crowd parted and allowed her to come forward. She looked at Raja and then started screaming, 'Oye, oye! You wicked man! How can you declare my cousin brother dead when he just got married the other day! Here, I can show you his wedding photograph. I brought it along as proof as soon as I heard his lies,' she said, waving a small photograph framed in yellow.

'Look, sahib, he has a moustache,' she cried. Raja looked sheepish and the senior policeman chewed on his pen thoughtfully. He turned the photograph over and then examined the back of the frame. 'Shall we cancel his name and address, sir?' the junior policeman asked.

The senior policeman, now examining his teeth in the van's rearview mirror, looked sternly at him and said. 'The dead body has no moustache, for certain. But you go and take a look, no harm in checking once more. I do not want a case of mistaken identity. But hurry up, because we need to get back to Simla.' The junior policeman opened the rear door of the van, and began rummaging in the plastic bundle. It took a while because he found he had opened the wrong end. He was silent for a moment and everyone held their breath. 'No, no moustache for sure, sir,' he announced and tied up the bundle again. The crowd, which had surged forward, hoping to catch another glimpse of the body fell back again.

Both the policemen now sat quietly staring at the hills. The crowd shuffled a bit and then a heavy silence fell, punctuated only by a raven calling. It was past siesta time and many were wondering whether to stay at the scene of crime or go back home for a quick nap. But then they did not want to miss anything now that the danger of 'post-mortem', whatever it meant, was over.

Lala looked around for a bit and then ordered some more tea and asked the policemen if they would like some hot pakoras. The two men did not say yes, but they did not say no either, which was the polite way of accepting. Lala shouted to the boys to bring some hot snacks. 'I have some freshly-made besan halwa, sir, you must taste a little,' he said and the senior policeman nodded with a faint smile. Besan halwa always deserved a response, he believed. 'All right, if you insist, but we must go back soon.'

They ate the halwa, walked around the street, checked the barber's shop once more, wrote down various things in a book and then, just when the day was fading, they decided to leave. 'We must get back before dark. Not safe to drive at night these days, a lot of bad characters about, but we will come again soon. You must inform us at once if you find anything suspicious,' the senior policeman said in a grave voice, looking at Tommy. Then they took a few bags of peanuts from Raja's shop, a packet of besan laddoos from Lala and got into the van.

Some people tried to complain about petty thefts that had taken place in the village, but the senior policeman said they did not have time for any new complaints today. Lala gave them a basket of freshly-picked cucumbers which they carefully placed on the black plastic body bag before they drove away. The dogs chased them all the way till the bridge and then came back panting happily, but Tommy stayed near Balu's shed. He seemed to be in a state of delayed shock.

Janak folded the bits of cloth lying on his table absent-mindedly. He had got away, but they might come back again. Who had killed the man? He could not help feeling sorry for the stranger. No one should die such a violent death. We should all die peacefully in our beds, surrounded by grieving relatives, he thought, offering a silent prayer for the dead man's soul and then a quick one for himself.

But he was relieved too. The police did not suspect him and now that the murder was over and done with, the third wife's dream would also vanish. Fate, happy and satisfied by the events, would sit quietly now and he could get on with his work.

He was not going to listen to any women any more,

not even his wife. No dreams, no revenge. He would go to the Badi Kothi and finish the curtains, and maybe the old lady would give him some more work. He liked sitting in the verandah, listening to the birds and sewing the old, expensive English cloth. Of course, there was the pink satin suit, waiting to be finished for the headman's whore, but it could wait a while.

It was only yesterday, but it seemed so long ago that he had cut the suit, given it a nice v-neck and frilled sleeves. He did not feel like stitching it any more. The pink satin reminded him of the bloodstained cloth in the barber's shop. The headman would want it soon, maybe even tomorrow, if he was going to Simla. It did not seem right, that the headman of Giripul should leave when there had just been a murder in the village. It was his duty to stay and protect the village. What if someone else was murdered tonight? Janak sighed. 'God, please protect Giripul from harm. And me too,' he added under his breath and touched his sewing machine for good luck.

Shyamala rose at dawn, quickly threw a shawl over her head and went out. She knew that Bengali Baba would be sitting at the temple below the bridge. This was a good time to talk to him, before all the women from the villages on top of the mountain arrived. She began walking faster, planning what to say to him in her mind.

She saw him as soon as she crossed the bridge. He was gathering some flowers from the wild bushes and she quickly bowed to him. Baba smiled and nodded to her as he continued to pluck flowers. Shyamala stood uncertainly with her head bowed and thought, should she speak to him? What if he was doing a silent prayer and did not want to be disturbed. Suddenly Baba spoke. 'What is it, beti? Why have you come to me at this early hour?' he asked as he plucked the red flowers and gently put them in his shawl. Shyamala quickly began telling him about her dream of beheading her husband, but before she could finish, he waved his hand and said, 'Why do you worry so much about a dream, beti? Dreams are just God's way of telling us stories. They never come true in this life, otherwise there would be chaos on earth. Dream your dreams and forget them.'

'But Babaji, this dream is so terrible. My husband, with his head chopped off,' said Shyamala as her eyes filled with tears.

'What else is bothering you? The dream is there, but there is something more, I can see it in your face,' he said, giving her a quick glance.

'There is Babaji. But ... but I do not know how to say it. I feel so ashamed.'

'I know. I know what is on you mind. Do not worry. All will be well soon. Throw away this anger towards your husband. Men stray sometimes, like, cattle but they always come home at dusk. Go home now,' he said, giving her a flower from his shawl.

'Now, listen. Light a diya and say these words at dusk,' he said and leaned forward and whispered in her ears.

Shyamala thought she heard him say, 'Brignala' and opened her mouth to repeat it.

'No, do not speak it aloud. Go home now,' said Baba and walked away.

'Leave fifty-one rupees under the stone and bring me a box of laddoos next time,' he shouted when he reached the bridge.

The next morning, the junior policeman returned, but sat in Lala's shop all day drinking free tea and chatting about the murders he had seen in his career. Lala listened carefully, but did not say anything.

'Our Lala here has also seen many murders,' said Shankar, eager to create trouble, but the policeman did not seem interested in what he had to say. After swiftly kicking Shankar under the table, Lala served the policeman another cup of tea.

'I like Giripul. I think I will buy some land here,' he said.

'Yes, the air is so much better in Giripul, much cleaner than in Simla. That town is too crowded now. Not what it used to be during the British days. Those days the streets were fragrant with ladies' perfume,' said the headman, watching the policeman warily.

Shankar rolled his eyes. 'He knows about Simla, does he not, especially about salons,' he whispered to Janak, who pinched him hard to shut him up.

Janak was weary now with all this talk. Shankar was enjoying the murder as if it was circus or a magic show and the headman was behaving rather strangely. He could feel his head throbbing with a nagging ache as he tried hard to stay alert. Let them come and take me, he thought. I am fed up. I will take my sewing machine and go to jail. He saw himself sitting in a cell, dressed in striped kurta pajama. He looked old and frail as if he had been there for many years.

'Many good hair dressers in Simla,' said the policeman, and Janak, Shankar and the headman froze. It may have been an innocent remark, but it went straight home and all of a sudden, the headman began to laugh for no reason.

Lala rose from the table, draped his shawl and offered to show the policeman around. 'I have a good piece of land which is for sale.' The policeman got up at once. He seemed to have forgotten about the murder and when Shankar mentioned it to him, he looked surprised. 'Yes, yes, the body is in the morgue. No one has come to claim it. We will carry on with our investigations. But these things take a long time. No clues have been found as yet. But something will turn up one of these days,' he said and putting his cap on, went out to inspect the land with Lala.

On the way back, he picked some ripe plums, tomatoes and cucumbers from the fields, then caught the evening bus, promising to return soon.

The magician, after performing an extra matinee show for the crowds that had turned up to see the dead body, packed up his tent, but decided to stay in Giripul for a few more days in case the albino boy came back. He had disappeared after the show. 'These boys are like stray dogs,' said the magician. Janak had hoped to see the boy again; he wanted to give him some clothes which were lying in his trunk in the shop. Shirts and pants people had ordered long ago, but had not picked up.

It was a pity he would never see the boy again. He seemed to be a gentle, quiet boy.

Rama made a row of dough dolls and began sticking hair pins in them. 'Give her a stomach ache,' she whispered. 'Give her lice in her hair.' As the pin pierced the soft dough, she smiled. Bengali Baba had told her to smile at least five times a day. 'Smile when you feel anger, smile when you feel jealous, smile when you feel hate,' he had said. 'Then the pain will dissolve like sugar in water.'

Bengali Baba was a great man and if he said something, one must obey him. She felt happy when she put the pins in the dough. It was more satisfying than just smiling, which made her jaws ache and her eyes twitch. Besides, Janak had been behaving himself and she had not seen the third wife in the shop at all.

If only her mother did not go on and on about Shyamala and all the other women making eyes at Janak, she would not even think about it. Her husband was such an ordinary, simple man, not the kind women would flock around. But he was a ladies' tailor who touched women all day and when your mother tells you something, you have to believe it, even when you know in your heart it is not true.

14

Many sleuths, many thoughts, many confessions; Janak tired and worried

Rama's mother was happy that her daughter had taken her advice and had decided to sit in the shop all day, cleaning rice and learning how to hem. 'Keep an eye on him at all times. Keep him under your nose, that is the only way to guard your property,' she had warned her before leaving Giripul.

As soon as she had heard about the murder in Giripul her suspicion had fallen on her son-in-law. He must be involved in all this she had thought at once, but kept silent because she did not want the women who had given her the news to report this when they went back to Giripul. News travelled so fast from village to village and one had to be careful, especially in front of Giripul people. They were all Rama's in-laws now in the village tradition.

She kept thinking over and over about what the women from Giripul had said while explaining the murder in great detail to her. It must have been a crime of passion. The poor, unfortunate creature must have come to Giripul to avenge his wife's honour. Little did he know he would meet his death. God only knew where his soul would roam. These were the kind of dead people who always turned into ghosts, thought Rama's mother. Now there would be yet another unfortunate shadow for the Shadow Chaser to deal with. She was on her way to see him. She was not happy with what he had told Rama. And wanted some advice for her. Bengali Baba had gone to the neighbouring village which was facing a shadow problem. It was a nice outing for her. Old widows like her could travel alone by bus, but they could only go to the temple or to meet holy men. They could not go off to the cinema or to see magic shows.

She stared at the hills and thought, where had the dead man come from? Fate had sent him here to die. Did he have a wife at home who was waiting for him? A faithless one probably, who had made eyes at the tailor. Was she getting his dinner ready, putting his plate and glass out like she had done so many years ago the day her poor husband died.

Everyone called her Rama's mother now, but earlier when she came to the village as a bride, she was called 'Masterin' – the teacher's wife.

Her late husband, may the gods keep him in peace, had never been a school teacher. In fact, he had never even finished school, but everyone in his village called him Masterji. Apparently a letter had come many years ago, wrongly addressed to a 'Master' Tula Ram, which was her late husband's name. The name stuck and he was known all his life as Masterji.

Later in life, he even began to believe that he was a school teacher and often went and sat in the classroom like the other teachers. No one minded his presence and the children always obeyed him when he told them to behave or to recite their tables.

If he was alive today, he would have told them who had murdered the stranger. Masterji had solved many such mysteries and people flocked to him from faraway villages when they needed something solved. A stolen cow, a bride who never spoke, a child who had too many nightmares, and milk that mysteriously turned sour. It was a pity he died before Janak's father disappeared, otherwise he would have certainly solved that mystery as well. A murder mystery had never come to him, but she was sure he would rise to the challenge.

The bus screeched to a halt and a group of holy men got in. All the passengers, including the driver, bowed to them and at once made room for them by sending some of the young men to sit on top of the bus. Rama's mother bowed too, but she did not like the look of them.

They seemed like fake sadhus, just out to make some quick, easy money, she thought, but put a coin in the bowl that was passed around by one of the sadhus, because she did not want to risk their wrath in case they turned out to be real.

She was sure that shifty-eyed Shankar also had something to do with the murder in Giripul. Her late husband always said that fishermen were very silent footed so that the fish could not hear them. He could have stabbed the stranger and then run away silently before anyone could catch him. Maybe Janak and Shankar had done it together and pushed the body into the barber's shop.

She would have to send a message to Rama to warn her. Birds of a feather flock together – a philanderer and a murderer would always walk arm in arm.

A flock of blossom-headed parakeets flew past and she suddenly remembered Mithoo. She missed the old bird, but he would be better looked after at Rama's house and she would go back soon to fetch him. Whatever the priest in the forest had said, her Mithoo was a boy, a sweet affectionate boy, better than any son a woman could have.

Shankar was certain it was the magician who had killed the stranger. Every afternoon, after Rama went home, he came and sat in Janak's shop to discuss the murder. He was trying to solve it before the police, but was not making much headway. 'How did the body turn up on your doorstep? There are no broken bottles or anything at all. The dead man must have put up a fight before he was killed. I find all this very confusing,' he said, chewing a bit of thread.

'Forget about it. Let the police solve it,' said Janak. His stomach churned with fear every time someone mentioned the murder.

'What do you mean? I am trying to help you. Well, if you would rather hang then ...' he said, looking very upset.

'They do not hang people any more. I found out,' muttered Janak, biting the thread off the button he was sewing. The pink satin lay crumpled in the trunk, but for some reason he was now afraid to touch it.

'I tell you, my friend, they can put you in jail for the rest of your life. You do not know you are sitting on a bag of gunpowder – a small matchstick can blow you up. Wake up and think. We must find out who did it or be ready to make chapattis in jail,' said Shankar peevishly.

They sat quietly for a while, the sound of the sewing machine filling the shop. The ravens called outside and Tommy gave a short bark. He was slowly recovering from his trauma, but still stayed close to Janak all the time. Balu allowed him to sleep inside his shed now, and had even put an old blanket for him in one corner. He felt safe there at night and did not go out even when the jackals howled.

Shankar suddenly jumped up. 'Janak, stop this sewing, come, let's go and search the field for clues – cigarette butts, bloodstains, anything,' he said.

'What for? The policemen have done all that and they found nothing,' said Janak.

'Yes, they found nothing because they were not really looking. You saw the younger one. All he did was pluck plums and look around for land to buy. We know the hillside better than they do. I want to check the place where the magic show was held. I have a feeling that magician is involved with this murder somehow,' he said in an excited voice and Janak reluctantly got up from his chair. Tommy shook himself and got up too. He did not want to be left alone.

They quickly went out on the street and then turned and walked down the hilly path towards the field, taking a shortcut through the headman's orchard. The peach and almond trees were in full bloom, promising a good crop of fruit unless hail struck before they could ripen. An old wild plum tree laden with tiny purple-black fruit stood in their path and they plucked a few as they walked past.

The breeze felt cool on his face and Janak now felt happy that he had come out of the shop. They would not find anything, but it was good to walk for a while on the hillside. The fresh air would clear his head. He knew he should stay alert and he was grateful to Shankar for helping him, but somehow the memory of the last few days was blurring and he felt it had happened to someone else.

When they were children, Shankar, Raja and he used to play cricket in this field, the only flat area in Giripul. Their bat was a roughly-hewed piece of deodar branch and the ball a tightly-stitched bundle of rags. After a few trial-and-error shots, they would get fed up and go and bathe in the stream. They went to school only if they felt like it. Most of the time their teacher was at home, nursing a hangover, and the children were free to play truant.

They would spend the rest of the day roaming about the hillside, looking for wild raspberries, jungle fowl's eggs and ripe fruit in the orchards. Raja could mimic a female partridge's call and the males would come running to them. He would catch one or two and put them in a bag and then sell them to Lala's father. When they felt thirsty, they drank from the spring or went into any of the village homes, where they would be given glasses of fresh milk. Life was good then and time passed smoothly, without any sudden jolts, without any nasty surprises. There was no talk of revenge or murder or a magic show even.

The field was covered with hundreds of wild daisies. They could see the exact place where the tent had been pitched because all the flowers had been trampled and were lying flat. A large mountain goat was inspecting the flowers and looked up at them belligerently. Tommy decided to ignore him. They had had many encounters which they both enjoyed greatly, but today he was not up to it. The handsome goat lowered his head and stared at Tommy for a few seconds, challenging him. Then he snorted and walked away with a disappointed look.

Janak looked up at the hills beyond. A huge vulture was circling right above them, its wings stretched wide, with the tip pointing like an accusing finger. It must have come in search of the dead body. Vultures always knew and told other vultures. But today there was only this lone one in the sky. Maybe the others were better informed and had followed the police van to Simla.

'Look, can you see something red in the grass there? Come and look from here,' Shankar said, pulling at Janak's arm. They went down the slope, Tommy running ahead.

It was a red leather wallet lying under a pile of stones, half hidden by a clump of dried grass.

Shankar quickly picked it up and opened it. There was one five-hundred-rupee note and a picture of a Chinese girl.

'Oh my god! It is the foreign woman! This is the headman's woman – the she-barber! This looks like a barber-versus-barber murder case,' cried Shankar.

'What do you mean? No barber has been murdered. Shankar, do not make these stupid jokes, you will hurt the dead man's feelings. He is listening to us, you know, from wherever he is now. Besides, this woman looks like an English lady to me. See, she has golden hair,' said Janak, holding the photograph up to catch the sunlight.

'Then this wallet belongs to an Englishman. He must have done this murder and run off to England,' cried Shankar, looking at him hopefully.

'The only problem is, Shankar, the last time an Englishman came here was in 1946,' said Janak, putting the photograph carefully back in the wallet.

'I know, the one who had an affair with Raja's grandmother, then later married her,' Shankar muttered in a distracted way.

'Yes, he planted all those apple trees in Raja's orchard,' said Janak, pointing to the orchard beyond the field as if reminding himself though he saw the trees everyday.

'He also built our school and then died peacefully in his bed forty years ago,' Shankar said in a sad voice. His case against an unknown Englishman was falling apart.

They sat down on the grass and thought quietly for a while, looking at the wallet, feeling its soft leather. The crickets called from the shrubs and then they too fell silent. A shimmering blue peacock butterfly floated past Tommy's head, but he did not look up.

'That tall Englishman did a lot in the short time he was in Giripul – had an affair, got married, planted so many apple trees, built a school and then died. Amazing man,' said Janak. Why did the Englishman travel so far away from his home? Maybe it was written that he should die in Giripul. Did the poor man's spirit still roam the hillsides, like his father's? Maybe they were friends – two lost souls.

'My grandmother, my father's mother, used to say that he did not die peacefully in his bed, but his wife pushed him off the cliff,' said Shankar, turning the wallet in his hands.

'Why?' asked Janak.

'Because he made her memorize English verbs everyday and she got fed up. She went back to her first husband as soon as the Englishman died. She did not even wait for his funeral, my grandmother said. But my mother said my grandmother was a big liar.'

Janak looked at the wallet again. 'So this cannot be the unfortunate Englishman's wallet. That much we know for certain.'

'But it is an important clue. We have got rid of one suspect. See, I told you the policemen were blind.'

'What should we do with the money?'

'I do not know. We should give it to the police.'

'No, never. They will think we stole it from the dead man. I don't want to go to the police. It is like asking a mad cow to come and gore you. I know what we'll do. We'll go and ask Balu. He always has the right answer, but whether he will talk to us or not, I am not sure,' said Janak.

They walked back to the street, stopping briefly to pluck some wild raspberries from the shrubs that grew near the steep edge of the path. The first sunlight at dawn fell on these shrubs and the berries here were always the sweetest. Lala saw them and came out of his tea shop, waving his hands, but Shankar did not want him to see the wallet, so he carried on ahead. He went into the shop and hid the wallet in the box with the buttons and hooks.

'Janak. I have been thinking. Do you think it was the magician who did it?' Lala asked as soon as he came into the shop. 'Maybe the dead man was an old enemy who came up to Giripul to settle old scores?' he continued, pushing the trunk with his foot. Shankar quickly moved the buttons-and-hooks box away from the table. Lala was one of those people who could never sit still. He had to open and shut doors, snap his fingers, juggle his keys or open any boxes he saw before him. It was a mistake to hide the wallet in a box, but now it was too late to take it out without Lala's beady eyes spotting it at once, Shankar thought, watching every move that Lala made. He seemed quite content just kicking the tin trunk and chatting with Janak.

'After all, old enemies are the worst kind, they say. They have years to plan revenge,' said Lala.

'No. He never left the stage, not even for a moment. The entire village saw him,' said Janak, taking out a new reel of thread. He must get on with his stitching, but there was hardly any room in the little shop to move. His cupboard and trunk were full of unstitched clothes. Once the murder fever left Giripul, all the women would start demanding their clothes. In fact, some of them who had come from distant villages to

Giripul yesterday to see the dead body had told him they would return soon with cloth for their suits. Life would go on as usual.

'But Janak, he is a magician, he can be in two or three places at the same time,' said Shankar, picking up a bit of thread and twisting it around his little finger. Then he winked at Janak.

'Why do we have to discuss the murder all the time,' said Janak irritably, spreading a new piece of cloth on the table. 'Move your arm, I have to cut this,' he told Lala.

Lala ordered some tea from his shop and when it came, he and Shankar went out and sat on the steps. Shankar was still wary of him, but he made a better companion than Janak, who was very sullen these days.

'I think we should tell the policemen that the magician did it. Maybe we can get a reward for solving the murder so fast,' said Lala.

Shankar did not respond, but he was alert now. If there was a reward, he should get it. Why should he share it with Lala? He found out about the murder much later and even after he came to the scene of the crime, he had fainted and then just sat there drinking rum. Just as well I hid the wallet, he thought.

In future he would be careful about sharing his clues with Lala. Once, when they were boys, Lala had stolen all their marbles by distracting them, pointing to the hills and shouting, 'Look, a two-headed eagle!' Janak, Raja and he had looked up at once and Lala had taken off with their best marbles. Then, Lala was not called Lala because he had not yet inherited his father's tea shop. He was called

Lekhi, and he was already selling them peanuts, which he stole from his mother's kitchen cupboard.

He would have to be careful, but Janak was trusting of everyone. That was his greatest flaw, and the fact that he was too generous. Anyone in the village could borrow money from him. Shankar, the fisherman who everyone thought was useless, was going to bring fame to Giripul by solving the murder, saving his friend and getting the reward, he thought and felt a deep sense of joy.

Lala was talking to Janak through the window, though he was getting no response from him at all. He went on and on about the magician as if he had a personal enmity with him and wanted to send him to jail somehow. They could hear the sewing machine turning at top speed inside the shop. After a while, Lala got up and left.

Shankar waited till Lala had gone a safe distance down the street and then he went into the shop and took out a pencil and a small notebook he had just bought from Raja's shop, and began to write. He paused after each word. He had not written anything since he had left school, eight years ago, except an occasional letter. Then he read it aloud.

Things we know:

1. Body found dead – placed in Barber's shop by us

2. Name unknown

3. Throat cut /stabbed

4. Wallet with woman's photo found on hillside

5. Chineeese/English.'

He paused and looked up. 'What else do we know?' he said, tapping his pencil in an official manner, like he had seen the senior policeman do. If only he had a red handkerchief to mop his brow.

Janak glanced at the list and said, 'You have spelt Chinese wrong.' Shankar moved the notebook away from him. He then began writing again, crossing out words and rewriting them, filling up all the pages of his torn notebook. Janak ignored him and continued to work on his machine. After a while Shankar stood up, yawned and put the notebook in his pocket.

'All this writing is giving me a headache. It is better to talk about the clues. You know Janak, I hate to say this, but it could be the headman. After all, you said he was not in his seat when you went to look for him. Look, I think it happened like this,' he said, settling down on the table once more.

'His Chinese woman's husband must have found out about him and come to Giripul to threaten him. The headman took him to the barber's shop; after all, he must be a barber too, being married to a she-barber. He could have offered him a free shave and then cut his throat with the razor. Then he quickly put some lather on his face and throat and threw a sheet on him, maybe he did that before he killed him, and then he came back to see the end of the magic show,' said Shankar with a triumphant look on his face.

Janak did not look up from his machine. Shankar could see he was not pleased about bringing the headman into this. But he was a suspect till the murder was solved. No man, however important, was above the law. 'Of course, he would have to lather the victim's face first before cutting his throat, otherwise there would be too much blood everywhere,' he continued.

Janak gave him an irritated look and said, 'You talk such rubbish. Why do you keep forgetting that it was we who put him in the barber's chair? I put the soap on his face. How do we know his throat was cut? You said yesterday it was stabbed. And why should the China-man agree to go to the barber shop when he had come to Giripul to fight with the headman, not for a free shave and haircut, which he can get at home for free,' said Janak. After a pause, he asked Shankar, 'You saw the dead man, did he have slit eyes?'

Shankar shook his head and then added defiantly. 'But after you are dead, your face changes. It swells up and your tongue turns blue.'

'Yes, but you do not become a China-man if you were not born one,' said Janak, waving his scissors in the air. Tommy looked up at them and sighed and tucked his head once more under the table. Why must they shout, these two? His ears hurt. Janak's shop used to be so peaceful, with only women coming and going, but now it was filled with quarrelling men.

'You are never satisfied with anything. I am just trying to help, to save your neck. It is a good thing you are a tailor and not a policeman. No murder would ever be solved in our country then. All murderers would be roaming around free and happy while you said, "No, no, not this one. No, no, not that one," like a woman buying vegetables,' said

Shankar, and went out angrily. He had forgotten all about the wallet in the buttons-and-hooks box.

Janak sighed and began hand stitching a small bag with the scraps of cloth lying under his table. It was not on order by any woman. He just felt like stitching something that did not require his full attention. He loved using up all the tiny bits of cloth, making them fit into a square; it was like trying to solve a puzzle. He worked for an hour and then got up and placed the finished, multi-coloured bag on the table to admire it, as if it were a fancy kurta. Maybe he would give it to Balu, but he had no belongings to put in a bag, even a tiny one like this. Balu would look at it and remember him if Janak was sent to jail.

Just when he was getting ready to shut the shop, Raja came and sat down on the steps without uttering a word. Janak was tired. He had hardly slept the night before. The stranger's face, alive, not dead, kept looming in front of him, followed by his wife's strange, smiling one. He suddenly wondered what had happened to the gold watch the man had been wearing. The policemen must have kept it.

'I was just shutting the shop,' he said, but Raja looked down at the ground and whispered in a mournful voice, 'I want to tell you a secret.' Janak sighed and sat down next to him. Everyone had secret stories to tell, so why not poor Raja.

'What is it, Raja?' he asked gently.

'Well, you know that sawing-me-into half bit? It was not really done,' Raja said, shrugging his shoulders in a funny way.

'What do you mean? Everyone saw it. Everyone except me,' said Janak, suddenly full of self-pity.

'There were two boxes. I was in one with my legs folded tightly – it was quite painful, you know. In the other box there was a small boy tucked away.'

'What? I cannot believe it! My wife said you were neatly cut in half in front of their eyes. She loved it, so did my mother-in-law!' Janak said. He wished Rama would praise him sometimes like she kept praising that magician.

'You mean to say it was all a clever trick to fool us? If I had seen it I would have found out at once that there were two boxes with two men,' said Janak.

'Yes. My body was in one, with my head sticking out for everyone to see and the boy's body in the other one. IIe quickly put my shoes on so that his feet could look like mine. When the magician held up his cape like a curtain, he jumped out of his box and ran off the stage while I stood up. I had no shoes on, but no one noticed. I got them back later, though,' Raja said, rubbing his hands over his eyes.

'Janak, please don't tell anyone. Not even my wife knows. She thinks I have been cut in half and then joined by magic. She really admires me now, but I just had to tell you.'

'I won't, my friend, I promise,' said Janak, patting him on the back. Raja grinned at him and then said in a cheerful voice, 'You know, I think Lala's new cook must have murdered the stranger. This man, Teera, is from a village in the plains. They say his father is a famous murderer. People pay him large sums of money to have someone killed. There is a waiting list, they say, to get a date with his father. Once you have this killing bug in your blood, you can never get rid of it. The murder thing becomes a habit. You need to commit a murder now and then or else you will go mad,' said Raja brightly.

'How do you know all this?' asked Janak.

'Teera told me. He comes to my shop often to buy toffees. He loves the milky ones, so I get them for him from Simla. He offered to have anyone killed for me if I ever wished. I could not think of anyone, but I did not want to hurt his feelings by refusing outright, so I said I would tell him later,' said Raja and then quickly got up. 'I must be going home now. My wife will be angry with me for staying out so late.'

'Raja, my wife said she saw your green pants sticking out of the box,' shouted Janak, but Raja had disappeared into the swirling evening mist.

That evening the house was in a quiet mood and Rama too seemed very thoughtful. After she had given him his dinner and put their son to bed, she came and sat next to him in the courtyard. They could hear the stream gushing below their land. Soon summer would be over and the clouds would gather on the high mountains. The days would get shorter and the evenings would fall suddenly, like a thick black blanket to cover Giripul. He must finish his work in Badi Kothi before the rains came and the hill paths became wet and dangerous.

'Do you think a woman could have killed that stranger?' said Rama in a soft voice, startling him. 'A strong woman can stab a man easily,' she said, watching his face, 'a strong, young woman, maybe like the third wife or Raja's wife.'

Rama wanted to see what Janak would say when she mentioned the third wife. She just threw in Raja's wife to show that she was not really accusing Shyamala, just wondering who could have stabbed the stranger. Janak sat very still. Something told him this was not an innocent question. It was a clever yet delicate trap, like the snake plant laid to trap flies. It would get him into deep trouble if he answered with a single wrong word.

Think very carefully. Don't say anything right now. This is a dangerous situation, he thought. Rama waited, cutting a piece of betel nut expertly with a cutter. She offered him some; Janak took a few slivers and chewed thoughtfully.

'Yes, could be a woman, but she would have to be very strong because the man would certainly struggle with her. He would not just sit in the chair and allow her to stab him,' he said and held his breath, hoping it was the right answer. Rama did not say anything for a while.

They could hear the crickets on the pine trees, their metallic clicks getting louder and louder as the sky got darker. A faint scent of honeysuckle floated in the air and a nightjar called on the hillside. How pleasant it was to sit like this with your wife. All the worries and cares of the world just vanished away in the cool, fragrant air. If only she would stop talking about the murder and just hold his hand.

Janak was tired of everyone coming to him with various theories about who had killed the stranger. He did not care any more and wished they would all forget about it, then Giripul would be normal again. He would be normal again.

Balu was the only one in Giripul not interested in the murder. 'People reap what they have sown in their past life. This man must have killed someone, so he got killed in return. In the next life, he will be the murderer and his murderer his victim. This play of life and death will go on forever till one of them gets free of this endless cycle of life and death,' he had said to Janak this morning, giving him some gur and channa to eat. 'Today's truck said, *Dusk is falling. My beloved is sad, I must go to her.* Maybe my time has come too,' he had said. 'Janak, I want you to find that albino boy and take care of him. He is a good soul, but must have done some bad deeds in the past and that is why he is a lost soul in this life – no home, no parents, no one at all.'

Rama suddenly turned to Janak and said, 'She could have drugged him, stabbed him and then put him in the barber's chair. Janak gave his wife a startled look. Had she been talking to Shankar? This sounded a bit like his theory, though he was confused about who had come up with which theory about the murder. There had been so many today.

Rama glanced at Janak. Well, well, he is looking scared. He is worried about the third wife being involved in the murder. Mother was right. There is something going on between them. She looked sharply at Janak again, narrowing her eyes. 'Yes, I think it was a woman, a strong, clever woman like the third wife – who all the

men in Giripul are running after like dogs,' she said and
went into the house. She slammed the door behind her
and an owl hooted an angry reply from the pine tree.

As Janak watched her in dismay, the house began to
close in. The windows started to rattle and the floor
beneath his feet trembled as if there was a monster
python awaking under the great Himalayan mountains.

15

Albino boy narrates his story; Murder mystery unravels; Balu adopts a child for Giripul

A week after the murder, Janak was sitting in his shop, enjoying the gentle morning breeze as he hemmed the satin suit. It was soothing to be away from his angry wife and the house, which seemed to want to choke him. Rama's terrible mood had forced him to stay at the shop all day and he had finally started working on the pink satin suit again. It was almost done now, except for the edge of the salwar. The soft material felt warm under his fingers and suddenly he wanted to see his wife and tell her how much he loved her.

You got married to a woman, a woman you had never seen before or even spoken to, and for the rest of your life, till you died, you loved her and took care of her. All men did that, it was their duty ordained by the gods. All men except his father, who left his wife for no reason and disappeared.

His poor mother had no one to look after her, but even then she brought him up, sent him to school, paid for his tailoring lessons in Simla, packed his lunch and gave his bus fare every morning. How she had managed he did not know. Maybe his father had left some money for her in the trunk which she always kept under her bed, locked with a big, brass lock.

It was still locked, safely under his bed. He did not have the heart to open it, even though his mother had been dead for two years. He was afraid the trunk would be full of memories that would fly out and attack him as soon as he opened the lid. Anyway, the key was lost and the nearest key-maker lived in Simla. One day he would get a new key cut and open the trunk.

Rama was in a strange mood these days and kept watching him suspiciously all the time. The other day he had found her going through his pockets. Maybe she suspected him and was looking for clues – a bloodstained handkerchief, or even a strand of hair. He did have a bloodstained handkerchief; his nose had bled copiously the other day. But would she believe him? Would she tell the police? No, never. She was his wife and a wife stood by her husband, even if he had committed murder. Well, at least, most wives did.

Janak looked out of the window. The hills were shining with fresh new grass which sprouted during late summer and a flock of sheep was scampering about. He counted ten baby lambs. If they sent him to jail, he would have to leave Giripul and go to Simla. That was the nearest jail as far as he knew. Maybe they had built a new one in Solan for this area.

Maybe he could stitch uniforms for the prisoners and send the money back to Rama. He did not want her to suffer because of something he had done or not done.

He saw himself sitting in front of a sewing machine, not his own, stitching a pile of striped kurtas. He had a ball and chain around one ankle.

Janak shook his legs to make sure he was free, then quickly got up from his chair to open the cupboard above the table and it was then that the snake moved. Janak froze, his hand hanging in midair. The snake raised its head and looked at him and Janak could not breathe. He saw the black and gold markings and knew at once it was a two-and-a-half snake. They called it that because once it sank its fangs into you, you had only two-and-a-half mintues to live. Or was it two-and-a-half hours, or seconds? Janak tried to remember as panic raced through his body and he began to tremble. The snake watched him and then moved an inch again. Janak wanted to pray, but his mind had gone blank. The snake had looked right into his eyes and cast a spell on him and now he was paralysed with fear. He knew at once that this snake was the spirit of the dead man who had come to seek revenge. He must know now that Janak had vowed to kill him. Once you died, you knew everything, his mother used to say. 'Please forgive me. I did not mean to harm you,' he tried to say, but no sound came out of his throat. He was slowly choking to death. Suddenly the snake moved forward and Janak shut his eyes. This is how death comes to you. Swiftly, without warning on a cool summer's day. He hoped Rama would be looked after by her mother, and his son would remember him a bit. He saw his picture hanging on the wall with a faded marigold garland around it. After what seemed a lifetime, Janak opened his eyes. The snake was slithering towards the window. As the sunlight fell on it, Janak saw it was a harmless grass snake. Its beautiful green skin shone in the light as it climbed swiftly over the window sill and then disappeared in the grass. Janak sat still for a long time waiting for his breathing to become normal. When he was feeling calmer, a sudden thought struck him. Was the snake trying to send him a message? Was it a clue from the dead man? Maybe he was trying to solve his own murder.

Janak heard a noise at the door and jumped up. He was still feeling a bit nervous. He saw the headman standing on the steps. Janak folded his hands to greet him and offered him his chair. 'No. I do not want to sit. I just wanted to talk to you,' he said, looking at the pink satin. Janak was about to apologize for the delay when the headman stopped him. 'Forget about it. I do not want it any more. The person who had ordered this has gone away forever ... to some faraway place and will never come back. But I will pay you for it. Here, will two hundred rupees be all right?' he asked in a low voice and put two hundred-rupee notes on the table. There was a worried look on the headman's handsome face. Janak had never seen him like this. Maybe he was upset because this Chinese woman was leaving him and going away very far, to China probably, forever.

'You know, Mukhiyaji, I can alter the measurements a bit and make the suit for your wife. Why waste such expensive cloth,' said Janak. The headman shook his head in a dejected way. 'Do as you wish. I do not care,' he said and sat down on the chair Janak had vacated for him. He began turning the handle of the sewing machine absent-mindedly.

Janak hated anyone touching his sewing machine. It was very sensitive and the slightest mishandling could ruin it, but he could not say anything to the headman. The poor man looked so troubled.

'The thing is, Janak, I might go to prison,' the headman said. Janak was so shocked that he sat down on the floor. The satin slipped and fell from the table. 'Why? Why do you say that ...' he managed to say. He felt a wave of fear hit him in the stomach. Had the headman killed the stranger? Oh, no! What a terrible thing to happen to Giripul. Their handsome, noble headman, a murderer! It could not be true.

All these days he had been worried that the headman would be killed, but now he turned out to be the a killer. Janak rubbed his hands over his face and gulped. He should be relieved at this confession, but he could not bring himself to believe it.

'Janak, I know you are horrified. I am only telling you and no one else about this. I have ... had a woman in Simla. You know how it is. We men, have our needs.' Janak nodded as if he understood.

'This woman had an evil uncle. I do not think he was a real uncle because he was quite black and she is fair and Chinese. Anyway, he found out about us and he had been blackmailing me for months, you know, asking for money, otherwise he threatened to tell my wife everything.' The headman paused, picked up the satin from the floor and began pulling out the threads. 'The other day I saw him near the Giripul bridge and we got into a fight. In fact, I gave him a good beating, cut his ear with one blow, I think.' He looked up at Janak, a triumphant smile on his face.

Janak quickly took the satin away from him and draped it over the trunk. 'It was my bad luck that this wretched, evil man was lurking in Giripul on the day of the magic show. He is the man you found on the chair. But I did not kill him ... I just tripped over him when I stepped out of the magician's tent to make water ... I suddenly tripped over this body and ... it was him ... I did not know what to do, then fear struck me. I knew the police would blame me for the crime, so I picked him up and put him on Lala's mule which was standing nearby. I wanted to send him ... the body, far away, so that the police would not find it,' he said quickly and got up from the chair shaking with fear. 'The mule just shot off in the dark ... I did not know where it went. How it dropped the body in Channa barber's chair, I do not know. But if the police find out, I am a doomed man.'

'Janak knew in his heart that this was an important moment in Giripul's history. He knew he had to protect the headman. The honour of Giripul depended on him now. He might have to go to jail to protect him, though neither of them had killed the stranger.

'So what? Even if he is the body in the chair, there is no proof that you stabbed the man. Is there a witness? No, there is not,' said Janak, surprised at how loud and firm he sounded, just like a hero in a film. The headman looked impressed too. 'Yes. Janak, you are right, but you know the police, they will come nosing around again and someone will tell them about our fight. There was quite a big crowd watching us and the afternoon bus also stopped for a few minutes to watch,' said the headman in a faintly boastful voice. Thank god he did not know that this was the man who had teased Rama and whom Janak had vowed to kill.

'No, rest assured, nothing will happen; no one in Giripul will give evidence against you. You are our respected headman, they all know that. I will make sure they remember that,' said Janak in his firm new voice.

They both looked at each other and there were tears in their eyes. They had been friends since childhood, though the headman was a very important man and Janak only a humble ladies' tailor, but at this moment they felt as close as blood brothers. Men in Giripul never cried openly, except at their father's funeral, but each understood the emotion raging in the other's heart. They were silent for a few minutes and then the headman sat down once more and said, 'I think this is how the murder happened.' Janak put his head down to listen patiently. 'This man, this terrible monster, must have come to Giripul to look for me. Then he must have followed me to the magic show. There, he must have got into an argument with the magician; maybe he was blackmailing him too. These, blackmailers have many people on their list. So many people have so many secrets to hide in this world. Anyway, the magician must have stabbed him during the interval with one of his many knives.' The headman looked at Janak for approval.

Janak was not sure what to say so he just nodded politely. This did not sound right because as far as he knew, the magician had never left the stage. Rama had told him that. But he did not want to disappoint the headman, who was now looking at him like a child begging for a sweet.

All night Janak tossed in bed, thinking, how did the body come to lie on his steps? The mule could not have brought it there. Maybe the man was still alive when the headman put him on the mule. But he would protest, would he not? You cannot just throw a grown man, a city man who wears expensive watches and shirts, on a mule and send him off into the hillside. It would not be easy. And what was the snake trying to tell him?

Rama snored gently next to him and he watched her for a while, trying to forget about the dead man. But when he finally fell asleep, the stranger came and sat by his bed. He was offering him his watch. Janak woke with a start and began looking on the bed for the watch.

'What are you doing? Why must you twist around in the bed like a top... Can I not get any rest even at night?' Rama muttered and turned her back to him.

Janak crawled out of bed and went outside. It was almost dawn, though the moon was still lurking in the sky, right above the forest. He decided to go to the shop, now that he had got up so early. He filled a bucket of water from the tap, taking care not to make any noise, but the brass bucket fell with a loud clang and he heard Rama's angry shout like a gunshot from within the house.

His hair was still wet when he opened the shutter and

went into the shop. He had to light the lamp since it was still dark outside, and then he saw the ghost.

Janak opened his mouth, but he felt the scream die in his throat. First the snake, now this spirit. Death was slowly, but surely coming to take him. There was nothing to do, but go forward to accept it. He lifted his head and the figure moved. Janak suddenly realized that it was a man, a tall man with his head covered by a shawl. He was standing at his table, his hands on the sewing machine.

Who was this now, Janak thought, his head spinning. Was he going to die or not?

The man turned around. 'Oh god, no! He is going to take my machine. Stop, you thief!' Janak shouted, suddenly finding his voice and surged forward to protect his sewing machine. Just then the man put his head in his hands and began to sob.

'Oh, tailorji... sir... I have five small children. Please save me. I did not do it ...' he howled, thumping his chest. A cloud of flour flew up and Janak realized it was Teera. The new cook at Lala's tea shop.

'All I did was brew some wine with the leftover rice, just enough for me, and then I went to sleep. I should have never gone to the magic show, magic frightens me. I was asleep when the mule kicked me. It kicked my stomach and then it dropped this body. It was a dead body... lying on top of me! I swear on my dead mother, sir, the man was dead when he fell on me. I got such a fright. I thought I had killed him in my sleep. You know, sir, killing is my family profession, though I have shunned it. I had to get rid of the body, so I dragged it out and put it on the steps of your honour's shop. Then I went to look for a spade to dig a grave for the poor dead man. You know, to get rid of him,' he sobbed.

'Save me, please! Believe me when I tell you this. When I came back, the body had walked up to the Channa barber's shop. Now the police will catch me. Save me, sir, I am innocent. I never killed him, even if I was dead drunk. I know this for sure, because it is a tradition in our family to kill only by strangling,' said Teera, wiping his face with a scrap of satin left over from the Chinese woman's suit, then he began to howl again.

Janak couldn't think of a suitable reply which would make Teera stop crying, yet not let him know the truth. That poor dead body had really travelled that night. First thrown out of the magician's tent, by someone then loaded on a mule by the headman, then dumped in Lala's kitchen courtyard by the mule. Then put on his shop's doorstep by Teera the cook, and finally carried by Shankar and himself to the barber's chair.

Who had killed him? Was there a murderer lurking in Giripul, waiting to strike again? Any one of them could be murdered any day or night.

Tommy began to growl. Janak looked around, but could not see anyone new on the street and started composing his reply again. But Tommy was whimpering now and trying to scrape the ground in front of the shop. There was an empty water tank there, left by the Water Supply Board last year. The pipes to fill water in it had been stolen long ago.

Tommy had not been the same since the murder and

kept whimpering and barking for no reason. But Janak trusted his dog, especially after the way he had led him to the dead man.

'I must see what Tommy wants,' he said to Teera, who looked a bit hurt at being left so abruptly. Janak followed Tommy to the water tank.

Then his heart froze. A thin white hand was sticking out from underneath the lid. 'Not again. God, please. Did you hear my thoughts about death waiting to strike, just now? It was not a wish, God. It was just a passing thought. One dead body is enough,' he cried and Tommy started to whimper again. He, too, could not take a second body in Giripul. It was too soon.

As the two of them watched, frozen with terror, the lid opened and the albino boy came out and bowed.

'Tailor, sir. Please ... I ... the murder ... Please, sir, water,' he whispered and sank in a heap on the ground. Tommy, overjoyed to see the boy was alive, began licking his face, and Janak, recovering quickly, bent over him.

'Oye! Boy!' he cried, shaking him, but the boy had fainted. He quickly picked him up and carried him in. Teera jumped up in alarm, toppling the chair.

Janak poured some water in a glass and cradling the boy's head, held it to his mouth. 'Here, drink this, boy.'

'He is alive – the ghost boy is alive!' muttered Teera.

Tommy barked again and they saw Balu at the door. 'I knew it was the pale boy. But keep silent, you lot. God has given him enough woes already,' he said. 'Go get some warm milk from Lala. He is starving, can't you see,' he said and went back to his shed.

The whole day the boy slept, safe in Balu's shed. The next day, Balu called Shankar, the headman and Janak to his shed. 'Come inside. The boy has something to tell you. Be quiet and listen to him,' he said, making room for them to sit in the tiny shed.

'My mother died soon after I was born, they said. An old woman who lived in our house hated me. She beat me all the time with a broom, with a stick, with a shoe, whatever she could find handy. She said I was touched by the devil and that is why my skin was sickly white. She got very angry if she saw me first thing in the morning. She said it was a bad omen. She often locked me up in the coal shed without any food or water if my father was not at home.

'One day I woke up at dawn because I needed to pee urgently and though it was dark, she saw me. She was doing her prayers at this time, so she was furious and gave me a terrible thrashing with an iron rod, calling me the devil's child. She broke my wrist. That night I stole some money from my father's pouch and ran away from home. I roamed the hills till I came to a town called Simla.

'I worked as a coolie there for a while at the railway station. There were many of us, all runaway boys from villages. We shared food and lived in an abandoned goods' coach near the railway yard. It was not a bad life. We earned ten or twenty rupees everyday and spent it all on food and sweets. Some boys smoked, but I did not. The boys teased me and called me a white ghost, but they never let anyone else abuse me or beat me.

'Then one day this man we called Mamoo, who lived near the station, came and offered me a job. "My magician friend needs a boy helper, an odd-looking one who will attract a crowd. You are a peculiar one, for sure," he said, pulling my hair and laughing, "He will pay well, but you have to give me half your earnings."

'I did not like Mamoo. He looked like a cruel man, but the money his friend offered was good, so I went off to train with the magician. He was a hard taskmaster, but I enjoyed the work. He only hit me when I made mistakes. And he gave me enough to eat and we travelled to many new places for shows. People loved our shows and I became quite good at helping him.

'But Mamoo followed me everywhere and took almost all my money. He often stole the magician's props too and then my magician master would scold me, saying I was careless. He never believed me when I told him about Mamoo. I think he was scared of him because everyone said Mamoo knew real magic which could make people disappear, or lame or blind.

'Mamoo would get drunk very often and he would turn up at the magician's place and beat me. I tried to run away once ore twice, but he always found me and dragged me back to the magician. He burnt my arms with his cigarette to teach me a lesson,' said the boy, showing Janak and Balu the scars. They looked like black holes on his white skin.

'Mamoo had come to Giripul, pretending he wanted to see the show. I told my master about Mamoo again, but he did not want to listen to me. "Do not complain to me, it spoils the magic. Life is full of sorrow, learn to bear it. Only in magic there is joy," was all he said.

'That day I was sitting backstage since I was not needed for the sawing-the-body act. Only that other boy who is very short and thin can do it. You have to fold yourself in half like a piece of rubber.

'I was sitting in the master's tent, cleaning his shoes when Mamoo suddenly came in and began demanding money. Before I could say anything, he started hitting me, slapping my face, punching me in my stomach. "Give me all the money you have hidden, you son of a shaitan!" he said.

'I gave him the few rupees I had to keep him quiet, but he would not go away. His eyes were red and puffy.

'He was smoking charas. I could smell it. His ear was cut badly. He kicked me and punched me, then suddenly he lost interest in me and began opening my master's trunks. I tried to stop him. Master hates anyone touching his things, he gets hysterical, and then we get a thrashing.

'But Mamoo gave me a hard knock on my chest and I fell. Then he tried to open the box in which we kept the knives. I tried again to stop him – Master's knives are very dangerous – but he gave me a kick. We struggled on the floor and then suddenly he saw the red velvet pouch that Master usually carried his cash in. He leapt up and before I could stop him, he put his hand in it.

'The cobra Master had just bought was sleeping in it. Master had decided the soft velvet pouch was the warmest and cosiest place for it. The snake rose and wrapped itself around his hand. Mamoo's eyes popped out in horror. He screamed, fell on the box of knives and the biggest one went straight into his neck. The snake vanished into the hillside.

'You see, the cobra was harmless; its fangs had been removed before we bought it for a new act, but Mamoo did not know that. He lay dead on the floor stabbed in the neck with Master's sharpest knife.'

The boy stopped and drank some water. Janak and the headman looked at him in stunned silence. Janak's heart went out to the boy. What a terrible life he had led. And all because his skin was discoloured. Janak could not listen to this any more. He wanted the boy to rest. He looked so tired and was breathing with difficulty, but the boy wanted to tell his story. 'Let him speak,' said Balu and put another blanket around the boy to stop him from shivering.

'My master was on stage, doing the sawing-the-body act and I could not call him. I did not know what to do. I was struck with fear. People would blame me. An albino like me always brings bad luck and is to be blamed for everything evil, they would say. No one would believe my story. The cobra had vanished and Mamoo was lying dead. His blood was all over me.

'I had to do something, so I quickly wrapped the body in Master's velvet cloak, put it in our big trunk and waited. When the sawing was going on, I dragged the trunk; it has wheels so that we can pull it on stage easily. No one saw me since everyone was at the magic show. But I tripped over a stone and the trunk rolled downhill. Mamoo's body now lay right outside the big tent. I was about to pick him up, but the headman came out just then. I was so scared I did not know what to do. I ran back into the tent to hide. I waited for the headman to go so that I could pick up Mamoo, but when I came back a few minutes later ... he ... the body was not there,' he said, rubbing his pale hands over his eyes.

'Tailor, sir, take me to the police station because I have no money for the bus fare. I am so tired,' he said and then shut his eyes. A few seconds later he was fast asleep.

Janak looked at the sleeping boy, his thin bruised face, and his heart filled with sorrow. How could God be so unkind to such a frail creature? He looked like a silver moth that lives only for a few days. Tommy sensed his sadness and licked his hands and Balu put his hand on the boy's head. Then he looked at them, his eyes blazing.

'Listen to me, you all, and listen carefully. The boy is innocent. He is under our protection from today. He is Giripul's child now and I will not let anyone touch a hair on his head.' Janak nodded and the headman folded his hands. They both offered a silent prayer to the gods. 'The boy must have had some connection with Giripul in his past life and that is why he came here. This black deed had to happen here and then be buried here forever,' said Balu. Then he began chanting a prayer softly.

The boy woke up and began to cry. He cried as if for the first time, while Janak held his head in his arms. 'Let him cry, it will cleanse him of all his sorrow. He needs to cry and then his heart will be new again,' Balu said and they sat near the boy, looking out at the hills till it got dark. Tommy laid his head on the boy's feet, his body shaking with the boy's sobs.

16

Policeman returns; Open and shut case declared; Boy gets a name; Leela gives him a home

All night Janak tossed and turned, thinking about the albino boy and the terrible life he had led. When he finally fell asleep, he dreamt that he was in the magician's tent, fighting with the dead man, while Rama sat on a swing outside and watched them. He woke up with a cry and quickly turned to see if he had disturbed Rama. She was still asleep. Janak got out of bed and went to the shed. He bathed in cold water because he did not want to light the fire in the kitchen. It would make a loud hissing noise since the wood was damp from last night's rain. He got dressed and came out of the house quietly before Rama could see him. Not that she would. She always slept with her face covered with a muslin cloth till he woke her up with a cup of strong, sweet tea.

He was the only man in the village who had to make tea for his wife; maybe he was the only man in the world who did that. But he did not mind, if it helped to keep her mood mellow.

Janak stepped out of the house into the empty street. 'Stop thinking about Rama all the time,' he said loudly to himself, scaring a flock of sparrows that had just settled down to feed on the raspberry shrub. Forget your wife and think about the poor boy. What should we do with him? How should we save him from the police? Janak stretched his arms above his head to wake himself up properly and then turned towards his shop. He began to walk faster to warm himself, and when he got to the shop, he said a quick prayer and lifted up the shutter. But he did not go in. He stood outside looking at the hills in the east, beyond the ridge from where the sun would soon rise. The sky had already painted itself pale orange to get ready for dawn, but the rest of the sky was still dark.

'I hope the boy is not taken away by the police. They will beat him till he confesses to the murder even though he is innocent. Poor creature. Why did God make him like this? All he had to do was give his skin a little bit of brown colour and the boy's life would have been so different. His family would not have treated him like a leper. He would be sitting at home today, loved by his family.

Janak felt his hands getting cold and he put them inside his pocket to warm them. The sky was lighter now and soon the first rays of sunlight would come rushing down from the mountains into Giripul. The days were getting cooler and the sun would gradually change direction. It would rise and set behind a different hill, cast longer shadows on the houses and the forest. The walnut tree behind his house would throw small green fruits down all day and the langurs would quietly emerge from the forest at dawn to steal them.

The musk roses, the raspberry bushes and the wild ginger plants would slowly wilt and die. The river would change its tune and flow with a loud gurgling song instead of the gentle murmur of summer. These changes in the hillside which he could predict easily always made him feel safe and secure. It was as if some order still existed in his turbulent world.

He knew the hills would not suddenly turn upon him and do something unexpected like spew fire or sink into the earth. They stood solidly, like they had done from the time the mighty Himalayas had risen from the heavenly sea to create the valleys and hills of Giripul.

Janak sat down on the steps and waited for the pigeons to arrive. So much had happened in the last few days. He was still trying to make sense of the boy's story. So much sadness heaped upon one poor child. He did not deserve such harsh treatment from fate. He had done nothing wrong. How could they make this boy's life easier? Janak thought over and over again, but he could not find an answer. For the first time in his life, he wished he had a big shop and could afford to employ half a dozen boys to cut and stitch. Then he could have easily given the boy a job. But there was no point in thinking of what was not. He must try to find a way to help him, they must all do something for him. Fate had sent him to Giripul and this was where he should live now. But what could the poor boy do here? He could milk cows and goats, or plough the fields for some farmer. But people in the village did not have extra money to pay. He could try to teach the boy how to sew or to cut simple patterns, but then what would Rama say? No, they must find something else for the boy to do. He needed to think and he could not do that later, with Rama sitting in the shop with him. She watched him like a hawk all the time. Her beautiful eyes lined with kohl followed him as he moved from his table to the door. The women who came to his shop now hardly spoke to him. No one showed him their belly button or spoke about their dreams. Rama sat still on the bench, her head raised like a guard dog, and they quickly left their cloth on the table and scuttled away. Luckily, he had all their measurements written down in his notebook or it would have been difficult for him.

He did not know why she had suddenly turned up at the shop last week and sat down on the floor with her knitting. Did she really suspect him of murder? He was her husband, the father of her son. He loved her more than anything else in the world and would even die for her. It was so strange that every woman in the village, including those who lived in the remote mountains, came to him clutching her bundle of hopes and poured her heart's deepest secrets out to him as he took their measurements. Everyone, except his beloved wife. She just sat and watched him, her rosebud mouth tightly shut and her large, doe-eyes glinting like steel. God's ways were strange. Janak sighed and rubbed his eyes.

Again he had let Rama distract him when he should be thinking of some way to find the boy a job, a place to live in Giripul. He could not sleep on the floor in Balu's shed forever.

Janak looked up at the sky. The orange was getting brighter every minute. Soon the sun would rise to bathe Giripul in its golden light. Janak folded his hands, closed his eyes and bowed to the east.

'O mighty Sun God. Keep all my loved ones safe. Keep my wife Rama happy and healthy. Bless my son and make this a day without danger.'

When he opened his eyes, Shankar was standing in front of him with two glasses of tea. He handed him one and sat down on the steps next to him. The pigeons swooped down at the same time for their breakfast seeds. His favourite one watched him from her perch on the water tank. She seemed a little less friendly this morning.

'I was thinking about the boy, poor soul. To be born with a skin like that and then to have such a cruel fate,' said Shankar, and took a noisy gulp of tea.

Janak nodded, 'I too have been thinking about the boy all night, wondering what to do to help him,' he said. He did not add that Rama and so many other stray thoughts kept distracting him. He was relieved that they knew how the stranger had died, but he also knew the police would not believe the boy.

'Yes, we have to think of what to do with him,' he said, pushing Rama from his mind for a while so that he could think clearly.

'We must help somehow, but what do we do with him? I could keep him at home, but I am not sure what my wife would say. I think we are going to have another baby soon, though my wife has not told me as yet, but I suspect it, since she has been getting sick in the morning. It will be difficult to feed all four of us with just my fish earnings, that too is not regular now,' he muttered sheepishly.

Janak nodded. 'I could take him in. Rama will get annoyed I know, but then she always is. Maybe she won't be. Who can tell with her? Anyway, it will be nice for my son to have some company. I can support them all. I don't mind working harder. There are so many women in Giripul wanting new clothes all the time. The wedding season is coming and then after that is Diwali. Maybe the boy can help me. But the problem is, the shop is too small for the two of us and now Rama sits here too. I dare not tell her to stay at home and I cannot afford to get a bigger place,' he said with a worried frown.

Both looked towards Balu's shed, where the boy was sleeping and said at the same time, 'The boy will not be sent back to his old life.' Janak looked at Shankar, his heart filled with pride. They had always thought alike from childhood, at least about the important things in life. There had not been many occasions when they had to take an important decision such as this and he felt a little nervous, but he said in a firm voice, 'No, that we will never allow, even if we have to eat only once a day.'

They sat quietly for a while sipping their tea. The cinnamon sparrows quarrelled amicably outside and the sunlight streamed into the shop, warming their hands. The pigeons had flown away to Lala's shop. Janak broke the silence. 'I am a bit worried. What if the police try to blame the boy for the death? We know now it was an accident, but they won't see it like that. They might try and beat a confession out of the boy.'

'Yes, everyone thinks it is Giripul's first *murder*,' said Shankar. 'It could have been you in handcuffs, but for the hand of fate,' he added. 'You did vow to kill him'.

'I wish you would not keep reminding me of that,' said Janak irritably, his warm feeling for his friend slowly disappearing.

'Luckily, the police seem to have forgotten about it for now. They are busy doing election duty, the bus driver from Simla told me yesterday. The junior policeman said he will be back soon, but no one has come to ask questions and it is already more than a week now,' Shankar said. Janak looked away from him, tilting his glass to finish the tea. It was lukewarm now, but still milky sweet and comforting.

'Balu has allowed the boy to stay in his shed and we can feed him, but it would be better if the case was closed. Then the boy can come out of hiding and look for work. We should go and tell the police what really happened,' he said after a while.

'No, no, never. You have had a narrow escape, now do not meddle. One should never go to the police, they hate people coming to them with any kind of information. It just creates more work for them and they get angry and lock up anyone who comes to report things,' said Shankar, suddenly looking like a sleuth again.

'What rubbish! Who told you this nonsense? People go all the time to the police station. I have always seen crowds waiting outside the Simla police station. Some people even take their bedding and cooking things and camp there for days,' said Janak. The pigeons suddenly flew down from Lala's tea shop roof, and the cinnamon sparrows scattered, chattering angrily. The white and brown pigeon, his beloved, flew down to perch on the steps. Janak held his breath. He knew that one day she would sit on his shoulder and nibble his ear.

The lame crow had finally become his friend after weeks of cajoling and at home Mithoo seemed more gentle and mild now that his mother-in-law had gone. Janak put some grain on the ground gently. If only his wife would love him like the birds did. But that day would come too. One day she would nibble his ears and coo at him and they would have a secret love affair which no one in the village would ever know about.

'I swear on my dead mother, I am telling you the truth. From my own personal family experience,' said Shankar in an agitated voice, jolting Janak out of his dream. 'It happened to an uncle of mine, a blood relative; my father's real brother. One day he was resting under a tree after ploughing his field and was about to open his lunch box when he looked up and saw a man being hacked to death with an axe in the neighbour's field. You know the uncle I am talking about, the one who owns two acres of good land on the other side of Giri. You remember, where a bus with the marriage party went down the khud?' said Shankar, pointing to the ravine beyond the bridge.

'Tell me about the police,' said Janak in weary voice.

'Oh, yes, the police. My uncle, went to the police station but he had his lunch first since he did not want to walk all the way on an empty stomach, and you know how expensive food is in Simla. Ask me about it. A cup of tea costs one rupee, and a samosa – rupees five! When I followed the headman to Simla, I ate only once, that too just a banana,' said Shankar.

Janak gave him a hard jab in the ribs. 'What did the police do to your uncle?' How he wished his quiet old friend would return and this garrulous sleuth would drown in the Giri river.

'Anyway, my uncle walked, took a bus to Simla, spending his own hard-earned money to report the murder, but what happened to him?' Shankar paused, looking up at the sky.

Janak did not say anything. He traced a pattern on the ground with his fingers, scattered a few more seeds to the pigeons. He would not ask. What did he care about Shankar's uncle. Then, after a moment of heavy silence, Shankar announced in a slow voice like a newsreader on the radio.

'He was locked up as soon as he told the police about the killing. He is still there for all I know ... and so you ...' Shankar stopped abruptly and sprang to his feet. Tommy gave a low growl and Janak looked up. A policeman, dressed in crisp khaki, was coming towards the shop. When he got closer, they saw he was the junior policeman, the one who had wanted to buy land and settle with his family in Giripul.

'Oh my god! Here come the police. You should not have mentioned their name,' Shankar whispered as he folded his palms in a namaste and bowed.

'Arey ... How are you two doing?' said the policeman,
smiling broadly as he wiped his face with a red
handkerchief. They all seemed to carry one, as if it
was a part of their uniform. 'Any news? I came by the
morning bus. I could not get a van today; they have all
gone on election duty. I thought I would come and see
what is happening here. My wife liked the cucumbers
and wants some more. I also brought an FIR form for
you to fill up, though no one has come to claim the body
as yet,' he said, settling down on the chair that Shankar
had quickly brought from Lala's tea shop.

A cup of tea arrived soon and Lala appeared with a
plate of hot samosas, followed by Raja who brought
a packet of biscuits. 'You Giripul people are too kind.
Actually, this FIR has to be done at the station because
we need an official stamp, but I thought why not be of
some service to you kind people. I will stamp it later,'
he said with a grin and brought out a folded paper from
his pocket. 'Bring one table and one more cup of this
delicious masala tea, made of creamy, pure milk, unlike
the milk and water mixture we get in Simla,' he said,
looking up at the hills and scratching his chin.

'You wish to drink milk, sir? Arey, chotu!' shouted Lala
and though the policeman coyly refused, a glass of hot
milk quickly appeared. It had a thick layer of cream on
it which the policeman lifted delicately with his index
finger and licked slowly. 'Forget all this sir, shir,' he said
and drank the milk in one quick gulp. Then, as they
watched, he wiped his mouth with his handkerchief and

burped. Lala nodded and smiled at him like a mother who had just finished feeding and burping her baby.

The FIR form was spread out on the small wooden table and the policeman, whose name Janak read on his lapel as Sunil Kumar, took out a pen from his other pocket. As he wrote on the table to test the pen, Janak watched him, trying to calm the fear rising in his heart. One wrong word and he could send the boy or himself to jail. He gulped and kept smiling bravely. The headman and Teera could also be in trouble for dragging the body about, but they were nowhere to be seen. Janak knew he had to carry the burden for all of them. He tried to stand up straight, but his knees began to wobble.

Constable Sunil Kumar took a sip of tea, noisily cleared his throat and turned to Janak.

'Name of the deceased?'

'Who is deceased, sir?'

'Arey, you have to tell me.'

'Deceased means what, sir?'

'Oh. It means dead. What was the name of the dead man? It was a man, we all remember that, don't we?' he said with an encouraging smile like a school teacher coaxing his students to give the correct answer.

'Yes, yes, we were sure it was a man, but we do not know the name, sir,' Janak whispered. So far he had spoken only the truth. 'All right. Deceased – Unknown,' Sunil Kumar repeated the words loudly as he wrote them down.

'Father's name?'

'We do not know that either, sir.'

'Deceased's father's name – Unknown,' he wrote and paused. 'Place of residence?'

'We do not know, sir. He was a stranger.'

'All right. Address not known,' he wrote, moving his head up and down like a puppet.

'Any identification marks?' Sunil Kumar asked, gazing into the distance where the cucumber fields were. Janak could see he was losing interest in the case and that was a good sign. The policeman would gather his cucumbers and leave, then he would soon be safely home. The gods were with him. He could feel their presence.

'You mean what, sir,' he said, his voice more confident now.

'I mean any scars, moles, an extra finger. You know people have all kinds of odd marks on their body.'

'Well, he had a scar on his throat, sahib,' said Janak hesitantly. 'Though it may have come after his death,' he added.

'Does not matter, a scar is a scar, dead or alive,' the policeman said. 'Now let us put down what happened, though we should have done this on the day itself. But you see, my boss had to rush off to his wife's niece's wedding function in Simla. In-laws, you know. You have to obey, even if you are a senior policeman,' he said, rolling his eyes.

Everyone clicked their tongues in sympathy. In-laws was a safe topic. You could not be sent to jail for discussing your in-laws, Janak thought and said, 'Yes, sir, we must always do what our wife's family asks.'

Before anyone could speak, Shankar said in a slow,

clear voice; his radio announcer's voice which he now used for special occasions, Janak had noticed. The policeman picked up a samosa and looked at him with interest as he began his story.

'Sir, it happened like this. The man, name and address unknown, was not murdered at all. A cobra snake bit him,' he said and paused.

'What? Here?' asked the policeman, lifting his legs off the ground.

'No, there. Where the magician's tent was pitched,' said Shankar, pointing to the empty patch on the hillside. They could see clumps of upturned soil where the tent had been pitched and a flock of meadow bunting were busy searching for seeds in the hollows. Though they were quite far, the birds sensed their collective stare and suddenly rose up in a flock and flew away.

'A magic snake? I have heard of these things, but I did not know your village had one. No one said it last time,' the policeman said, shifting in his chair nervously.

'No, no, sir, not a magic snake, but a snake in the magic-show tent. It was a real snake – a cobra brought here by the magician for a new trick,' said Shankar, speaking slowly and clearly. Janak could not help feeling impressed by him. When he wanted to, Shankar could be quite smart and bold.

'You know, I have always wanted to see a magic show, but never got the chance. A policeman has no time for enjoyment. I have heard they cut a body in half, yet the man came out alive and whole,' said Sunil Kumar, drumming his fingers on the table like policemen do in films.

'Yes, sir, Raja here was cut in half,' said Janak and Raja was pushed forward. He stood in front of the table, grinning and pulling at the seat of his trousers like he always did. Janak could see the murder case receding further and further away from Sunil Kumar's mind.

The policeman rubbed his chin and looked at Raja thoughtfully.

'Did it hurt?' he asked.

'No sir, just tickled a bit,' said Raja and then quickly added, 'Though it was quite dangerous and I had to lie very still.' Before he could narrate his story of being sawed in half, Janak came forward.

'So, no murder then, sir.'

'Well, you people say this unknown man was bitten by a cobra – where?'

'In Giripul, sir, in the magician's tent,' said Raja loudly. They were not afraid of the policeman any more. He seemed a harmless man and not very clever. Not like the cops in films who could read everyone's minds and put criminals behind bars in a minute.

'No, where on his body? The snake bit him where? Head, arm, legs?' Sunil Kumar asked, looking down at the ground below his chair.

'Throat, sir,' Janak said before Raja could say anything; he too was feeling quite bold now. The danger of the boy being arrested seemed to have disappeared totally. Wtih God's blessings they were going to get away with this.

'So he was bitten where the scar is?' asked the policeman.

'More or less there,' Janak replied.

'And he died at once, you think? Why was there blood on the sheet?' asked Sunil Kumar, narrowing his eyes.

'Yes, sir, a cobra bite kills you in one minute, before you can say your own name, they say,' said Lala, appearing once again with a plate of sweets. The brief moment of danger had passed. The policeman forgot about the bloodstained sheet and took two laddoos. He popped one in his mouth and kept one on the table.

'Well, I am writing here, death of unknown party by snake bite. Cobra snake brought from outside Giripul. One of you can sign it.'

Janak hesitated, but then took the pen and wrote his name down. He felt a little scared, putting his name on an official form recklessly like this, but it had to be done to save the boy's life. A gentle breeze floated down and made the paper flutter. Sunil Kumar picked up the FIR form and began reading it while they waited. He read for what seemed a long time, though it was only a single sheet. He paused, chewed the laddoo thoughtfully, and then began reading again, moving his lips. Humming under his breath, he quickly wrote something, folded the paper neatly and put it in his breast pocket along with the pen. He popped the second laddoo in his mouth.

'So, that is that,' he said after he had finished eating. 'In any case, if the snake was brought from outside, it does not fall in our official area. No one has claimed the body. The case will be closed,' he said and Janak almost burst into tears.

They accompanied the policeman in an orderly line to the waiting two o'clock bus. He settled down on the front seat, which was vacated for him and quickly dusted by the driver. A basket of cucumbers, a ripe pumpkin and a box of laddoos was carefully placed near his feet. 'The case will be closed,' he repeated, 'Who can catch a magic snake, that too from outside our territory?'

'Look out for a good piece of land for me, where my wife can grow cucumbers,' he shouted as the bus lurched forward. They never saw him again.

It was Balu ho decided to give the albino boy a new name.

'He has to have a real name,' he said, 'He cannot be called Choomantar any more, or Chotu. He must have a new name to begin his new life in Giripul.' Before anyone could say anything, Balu said, 'We will call him Albela – he is unique, different from us, and so his name will mean just that.' Everyone agreed. 'Go bring some raw rice and some gur. We must sprinkle some holy water. There is no Ganga water here so we will just use water from our river.'

'That is holy water too, sahib, it fell from Shivji's water pot, that is why it is called Giri,' the boy said, looking at his feet.

'How do you know that, boy?' asked Balu, surprised.

'When I worked at the Simla railway station as a coolie, there was a sadhu who lived on the platform too. He told me stories about the gods and goddesses. I cleaned his hut and washed and mended his clothes.'

'What else can you do, boy? Albela, I mean,' asked Janak, pleased that the boy could stitch.

'I can do a little bit of everything. I begged at the holy river for a while with the sadhu, diving into the water to pick up the coins people threw. He taught me to read a little and chant a few hymns. I can also do many magic tricks my master taught me. I can knead dough quite well and I can dig too, because I worked on a road building site for a few months. If I have a good spade, I can dig really fast,' he said, looking eager and bright now.

'How much you have done in such a young life,' muttered Balu. 'Digging is a great skill. If you can dig well, you can find work anywhere. A man who digs will never starve.'

It was rare for him to stay out of the shed for so long, but he seemed to have adopted Albela. He had brought out an old shirt for him and put a cloth cap on his head. Janak was surprised to see how much the boy had changed in two days. He no longer looked scared and half starved. Shankar and Janak got him hot chapattis from home and he ate them quite happily with only garlic and chilli chutney. When he brought him dal and sabzi, the boy looked up at him with surprise.

'For me? All this food is for me?' he asked and then looked at Balu to make sure.

'Eat, boy, eat. You have a lot of catching up to do,' Balu said and went into his shed.

Janak watched the boy eat and then suddenly sat up. 'I have an idea. If he can dig so well, he can dig in Badi Kothi. There is so much digging to be done in that garden. We can go and ask bibiji,' said Janak in an excited voice.

Shankar nodded and slapped his back. 'What a great idea, quite a new thing for you, Janak. You know what? I was just going to say the same thing. But let us go there while the sunlight is bright. I do not like to walk there in the dark.'

They decided to set off at once. 'Go, go. Gods will smile on you,' shouted Balu from inside the shed. He was exhausted with so much involvement in the goings-on in Giripul and needed to rest for a long time.

The hill barbet called incessantly, though summer had almost ended. Leela wondered which tree it was on, was it the coral which had just a few flowers left on it, or was it the kachnar which was about to flower, but she did not feel like opening her eyes. Once, long ago, she had seen the hill barbet swoop down and pick up an insect and then spit it out at once as if it tasted bitter. The poor, unfortunate insect had been digging furiously all morning to make a tiny hole in the earth under the oleander shrub. It was a funny, slim-waisted insect, almost like a wasp, with a big amber head. After digging for a while, it flew away and then came back dragging a spider. The spider was not quite dead. She saw it was waving its legs drunkenly. The insect tried to put the spider in the hole it had dug, but it would not fit. It put the spider aside and began digging again; then it paused for a moment as if thinking of something, and began digging again.

This time the mouth of the hole was big enough to fit the inert body of the spider. Now the insect disappeared into the hole, dragging the spider behind it. Leela waited patiently. Would it come out or stay there with the comatose spider? Just when she was about to walk away, she saw the amber head emerge waving its front legs.

It began to work again, covering up the hole by turning around and kicking back the earth it had dug out. For a small insect, it had powerful hind legs. It only took a few seconds and the ground was smooth again. Then it flew away without a backward glance.

What was the point of all this exhausting work? Then many years later, she read somewhere that the insect was called a spider-hunting wasp. It dug a hole and laid an egg in it, and the spider, stung into a comatose state by the wasp, was fresh food for the larva when it emerged. It was all very efficiently thought out.

If she had conceived and had had a baby, would she leave it in a hole with a chunk of meat and never looked back at it ever again? First of all, she was vegetarian, so that would be a problem, you cannot leave a cauliflower or beans like that. Maybe a pot of yoghurt would be all right. Yoghurt stays fresh for a long time, though it does get sour. Anyway there was no point in thinking all this. She had never carried a baby in her womb and that was that.

Leela heard the sound of foot steps and opened her eyes. A pale white face, not too high from the ground, peered at her from behind the tree; a child's face, not a ghost's. Had it come from heaven to fetch her? If she was dead, it did not feel any different. Surely there would be more drama in death and not just this silent, sleepy passing on?

She could still hear the barbet calling. She tried to wriggle her toes, but her feet felt numb. A gentle burp rose in her throat and she could hear her breath rise and fall. No, she was not dead. Not today.

The face had disappeared. She could hear some low voices behind the shrubs. Leela shut her eyes and waited; nothing else to do now but wait. Something always happened if you lay very still and waited. Either Kammo would bring her lunch, or the pale creature would take her hand and lead her away to cross the river of death.

Life was all about waiting. Seeds waited for rain, babies waited to be fed, wives waited for their husbands to come home, husbands waited for sons, and finally they all waited for death. The biggest problem was how to pass the time between birth and death – this long river of time with no end in sight. Leela burped again. Rajma dal always gave her wind. 'You dal eating, farting Indians,' Robert had said to her many years ago. So many years ago that it seemed like another lifetime. Why had she thought of him now? She never allowed herself to think of him during the day. As if people could see what was going through her mind. But who was there to see any more?

His face was so close to hers, his grey eyes twinkling as he rubbed her bare midriff. She could smell his strange English smell of tobacco and soap. 'What are you doing? Someone will see us,' she heard herself say as she ran down the hillside, her sari trailing behind her. He ran behind her, laughing. The deodar trees shook and trembled in the breeze. 'Stop. You must not run. You must not run shamelessly like this with a white sahib,' she heard them whisper. She was afraid, but she kept running, knowing he would follow her.

'Is she dead?' asked Shankar in a whisper, hiding behind the kachnar tree.

'Not again ...' hissed Janak, feeling a bit nervous himself. Bibiji was so still, he had never seen her like this.

She was an old woman, nearly hundred, they said in the village. But he did not want her to go like this, so suddenly, so quietly. Then she wriggled her toes and burped gently. Startled, they all took a step back, Shankar, Janak and Albela.

'Bibiji is alive and burping. All will be well,' whispered Janak.

Though the old mali was not pleased, he agreed to, take Albela on as a helper because bibiji told him to and he did need someone who could dig. His back gave him trouble now and the garden was too big for him to manage alone. This pale, ugly boy looked like a ghost, but he seemed obedient and willing and that was rare in young people, including his sons. The old mali wished he could give them all a good thrashing.

Bibiji liked the boy at once and asked him many questions to which he replied quite smartly. 'You can help in the garden in the morning, maybe we can grow some vegetables now, and you can study in the afternoon. I will get some books for you,' she said and smiled at them, her eyes strangely bright in her old wrinkled face. Then she sighed and went back to sleep.

'What will he grow, this strange looking boy with white eyelashes. Anyway, the monkeys will eat it all, you mark my words,' the old mali said to his wife who was deaf, but she could lip read what her husband said. He had been saying the same things for the past fifty years they had been married, so she just nodded as usual. 'Albela, what a name,' the mali grumbled. 'Maybe his funny face will frighten the monkeys away. Looks like a langur himself. He is albela all right.'

The monkeys came to check this new bandar guard and were surprised to see how small he was. They were more amazed when he shot at them with his catapult, almost hitting their leader. After a conference, the senior monkey decided the boy was too dangerous and they would move to the higher mountains where the wild berries were about to ripen. In any case, there was nothing but sour fruit in this wild, weed-filled garden.

Albela soon settled down at the Badi Kothi despite the fact that the old mali often shouted at him and clipped him behind the ears for no reason. When the old mali called him a lazy donkey or an owl's son, he burst out laughing because these words sounded like endearments after all the cruel abuses he had heard till now.

He dug furiously all day and when the old mali went home for his siesta, he explored the garden. Most of it was overgrown with weeds and wild rose creepers.

There were three old deodar trees which stood like pillars, spreading their branches down to the ground and near them there was a broken bench, half covered with ivy. The forest seemed to be crawling into the garden bit by bit, to claim the land that had once belonged to it.

In one corner, where the garden almost merged into the forest, there were a dozen peach trees laden with tiny fruits, but the branches had vines trailing all over them. He decided to do something soon to free the helpless trees.

The old sadhu who had taught him to read and write had also told him about wild plants that could cure coughs and colds and other ailments, though he never taught him the secret of making medicinal oils. He searched the wild undergrowth everyday for these herbs because Balu had a bad cough and the herbs could help. He knew that black tulsi that grew near rocks could cure a cold and wild ginger could soothe a stomach ache. He ran his hands over the grass and tried to remember which other plants the sadhu had taught him to collect when they went into the forest, but he could not remember.

Suddenly Mamoo's face, black with rage and covered with blood, jumped out of the shadows. Albela stood frozen as the shape hovered over him, spreading itself wider and wider. He could not breathe and his body, strangely heavy now, was slowly being dragged down to the earth. The shadow became bigger and bigger, smothering his face with its wet clammy fingers. He was falling. He forced himself to shake it off and then opened his mouth to scream. There was no sound, yet he tried and tried till he heard a faint cry. It was his own voice. He screamed louder and ran towards the house. He was covered with cold sweat. He stumbled and fell on the grass. With trembling hands he began pulling the weeds out and talked softly to himself. 'He will not come back. He will not harm me. Janak chacha, Balu baba will save me. I am safe. I have a home now.' For an hour he pulled the weeds and then, when a large corner of the lawn had been cleared, his hands stopped trembling and he looked up at the sky without fear.

For the next week he stayed near the house and dug the vegetable patch, glancing nervously at the dark shadows under the trees. Then one day he forced himself to go to the orchard and sat down under the old peach tree. He waited and waited for the demons to come out of the shadows. He would face them, look straight into their eyes like baba had told him to do, and they would go away forever. But though he sat there for an hour, cleaning all the stones and wild shrubs from underneath the trees, nothing happened. The sun shone above his head and the sky remained a clear blue with a few gentle wisps of clouds. A group of langurs came by to inspect him, but they did not stay long when they saw there was nothing much to eat. A cool breeze carried the scent of honeysuckle to him and he knew he had won the battle with darkness.

While working in the verandah on his sewing machine, Janak often saw Albela digging furiously in the far corner of the garden. He looked like a little mole digging itself a new home. He was still very thin and jumped if you spoke to him suddenly, but time would heal the wounds that were hidden inside him. He did not run and leap about like other boys of his age, and sometimes Janak thought he looked like a weary old man. Janak could tell that the boy had some fear hidden in his heart which dragged him down. He understood what it was to be afraid, but he did not know how to talk to the boy. Maybe he would come one day to his shop and talk to him like the people of Giripul did.

Janak suddenly thought of the third wife's dream. It all seemed so long ago. She must have forgotten all about her beheading nightmare since she looked quite happy and went about the village smiling. The headman had bought a colour TV and Rama said that the third wife was boasting about it all the time.

Janak knew the TV would cause a lot of problems in the village, especially with the women who would now see all kinds of new things which were unknown in Giripul. But what could one do? Giripul would soon be touched by the outside world. Old ways would change.

Albela grew stronger as the days went by. Though he still felt shy when people from the village tried to talk to him, he was no longer afraid of the shadow. He began going further and further into the garden, right upto where the forest began. He no longer looked over his shoulder as he cleared the weeds. He cut all the tall grass. He pulled down all the strange creepers that covered the fruit trees like green cobwebs. He found a row of apple trees and a strawberry patch too. Sometimes, at dusk, a faint tinge of fear touched his heart or a voice hissed at him, but he laughed and lashed at the weeds harder. He worked hard all day to make bibiji's garden so beautiful that she would say to him, 'Albela you have done a good job.' That would make him really happy.

Bit by bit, the lost orchard appeared. He found two more peach trees and two plum trees with tiny fruits on their branches. Albela now began making a path from the house to the orchard by digging up the earth and then stamping it down so that bibiji could walk to the orchard if she wished.

The old mali was against it. 'She can never walk so far,' he said, 'you are just making extra work for us.' But Albela worked early morning and then in the evening till the sun set. He was not afraid of the forest at twilight any more.

He was sure that if he made the path smooth and even, bibiji could walk right upto the peach trees. He wanted very much to finish the path and line it with white pebbles before the rains came. The first crop of peaches would come with the rains and he would give the biggest peach to bibiji who had saved his life.

They had all saved his life – Janak, Balu, Shankar, Raja and Lala. Giripul had given him a new name and a new life. He must show them that he was worth the trouble.

It was late in July, almost two months after Giripul had been shaken by the murder, that the peaches finally turned golden. They were not too big and many of them had brown spots on them. Albela carefully sorted out the best ones, washed them under the tap in the garden, and arranged them in a bowl with some marigold leaves. Then he placed a pink rose from the garden on top of the peaches.

The old mali had been right, bibiji could not walk up the path. But she was very happy when she saw it was finally finished, and clapped her hands like a child. 'Well done, Albela! You have built a grand highway. Maybe I can drive down in my car one day,' she said, laughing. They all knew she could never do that, but they laughed too.

The morning sunlight was making the garden gleam as he walked down the path to the verandah where bibiji was dozing. He placed the peaches on a table near her and sat down to wait on the steps. An orange butterfly came and sat on his arm and though it tickled him, he let it stay.

Her father had sent Robert an invitation card when she got married. She did not know why he had done that. After Robert left Simla in 1947 along with all the British families, there was no need to keep in touch. Maybe he had suspected something. That was not possible, they had been so careful. They only met in the old ruined house beyond the Jhakhu hills. Only the monkeys knew about their love. He had only kissed her a few times, that was all. But for her it had been a lifetime of love.

A few innocent kisses; a lifetime of love which had sustained her till now. She had been a silly young girl, so madly in love with a man she hardly knew or understood. Half a century later, she still felt the same way about him, maybe understood him better, though they had not seen each other for fifty-odd years. Sometimes she felt a desperate need to talk to someone about Robert, just a few sentences which would make him come alive once more for her. Who was there to talk to? The only person she knew here, besides the servants and Janak, was her neighbour Rati. A gentle, thoughtful woman, but very reserved. Could she talk to her one day, tell her about Robert? Nothing romantic or sentimental, just ordinary things like how he had taught her the names of all the birds, the way he would tease her about her lack of knowledge about her own land. Yes, maybe one day she would talk to Rati, but when her husband, the boisterous but charming Raja, was not around. Maybe she would tell her about her secret love too. She had to tell someone before she died.

Albela had been waiting for an hour and just when he thought he should go back to dig the vegetable patch, bibiji opened her eyes and smiled. 'Oh! Robert, look, peaches,' she said and put her hands out to touch them. 'Where did you get them from, not from our garden?' Albela nodded his head, suddenly feeling too shy to speak. 'You are a clever boy. Are they magic peaches? Let me see if they vanish. Here, Albela. You have one too,' she said. But he hesitated and moved back.

'Don't be afraid. Come on, take one,' she said and when he came forward to take the peach, she laughed and ruffled his hair. She was the first woman who had touched him like this, with affection and not in anger, and Albela ran away before she could see him crying. Later, when he ate the peach sitting under the tree, it tasted sweet and a little salty with his tears.

Summer had long gone. The rains came on time, turning the Giri river into a raging torrent and then as it flowed down thousands of miles to the sea, the skies filled it with rain again. Finally, after two months the clouds floated away and the skies cleared. The hills were emerald green and sparkled in the soothing autumn sunshine.

People brought out all their winter clothes and put them out in the mild sunshine to get rid of the mildew the rains had sprouted. But soon the sun began to lose its warmth and the days got longer. The wheat and corn had been harvested and now only garlic grew in the terraced fields. The air smelled of firewood.

Winter was waiting around the corner, but at Lala's tea shop they still discussed the murder. Since only Janak, Shankar, Lala and Balu knew the facts, the rest of them were still trying to solve the mystery. Everyone added their own bits and the story grew with each telling.

The only real fact that remained unchanged was that a stranger's body had been found in the barber's shop with its throat cut. The grey areas were filled in with much enthusiasm and no one cared much for the truth, as long as the story held their attention.

The women discussed it as they walked to the spring to fetch water and the men as they sat in the tea shop. Bus passengers talked about it as they passed Giripul and the driver always added his own bit to the tale. When relatives came to visit, they were taken to the barber's shop and shown the chair where the body had been found.

Channa the barber had kept the chair aside in the beginning, but his wife said it was a waste of a good chair and since there were only two chairs in the shop, he decided to use it again. No one seemed to mind. In fact some people said they got a real thrill getting their head massaged while sitting in what was now called the 'murder chair'.

The stories got more and more complicated and now that they had all heard what everyone had to say, they longed for a new listener who would be thrilled and awed like they had been during the first week of the murder. 'It is a pity we never got to know who the wretched fellow was,' they often said and Janak, Shankar and Lala just nodded.

Raja who only knew bits and pieces of the true story, loved weaving long yarns to any customer he could stop at his shop. People got so fed up of him that they complained to his wife and she put an end to his stories by saying she would go away to her mother's house. She also wisely pointed out how sales were falling because people had started avoiding his shop and going to the next village to buy essential things. This made Raja stop at once.

Balu never participated in these discussions and remained in his shed. Though, when Albela came down from Badi Kothi to meet him, bringing some vegetable or fruit he had grown, he seemed very pleased and talked to him for a long time.

Janak hummed a tune as he turned the sewing machine handle. Next week he would get a new sewing machine, one that had a foot pedal and an embroidery attachment. It was called 'zig zag' and it could do a variety of complicated stitches like button hole, daisy and blanket. He was going to pay for it in instalments – fifty rupees a month for three years, but it was worth it because now he had a lot of work.

Bibiji had ordered uniforms to be made for all the school children in Giripul. They had discovered fifty nearly new sheets in a trunk and he was going to cut them up to make shirts for the boys. For the girls they would buy twenty metres of cloth from Simla; pink for the kurta and black for the salwar. There was so much work now, and no dreams were going to complicate his life.

The house was quiet, its walls steady and the floor even, and Rama too seemed content; she was getting quite good at hemming and stitching buttons and so far had not shown any interest in his sewing machine. And that strange smile of hers now only appeared when there were women customers in the shop.

She stood at the door and guarded the shop along with Tommy. The women quickly gave their measurements to her and left, not wasting time in idle chatter any more. Janak missed their friendly voices talking about things a man would never know, but you could not have everything in life. It was better to have peace and quiet in your life even if it was boring at times.

Rama liked being in the shop, not just to keep an eye on Janak, but because she actually enjoyed hemming and creating neatly-stitched holes for buttons. Her mind rested on each button as if it were the centre of the world and she felt calm and at peace.

The flour dough dolls she had made to stick pins in now lay forgotten and the mice from Lala's shop carried them away one by one. Their mates were delighted with this unexpected bounty and quickly produced a bigger brood.

Shankar started going down to the river once more, but he gave all his fish to Lala to keep in the new fridge – the first one in Giripul. He and Albela now sold cucumbers, tomatoes and peaches to the bus passengers, charging them high rates, but they did not seem to mind. They gave Balu whatever was left each evening.

The headman got a telephone connection for Giripul, but the telephone was kept in his house, draped with a white napkin which his wife had crocheted, next to the TV. He stopped going to Simla and sent Raja, who had been appointed his deputy, for all the panchayat meetings. He never picked up the pink satin suit, though he had paid Janak for it. It hung brazenly in the cupboard since there was no need for secrecy any more and all the women who came to the shop stared at it with awe.

'Who is it for?' they asked.

'Some foreign lady,' Janak would say truthfully and even Rama was impressed.

'Which foreign lady?' she asked once or twice, but then lost interest.

Women had short memories when something did not touch them directly, but God forbid if they or their children were involved. Then they would remember things even from their past lives.

Finally Janak cut up the suit and used the buttons, lace and trimming for other suits. It gave him a thrill each time he took the pink satin in his hands to cut it. It was as if he was cutting up the headman's she-barber, bit by bit, till she disappeared.

The third wife was expecting her first child and sat at home praying for a son though she often said a daughter would be fine too, as long as she was fair like her husband and not dusky like her.

She came to the shop and started telling Janak about her new dream. It was about a baby – a fair, plump baby boy who had the headman's eyes and her nose, but Rama had cut her short. 'Give, your measurements, sister, and go,' she had said, not looking up from her hemming.

Janak suddenly saw Rama leap up and rush out. She ran behind the third wife shouting, 'Shyamala, you bitch! Don't you dare make owl eyes at my husband. I will scratch your eyes out!' she screamed. The third wife turned around and smiled. She stuck her tongue out at Rama and showed her her thumb. 'Your husband? Hah! Ask him who he loves most,' she said, pointing to his door. Janak could not believe it. What a liar! Rama paused for a moment to absorb her words and then jumped up and pushed her to the ground. The third wife caught hold of Rama's long plait and pulled as she screamed and screamed. Rama put her fist through the third wife's cheek and there was blood all over her face. 'Oh no! Stop!' cried Janak and ran out to pull Rama away from the third wife. She was about to strangle her with both her hands. How ferocious she looked, her eyes blazing, her hair streaming down like Durga.

Mithoo gave a terrified screech and Janak looked back. Rama was sitting quietly hemming a kurta. The third wife was nowhere to be seen. Janak wiped the sweat from his face and whispered to Mithoo, 'I must not imagine these things. Please warn me next time it happens, Mithoo, my friend.' Rama gave him a quick glance, but did not say anything. Mithoo began to recite the 108 names of Durga. As he listened, feeling calmer, Janak knew the old bird had understood his every word and was trying to help him.

Janak's mother-in-law had still not come back to fetch Mithoo, and Janak was happy. He brought the old bird with him to the shop everyday. He came out of the cage and sat near the sewing machine, watching the women with beady eyes. But now Janak saw there was no evil in those eyes, just curiosity. Despite what the priest had said, he was sure Mithoo was a male bird. It was an old male bird who was harmlessly watching the world go by.

How could he ever have thought him an evil bird? All evil, or sorrow, or fear is sitting in our heads, from where it pours into our hearts whenever it gets a chance. If we keep our heads clear and clean, all will be well, he thought, cutting bits of thread from a new blouse.

The sun rose in the east every dawn, gifting them a new day, and then set behind the hill, casting a serene light on Giripul, like a blessing. Life was safe and good, life was peaceful. And then the magician came back.

Janak was sitting in the shop, cutting a new suit, when he heard a loud scream. He dropped his scissors and rushed out.

At first he could not make out what had happened and then he looked down and saw the magician. He was clinging to the topmost branch of the pine tree just on the edge of the hillside and screaming in a shrill, she-demon like voice, 'Bachao, bachao!'

Janak quickly went right to the edge of the khud and peered down. The magician was stuck half-way down the hill. If he let go of the branch, he would fall fifty feet down, right into the river. Janak did not know what to do. Someone would have to go down the khud.

Lala and Shankar appeared behind him. 'The man is going to fall. He will fall straight to his death,' said Shankar, picking his teeth with a twig.

'Do not talk rubbish and scare him even more,' shouted

Janak. 'We must save him,' he said and waved to the magician.

'We are bringing help. Hang on. Stay calm,' he shouted.

'Someone should climb down the hill and pull him up before the branch breaks,' he said, looking at Shankar and Lala.

'I cannot, I am too fat and I have just had my lunch,' said Lala, backing away.

'I am scared of heights,' said Shankar, staring down the khud to the river below.

'Don't lie. You go down the steep path everyday to the river,' said Raja who had come to watch.

'Help, please, help me!' shouted the magician.

'You are a great magician. Why don't you fly down to the ground?' said Raja.

'Shut up all of you,' said Janak. 'Can't you see how scared he is?' He paused, took a deep breath and then said, 'I will go. I will do down and bring him up.'

'You!' said Lala, Shankar and Raja together.

'Yes. I will go,' he said loudly.

There comes a time in a man's life when he has to overcome fear. He has to stop his heart from beating in a cowardly beat and rise to face a challenge. Janak took his cap off and put it on the ground and as the others watched, he slowly began the descend into the deep khud. He waited for his heart to start thumping in fear, but nothing happened. He felt quite calm as he went down the slippery hillside, clinging to the shrubs to keep his balance. The river glinted in the sunshine far below and a cool breeze drifted over his head. The magician saw him coming and began to cry. 'Save me, brother, save me.'

Janak stopped next to the pine tree and, keeping his feet firmly on the soft earth, he reached out his hand.

'Come, just hold my hand,' he said.

'No, no... I will fall,' the magician sobbed.

'You will not. I am here. Just shut your eyes and stretch your arm out to me,' Janak said in a firm voice which sounded unfamiliar to his own ears.

'Durga, Vishnu, Shiva,' chanted the magician with his eyes tightly shut, and then put his arm out.

'Janak... Janak... Janak... Waah... Shabash...' shouted all the people who had gathered to watch as Janak carried the magician on his back and climbed up the hill.

'You are a hero, my friend,' cried Shankar, patting him on the arm. Janak put the magician on the ground and stood still, trying to catch his breath. 'Janak, you are a tiger! The tiger of Girpul', said Lala. 'Bring tea and samosas for everyone!' he shouted.

'It was nothing. Once you cast aside the fear in your heart, everything becomes so easy,' he said, but no one was listening to him. 'Janak, Janak, Janak! Our tailor is a hero,' they shouted and thumped his back till he started coughing.

Rama was washing the dishes when he walked into the courtyard to wash his hands. His kurta was torn where the thorns in the shrubs had caught it and there were a few tiny scratches on his hands. He opened his mouth to explain when Rama smiled at him. 'So, the hero of Giripul has come home,' she said. Janak stared at her face, trying to make out her mood. Was she simmering with anger or was she pleased? The house seemed quiet. 'My hero,' she said and the stars came out to dance above his head. Dizzy and overjoyed, he reached out for her hand. Then he remembered the money in his pocket – five thousand-one rupees that the magician had given him. 'You saved my life, brother. This is just a token, just a small token...' he had said, putting the notes on his table.

'The magician gave this to me. Look ... ' he said, pulling out the crisp notes.

'The magician ... do not talk to me about him. What a sissy. They said he could not climb down from the tree. You had to risk your life and fetch him. My hero,' she said again and looked at him. Janak had never seen her look at him like that. He felt a surge of joy rush into his heart and he had to sit down at once on the floor. Rama went back to scrubbing the pots.

That night Janak stayed awake long after Rama had gone to sleep and thought about the many strange things that had happened in Giripul in the last few months. Evil things, and good things too. Fate was playing games with them. Then he thought of the money that had suddenly come to him. 'You are a kind man, a good man,' the magician had said, 'People will always come to you for help. You know why? Because they can trust you,' he had said and vanished. He thought of all the wonderful things he would buy with the money the magician had given him. He could get a TV for Rama and new shoes for his son. After that he could not think of anything else to buy and soon fell asleep. The thunder clouds roared far away on the hills. The rains filled the springs, made the maize grow faster. The trees whispered gently, as the easterly wind swept over Giripul, bringing peace and happiness once more.

But on the other side of the mountain where the river broadened out into a deep valley, fate, restless as ever, was waiting to strike.

Sitting quietly on the get-sick side of the afternoon bus was Janak's long-lost father and his beautiful young bride. Soon they would arrive in Giripul with nothing except a bag of old rice and twenty-one stolen gold coins.